JOAN FLE

When I Grow Rich

A COLLIER MYSTERY CLASSIC

With an Introduction by

ANTHONY BOUCHER, General Editor

COLLIER BOOKS, *NEW YORK*

Library of Congress Catalog Card Number: 64-22681

First Collier Books Edition 1965
Second Printing 1966

This Collier Books edition is published by arrangement with Ives Washburn, Inc.

The author and publishers wish to express their gratitude for permission to quote from *All Trivia* by Logan Pearsall Smith (Constable and Company Limited).

The Macmillan Company, New York
Printed in the United States of America

To Penelope who helped

Introduction

BOTH COLLIER BOOKS and I believe that this series of Mystery Classics should, for liveliness and variety, include an occasional recent book, such as Charlotte Jay's *Arms for Adonis* (AS 418V), even though the "classic" status of anything hot from the presses is all but impossible to determine.

Nevertheless, even though time and perspective may be essential to sober judgment, I am still willing to take a critic's gamble in the case of the novel you are about to read, and to assert firmly that Joan Fleming's *When I Grow Rich* (1962) will be recognized as a classic of the crime novel in 1972 or 1982—both because it is, in itself, an unusual and excellent work, and because it marks the highpoint (to date) of a highly interesting but largely underrated writer.

Joan Margaret Fleming wrote a number of books for girls in the 1940's, and in 1949 published her first adult novel (which has never appeared in this country). In a little over a dozen years she has brought forth fifteen novels, twelve of them published here*; their average quality has been exceedingly high; and yet she is hardly ever mentioned (except by me) among the leading practitioners of the contemporary English crime novel.

This would seem to result, at least in part, from the fact that her work is so inexhaustibly various. There is no neat commercial package labeled "characteristic Fleming novel." She writes comedy or tragedy, detection or character study, with equal readiness and skill; her settings may be any part of England or the Continent; her plots regularly spring from fresh and unpredictable premises; and no two of her novels resemble each other in anything save artistry.

In the analogous case of Andrew Garve, the public has finally learned that his by-line, despite his refusal ever to write the same book twice, is a sure guarantee of quality;

* See checklist p. 9

and I predict that readers will soon recognize the same assurance in the by-line of Joan Fleming. In the meantime, this is the first and only Fleming paperback; if it stimulates you to hunt out her earlier books (which will not disappoint you), you'll have to find them in libraries or second-hand bookstores.

What sort of novel has Miss Fleming gone and written in her fifteenth try? Well, it is a book which demonstrates, I think, just how far the boundaries of "the suspense novel" extend in the 1960's; twenty or possibly even ten years ago this would have been published as a straight mainstream novel. For it deals, to be sure, with crime; but there is little mystery and no detection and no hyped-up pursuit-suspense-chase.

This is, in essence, a novel about a place and time (Istanbul in 1960, with the Bosphorus coursing through the book like a serpentine symbol of terror), and about four people, all a little larger than life and each in his way unique. The inconsolable eunuch Hadji, the magnificently evil Mme. Miasma, the lost and rootless Jenny Bolton, and the naïf yet wise Nuri bey, the philosopher forced to become a man of action, are people you will long remember; and the novel's plot, beautifully calculated though it is from a technical point of view, is nothing more than the inevitable result of the interaction of these beings.

This is a warm, a colorful, a rich novel. 1962 was by no means an indifferent year in the crime novel; but if I were forced to pick my one single favorite book of the year, this would be it.

ANTHONY BOUCHER

The leading British mystery reviewers apparently agree with me. Between the writing of this introduction and its publication, a jury of major critics chose *When I Grow Rich* for the Crime Writers Association's annual award (equivalent to America's Edgars) to the best crime novel of the year.

A. B.

The Novels of Joan Fleming

(Published in London by Hutchinson through 1955, since then by Collins; American publishers in brackets.)

Chapter 1

BETWEEN THE two concrete blocks of new flats, separated by a small stretch of hard-trodden earth and half a dozen fine plane trees, stood a decrepit old wooden house. A fair size, it was built of horizontally-placed planks of wood; beaten by the sun, smoothed by the wind and shaken by earthquakes, its silvery-grey uneven walls rose to a second story and were capped by a turret, or look-out room, perched absurdly on the extreme northern corner, where it was possible to stand, like Sister Anne, scanning the horizon, a few feet away: a wall of not very solid concrete.

Inside the house, Nuri bey stood in his wreck of a kitchen and ate yoghourt from a shallow bowl. He had spent a profitable day completing his own analysis of St. Paul's preaching of the gospel at Konia. That no one would ever read it, or show the slightest interest in it, was of no concern to the author; he was satisfied that it was a scholarly piece of work.

If asked point-blank, Nuri bey would say that he was neither a Moslem nor a Christian nor a Buddhist but a philosopher who had acquired some of the habit of thought of all three. But because he had drawn in the teachings of the Koran with his mother's milk, he was aware that Allah is closer to a man than the vein in his neck and therefore he did nothing deliberately of which he knew Allah would not approve. Though his personal cleanliness was exquisite, his kitchen was pretty filthy and, when he had finished the yoghourt, he tossed the container down amongst a pile of similar bowls, tea glasses and other unwashed dishes where it would lie, walked over by flies, until such time as there were no clean utensils left and he would be obliged to wash up.

The large narrow table in the centre of his wide hall

was covered with a cloth of pale green satin, exquisitely embroidered with silver and gold thread and many-coloured silks. Upon it lay a three-hundred-year-old copy of the Koran, a small engraved dagger, a copy of *The Weekly Times* still wrapped in the covering in which it had travelled from London, a similarly-wrapped copy of the *New Statesman* and *Paris Soir*.

With the dagger, Nuri bey neatly ripped the covers off, smoothed the periodicals flat and slipped them into his shabby leather dispatch-case. Briskly he buttoned the front of his brown double-breasted jacket; too briskly, one of the buttons flew off, shooting several yards away and disappearing beneath a great metal-studded chest. Down on his knees, with the aid of the dagger, he retrieved it and, finding a needle and thread, laboriously sewed the button into place.

Everything now under control, he stood by the front door and took a look round his hall. Deeply superstitious, Nuri bey afterwards believed that Allah was at that moment telling him something, warning him of impending disaster, but that he, Nuri bey, being neither a good Moslem nor anything else, had not heeded. After many years of uneventful and tranquil existence, everything was about to be changed; never again would his home be quite the same inviolable place.

He locked his front door carefully and ran down the front steps. Tall for a Turk (but descended on his mother's side from a Circassian youth, who had grown immensely tall through being breast-fed by a series of wet-nurses till he was ten), he strode along the street with the dispatch-case tucked under his arm in a business-like way. His face was smooth and a pale silvery-tan colour, with the texture of a hazel-nut. His hair was hardly hair at all, being a grey scrubby growth, like lichen on a barn roof and growing a long way back from his smooth tan forehead. His lips were thin and, though the kindest and gentlest of men, he had inherited a cruel line to his mouth from another of his warrior forebears. He had abnormally big eyes, the colour of motor oil in a large tin container, heavily lashed and oddly luminous. This strange luminosity was not the result of applied drugs nor any secret vice but simply his soul or his spirit, overstimulated by continuous contact with the writings of the great minds of the world's thinkers and prophets, shining out. So grand a light shone in his head that he was neither observant nor curious. His eyes were so constantly fixed upon the stars that he tripped and stumbled along the familiar uneven streets of his native city and quite often trod on a starving kitten or bumped into a concrete lamp-post.

He leaped on to a tram, crowded to boiling point, and clung to its perimeter as it swayed and lurched down through the narrow streets of Pera to the Galata Bridge where he ran to catch a ferry across the Bosphorus to Uskudar, on the Asia side, and then a bus going north.

Most large wooden houses on the Bosphorus are called either *yalis* or palaces, whilst the cheaper and shabbier hotels are called *palas*. The *yali* or villa of his friend Madame Miasma, was some distance up the Bosphorus beyond the Sweet Waters of Asia, a stretch where the current ran strong and deep and where anchorage was almost impossible. The bus stopped short of the front gate on the main road, from which one descended some few shallow steps into a cool, tree-shaded, flagged courtyard.

Nuri bey had made the journey hundreds of times. Weekly for years he called upon his elderly friend and spent the afternoon and early evening reading the papers he brought with him, translating the news of the world for her into Turkish and discussing world affairs with her over glasses of tea and slices of dry bread.

But to-day, the moment he had stepped from the bus and turned towards her gateway, he could see that something was wrong. From a distance, what looked like bundles or sacks of rags seemed to be piled up by the great metal gates, all over the pavement and overflowing into the road so that the bus made a sharp detour to avoid them. As he approached, Nuri bey's heart lurched into his throat and nearly choked him. The sacks of rags were human beings and they were chanting from the thirty-sixth chapter of the Koran which is sung when a death occurs . . . *We have ordained phases for the moon, which daily wanes and in the end appears as a bent and withered twig . . . .*

In the few seconds it took to walk amongst the small crowd of squatters, push open the gates, descend the three shallow steps and walk across the courtyard, Nuri bey became a visionary, no longer aware of his surroundings: he was in Oxford, England, walking along High Street as depicted in the picture postcard, photographed from Magdalen Bridge, which he kept in a prominent position in his drawing-room. His companion was Professor Toynbee and they were deep in discussion.

Nuri bey had never been outside his country. He lived on the income from renting a few old wooden houses. But he had known for many years, because she had more or less said so, that when Miasma died there would be enough money for him to achieve the ambition of his life. Though he had never so much as formed the thought into words in his mind: *when she dies I shall go to Oxford,* the whole great glory of it broke over him and transfigured his face so that, unsuitably, he burst radiant, into the house, to find Hadji the chauffeur kneeling, in the hall, prostrate in prayer.

For once Nuri bey joined in the prayer, kneeling beside the servant, turned towards Mecca, and prostrating himself likewise, and from him rose a prayer of thanksgiving.

Having finished his prayers, the chauffeur broke into soft eerie chanting. Nuri bey got up. The hall was a broad place with a marble flagged floor from which rose, in two shallow sweeps, a wooden staircase which turned back on itself, showing its carved underside to the hall and joining the first floor in a great commotion of carving against the hall ceiling. Under the small bridge-like landing where the staircases met, two great mirror-doors opened into a big room which was so close to the Bosphorous that it was like an underwater room full of lucent green shifting light, the long windows on the water side now fringed with creeper.

The walls were painted with what had once been elaborate murals of flowers and creeper and more flowers, now faded and stained and the lower part obscured by bird-cages all around the room which both looked and sounded untidy. The gaily coloured birds inside filled the air with cheeps and twitters and pipings, and threw scraps of seed and sand out on to the floor. In the centre stood a round Victorian back-to-back sofa or love-seat, covered in purple brocade, shabby and worn now, the stuffing bursting out between the frequent buttons which battened it to the frame.

The balcony of Miasma's bedroom above jutted out and deprived the great room below of any sky-light; all the light it had was reflected from the water. *A hateful room,* Nuri bey thought, and realised that he had always thought so but had never dared to admit it.

He put down his dispatch-case and walked over to the double french windows, now wide open. A few feet away the fierce alien water, river water from the great Russian rivers, rushed past purposefully. In earlier days caiques or gaily coloured gondola-like boats, would bring arrivals at the *yali* to the marble steps and two stalwart slaves would hold it firmly to the bank whilst the passengers disembarked. But now people no longer arrived by boat. Nuri bey stared down into the water, black and almost soundless as it slipped by.

Money, money, money . . . he was thinking. How he despised it! Yet how he treasured that which money could bring! With money he could buy occasionally from the old man in the second-hand bookshop down by the mosque of Bayazlt II, the rare, almost priceless, illuminated Koran; old Sanskrit writings; treasures of ancient Buddhist philosophy.

And now . . . Oxford and the books in the Bodleian Library. He would go by train because then he would be sure of getting there; first he would get a room at a small hotel in St. Giles and then he would go to the Ashmolean where he would look at the things which he had dreamed of seeing, King Alfred's jewel for instance, then he would go to one of the colleges where he would ask for the young Prince, as he still called him, a great-grandson of the Sultan Ahmed II, and a relation of Nuri bey, and this young man who excelled in the sport of rowing

(Nuri bey believed he was called a *cox*), would take Nuri bey round and show him the splendours and the glories of that fabled city. Then he and Nuri bey would have a *hot dog* and perhaps two, and many many days of such delight would lie ahead. Allah be praised! All this and perhaps Professor Toynbee, too!

With an optimism which was undiminished over the years, Nuri bey kept an up-to-date passport in his breast pocket in case, rather like the Mad Hatter who always took a plate in case he found a plum cake.

Smiling, he turned round to go back to the bird-room. His lips remained stretched in a smile but his eyes lost their light and became mere holes for seeing through.

There she was, very much alive, standing before a bird-cage thrusting scraps of lettuce between the bars and making her absurd tiny chittering sounds, like someone insane *who with age and envy was grown into a hoop* . . . or was it her ghost?

Was it perhaps that his eye had registered this sight so often that he could still see that which was not there? Alas, no!

Without turning her head she said in Turkish: "You have heard the bad news, my lion?"

Nuri bey could say nothing. His throat moved but no words came. He walked across and kissed her hand.

"A sad day. A disaster! My friend of a lifetime, and servant, gone, by the will of Allah!"

Valance, the shadow of Miasma upon earth, had evidently died. Valance, the French companion, grown old but unstaid and skittish in spite of her years, with her wrinkled face, her slim figure and still unfaded blue eyes, her inability to speak a word of the Turkish language, her coy mannerisms, her loyalty to her mistress, her unfailing cheerfulness, her robust good health, her endless talk about her many relatives in France and her annual holiday in Paris, her dislike of Turkish food, manners, men . . . evidently dead.

Nuri bey could make no reply. He walked slowly to the sofa, picked up his dispatch-case and drew out the newspapers thoughtfully.

Miasma moved from cage to cage, tearing at the lettuce she held and pushed the mutilated fragments towards her eager birds.

"Have you nothing to say, Nuri bey?"

"Of course. I'm sorry. You will miss her."

"Miss her!" Miasma repeated bitterly. "I do not know how I can live my life without her. I shall have to leave here."

"How can you possibly leave here?"

"And go and live in a hotel . . . maybe."

"That is a fantasy! You . . . live in a hotel!" Nuri bey shook his head, smiling sadly, a shadow of his former smile.

"Valance has been with me, with the exception of the one month out of every year when she went home, for a long time and during all those days, weeks, months, years I have never dressed nor undressed, nor made my bed, had a meal, nor brushed my hair, nor threaded a needle, nor made a single stitch with the thread, nor put on my shoes, nor gone to the *hamam*"—she closed her eyes for several moments—"without her."

Still far from fluent, Nuri bey stood before her with hands outstretched as though asking what was to be done.

"You will be telling me to get a temporary maid; I do not like to have a servant always with me; Valance was more than a maid, she was my companion. Hadji and I will have to go to Beirut, to the hotel where I often stay when Valance is away. But I do not like Beirut very much and the woman there does not look after me very well, though she thinks she does!"

And how had Valance died?

With all the talkativeness and attention to detail of those who have come through some sudden disaster Madame told how Valance had died. She had seemed perfectly well yesterday. They had spent the day as usual and during the afternoon had taken a taxi to a cinema where they had seen a cowboy film which they had both much enjoyed. On the return, Hadji had met them at Uskudar and driven them home. Valance had brought her supper which Madame had taken here, in the bird-room, on a tray at that small table. After supper she had dozed a little, sitting here on the sofa but later she had walked in the garden. It was a beautiful evening and the Bosphorus was looking its best. She had strolled in the garden for a few minutes, wrapped up in her sables. Valance had called from the steps of the bird-room: "Madame, dear Madame! You will take cold. Come in now, *chérie*."

She had walked back and stood for a moment there— she pointed—just there on the steps, where Nuri bey had been standing a few minutes ago, overlooking the water. Valance had come out to stand beside her and together they had discussed what they were going to do to-day, Monday. Valance had said suddenly that she did not feel well. She put her hands to her head and said that a great pain had struck her in the head. She had never complained of pain or fatigue or of any physical symptom in all the years Miasma had known her and now she cried aloud with pain. Miasma had gone back into the bird-room, now lighted, and taken the flask of brandy (which she took medicinally) from her supper tray and returned . . . but Valance had gone. Calling her, Miasma had followed her, as she thought, into the garden round the side of the house.

"Valance! Valance! Where are you, old woman? Come and have some of this fine old brandy." Miasma's hands fell to her sides, palms forwards. "It was too late. A stroke, they say, an attack of dizziness, the pain, sudden death. She fell forwards into the water. . . ."

Nuri bey caught his breath sharply. "So the old woman drowned!"

"They think not, they think perhaps she died as she entered the water. Struck down by the hand of Allah," she added piously. "They found her early this morning, down in the shallows by the Sweet Waters of Asia. She was taken to the mortuary where they examined her. I telephoned for Dr. MacPherson, who went at once and saw her body. Later we had a long talk, he and I. He said there was no doubt she died of a stroke; the severe headache she complained of proved that she had a condition which is well known in the medical profession, I cannot remember what he called it."

"They brought her body back here?"

"Yes. Hadji cleared the marble table in the salon, and she lies there. The *imam* is with her now."

Nuri bey gave a cry of distress. "But she is a Christian!"

The *imam* is the parish priest of the Moslems; he has no supernatural powers and wears no robes of office but he is concerned for the individuals of his flock much as a Christian minister of the church. When he receives the name of the dead person, he goes to the house accompanied by the *muezzin* (whose duty it is to call the Faithful to prayer) and an assistant. After the body has been washed he annoints those eight parts which touch the ground in prayer, the forehead, tip of nose, palms of hands, knees and feet, with camphor. Then the body is wrapped tightly in a winding sheet in the manner of the wrapping of the newly born baby in swaddling clothes, except that the head is also covered. It is then laid upon a bier which has been brought to the house for the purpose, with the right side focused upon the Mecca beam and covered with a pale green cloth, the death-colour of Islam, and the Prophet's own colour. It is hurried to the grave at the earliest possible moment because the Prophet said: "If the deceased be of the elect it is meet to convey him with speed to the goal." And if the dead were not of the elect: "If he be one of the accursed, it is equally meritorious to get rid of him with expedition." The weepers stay around, hurrying forward to help in the removal of the bier from the house because Mohammed said that assistance in carrying the body forty steps towards the grave helps to expiate a mortal sin.

If the graveyard is nearby, the bier is carried by four bearers and followed by the *imam* and the immediate family, the professional mourners having done all that is required of them. If the graveyard is some distance away, the bier is carried on a pale green hearse with the rather jolly look of an old-fashioned ice-cream cart.

Miasma smiled thinly. "My dear Nuri bey, at home, perhaps, Valance was a Christian, but here she was as I am." Many times she had accompanied her mistress to the mosque and had prayed beside her and with her in one of the niches along the walls reserved for the women, for the women may not pray with the men on the great flat stretch of beautifully carpeted floor upon which the men prostrate themselves in absolute humility before Allah.

"I have, many years ago, bought a grave for myself up there." Madame pointed towards the back of the house behind which, on the other side of the road, a cemetery ran up and up the hillside for nearly a mile. "I have arranged that Valance shall be buried there and when my time comes I shall lie beside her. I am arranging for her to be treated in death exactly as I would wish to be treated. The *imam* thinks she is a Moslem, and I do not wish that he should think otherwise, Nuri bey. The only way in which I must transgress is in regard to the name of her mother, in order that the *imam* may cry it aloud as she is put into the grave; as I do not know the name of her mother, and Valance's name was Marie, which is Christian, I shall tell the *imam* her mother's name was Fatima!"

"That, also, is a Christian name!"

"You see," Madame said benevolently, "even that! I cannot do more for my poor maid."

"Her people?"

"Hadji sent a wire immediately to her people in France and later, when we are not so busy, you will write a long letter to them, Nuri bey, under my guidance; we will tell them about her beautiful funeral."

She wandered towards the cages, lips compressed. "I understand them to be an avaricious lot. They will demand the return of all her personal possessions. I may tell you that Valance never spent a *lira* here. She smuggled all the money she earned in a year out of the country, when she went on her annual holiday, inside her stays, the old rascal!"

It was against Nuri bey's principles to sit when a woman was standing but his reaction to the shock caused an unaccustomed weakness; he sank on to the love seat, feeling as though all the stuffing had gone out of him. It was exhausting to travel in the flick of a bird's wing, to the heights and back again in as short a time. He brought out his handkerchief and wiped the palms of his hands which felt unpleasantly moist and clammy.

"A fine death, my lion, do you not think?" she murmured at last.

No, Nuri bey did not agree. He thought it a fearful death; it reminded him too strongly of the many, many women, young and middle-aged and old, who had died by unavoidably filling their lungs with the icy water of the Bosphorus. Such deaths belonged to the bad days of old Turkey when human life counted for nothing and intrigue and jealousy and ambition regulated human behaviour.

"Come, my friend, admit truthfully that if one must die in a foreign country, and as a servant in that country, it is better to have the ceremonies of that country attend one's funeral rather than be bundled out of the house like a mere dead rat. Mourners have been hired. Hadji will pin the notice to the front door, the *imam* will be paid handsomely for his services and to-morrow morning soon after daylight she will be safely in the good ground. It is costing me a fine lot, I can tell you. What more could I do for my faithful friend and servant?"

Nuri bey composed himself more comfortably. He opened *The Times* and said: "We have much to discuss this week. The American Election draws near and it is time for us to examine the qualities of the respective candidates. . . ."

"No. No. Not to-day. I am not in the mood. There are more urgent things to be discussed."

The *imam* being in the house, Madame was wearing her best day dress, a bright brown satin from a Paris house, heavily embroidered with beads and giving her bent and shapeless figure a certain dignity and even splendour. She was wearing a number of rings on her fingers and a dirty diamond necklace. She turned from the bird-cages and hobbled across the room, standing before Nuri bey and putting her chilly bird-like claws on his already cold hands.

"My friend, my lion, there is a small favour that I

must ask of you now that my poor Valance is gone. Will you go to the airport and deliver something for me to a young friend passing through?"

"To-night?"

"He arrives by the Comet from England at eight o'clock this evening."

He had been invited for coffee with an English friend from the British Council. He hesitated.

"I am in great trouble," the old woman pleaded. "I cannot leave the house with the corpse of my poor companion waiting for burial, in torment."

"Hadji could go!"

"And leave me alone here with the corpse? Nuri bey, how could you suggest so cruel a thing? Alone here with my dead Valance!"

Though Nuri bey was unconvinced that Miasma would turn a hair at such an experience, he could understand that it was conventionally undesirable but still he hesitated. "I would have time, indeed, I would make time, in the morning. . . ."

She stamped her foot impatiently. "The aeroplane of Zenobia Airlines is passing through. It goes on to Hong Kong. I have something all ready to send to my great friend there."

Because he knew that she could make life pretty unbearable for the person of whom she asked a favour if they did not instantly comply, Nuri bey agreed.

Why did anyone bother to do anything for her? he asked himself unhappily. She was not charming, nor kind, nor generous, nor beautiful, nor appealing, nor pathetically in need of help. She appeared to be neither greatly upset nor seriously stricken by the death of her personal servant and friend. But she had a regal autocracy that was very difficult to stand up to. She acted upon a kind of divine right to demand and receive from people instant sacrifice and there would seem to be no getting away from it.

In the entrance hall at the airport he would see a thin young Englishman of medium height with dark hair; he would give him a small fibre case with Madame Miasma's compliments. As the young man would be looking for

Valance, Nuri bey must appear to be waiting for someone, it might be that he would have to be the first to speak. All he would need to say was that Madame Miasma had asked him to come. There was no need to mention death or disaster.

"You understand, Nuri bey? That is all that is necessary. He will take my case from you and return to the aeroplane. You will have done me a very great favour and one day, as I have said before, one day, my lion, you will be rewarded!"

When Nuri bey left the house, the *imam* and his staff had done their duties. The bier stood in the entrance hall, by the front door, almost athwart the entrance, at the requisite angle to Mecca, so that Nuri bey had to skirt it as he made his way out. For a moment he stood and looked down at the earthly remains of the French maid Valance, now a mere corpse, strangely slim and absolutely anonymous beneath the pale green pall.

This hurry to bury the dead, he thought as he gently closed the front door behind him and stepped amongst the mourners on his way out, how could one be sure that one was not buried alive?

Chapter 2

. . . AND YET, he thought, as he sat in the bus rattling along the Ataturk Boulevard, under the aqueduct and through the Southend-Road-like countryside of Thrace, Miasma had any number of friends. For one short glorious period before the First World War she had been married to a Greek ship owner and had known a variety of international celebrities. She had met and talked to the Czar of Russia, the Kaiser, and the Prince of Wales but the beginning of the war had put a sudden end to these halcyon days. Turkey and Greece had been on different sides; she had returned to Istanbul or, as one of her enemies had crudely put it: "The Greeks kicked her out."

The *yali* on the Bosphorus had belonged to a Vizier of the Sultan's court and in the dark days of the first war she had been able to buy it at a bargain price. She settled in with the two plums she had picked from the Greek pie: the French personal maid Valance and a De Dion Bouton motor car or limousine as it was then called, with glass windows which let down with leather straps and brass oil lamps with coloured glass panels at the sides.

Between the wars when Ataturk was wreaking havoc with all the old Turkish shibboleths and Moslem principles were being knocked down as carelessly as fezes were knocked off heads and veils torn from the women's faces, Madame Miasma's house became a little haven of stability. Anyone coming new to Istanbul, anxious to get to know people, having a letter of introduction to Madame, would be sure of being accepted into one or two of the best Turkish households.

With the Second World War, the rise of young Turkey and the new capital of Ankara, Madame's influence waned as Istanbul's importance as a capital decreased. As the face of her city aged, so did she; now both were showing signs of decrepitude. Unlike Cleopatra, age had withered her and custom had staled her, and in any case she had no infinite variety, she was always the same.

Valance had gone; next it would be the De Dion Bouton which used a great deal of gasoline and was expensive to maintain.

He would have to be careful, Nuri bey mused. Now Valance was gone, he could see himself being charged with all sort of duties which the Frenchwoman had performed in the past, as, for instance, this unwanted trip to the airport. He would have liked to assure himself that he would never have agreed to it had it not been for the exceptional circumstances but he knew, in his passion for the absolute truth, that he would do anything which Miasma requested of him.

The bus was almost full of American women who seemed to have about three husbands among the lot. They had been staying at the American Hilton Hotel for two days, had done Istanbul and were now going to do the Far

East, staying a night or two in Hong Kong, on to Tokyo and home via the Pacific; the world in a fortnight.

Hatless, in his best brown pin-striped suit which was worn to the point of shininess and with the shabby fibre overnight case which Miasma had given him, Nuri bey looked like their courier, though the thought would never have occurred to him. When the bus arrived they stood up and created a great bustle and fuss lifting the hand luggage down from the rack, calling to one another and talking incessantly in what Nuri bey privately thought of as their parrot-like tones of voice. Surely, he thought, their tongues must be differently shaped from those of other mortals. From their chatter he gathered that the Zenobia Airways Comet had arrived from London and that, when through the customs, they would all join the passengers in the transit lounge before embarking.

He walked into the reception hall, standing some few paces from the main entrance. Was it not over-optimistic to be sure that he would meet the young friend of Miasma? As soon as this thought had passed through his mind, he saw a young man, alone, sauntering to and fro at the far end of the hall. He was watching everyone who came from the bus. Nuri bey watched him. He was clearly waiting for someone and when all the travellers had passed, chattering and laughing and making all the sounds of confusion that travellers in such circumstances make, there was no one left in the reception hall who was so obviously waiting for someone as Nuri bey. The young man looked at him. Not directly but casually, he made his way across and, when he was near enough, Nuri bey could see him staring fixedly at the case in his hand.

Presently, having reassured himself, he came up.

"Madame Miasma? You are from Madame Miasma?"

Relieved beyond expression, Nuri bey agreed eagerly that he was, indeed, from Madame Miasma. He said that her French companion, Valance, was unable to come to the airport, and as it was too late to alter the arrangement, Madame had asked him to come instead. If he would kindly deliver this case to Madame's friend in Hong Kong . . . Nuri bey had heard the name of Madame's friend from time to time but at the moment it eluded him.

The young man made a face. He was hatless and wore a sports jacket over a pair of smart tapered black trousers. He was smoking, pulling nervously at his cigarette.

"Is the old woman ill or something?"

"Which old woman?"

"The . . . er . . . the French companion?"

She had said that all he would need to say was that Madame Miasma had asked him to come. She had asked if he understood and he realised that she had meant he was not to mention, under any circumstances, her death. He hesitated.

"It she ill?"

Nuri bey still hesitated. He could not say *yes,* he equally could not say *no.* He compromised in a shrug, the very essence of the Levant which the French epitomise so well with the expression: *ni l'un, ni l'autre.*

The young man seemed to understand. "Just one of those things," he said.

Nuri bey looked puzzled. "One of what things?" he asked, preparing for an informative discussion.

The young man took the case and dropped his cigarette stub on the ground, pressing it out with his foot. "Well . . . thanks a lot, Mr.—er—" He gave Nuri bey a brisk nod, "Be seeing you," and hurried away.

Incurious about his immediate surroundings though he was, certain questions did rear their ugly heads in Nuri bey's mind, only to be discouraged. Anyway, it was now no further business of his.

Be seeing you . . . what did that mean? Was it a brand new idiom?

And now to the return bus. It was almost completely dark, in the time after sunset and before moonrise. Nuri bey was about to go out through the doors to find the return bus when there was the sound of a shot, at least he thought it was a shot, and when it was followed by a series of shots he paused, knowing that something serious must be happening in the transit lounge behind the big double doors.

The girl selling sweetmeats at a kiosk, two airport

officials, a couple of porters and Nuri bey ran across the reception hall and through the big double doors, down the stairs. In the transit lounge the noise and confusion reminded Nuri bey of the fuss made by a lot of laying hens when disturbed. An American matron rushed up to him hysterically and clung to his arm.

"Oh, oh! Help! Mur . . . r . . . der!"

"What happens?" Nuri bey asked.

"There's an assassin around here . . ." she shrieked. All the males in the place seemed to have run out on to the tarmac, except one, a smallish square figure lying by the bar and the two bartenders who had climbed over the bar and were pulling at him in an evident attempt to be helpful. Several women who had thrown themselves flat on their faces at the sound of shooting were now picking themselves up and checking that they still had their handbags.

Then spying a friend, she yelled: "Leonore, hi there, Leonore!" and released Nuri bey for whom she had no further use. "You all right, honey?" he heard her anxiously asking her friend.

Nuri bey turned away and slowly mounted the stairs, feeling unutterably sad and melancholy. A terrible depression descended upon him because human beings did not know how to live their lives. Shouting and shrieking and shooting and hurting each other when it was all so unnecessary.

The entrance hall was completely deserted, even the bus drivers had run to the scene of action. Nuri bey walked up and down the line of some half-dozen buses, decided to take the one that was lighted and was about to pull himself up into it when someone sped out of the reception hall and stood in the exit, poised like a bird in flight, alighting for a moment, wondering which way to go.

She caused a strange sensation in Nuri bey's heart because she was young and to be young is to be beautiful and it is beautiful to be young, or so Nuri bey had always thought.

And in her hand, he could see clearly in the light shining from the lamp above her, she was carrying the overnight case which he had brought to the airport with him.

At least, he thought it was. He moved a little closer. It was an anonymous-looking case with nothing distinguished about it other than that it was clearly an English-made case, or rather a case not made in Turkey. Shabby, plain and perfectly ordinary, it was certainly the case which Miasma had handed to him a few hours ago.

Any ordinary man would have cried: "Hi, what are you doing with that case?" But Nuri bey was no ordinary man. It was his habit not to ask a direct question unless absolutely necessary and he did not consider it necessary to do so now. If he waited patiently, in time the answer to most questions would be forthcoming.

She was behaving as he would expect anyone to behave who had just witnessed a shooting incident; breathless, the pupils of her eyes enormous, the handbag on her arm hanging open displayed an untidy jumble of letters, passport and articles of make-up. Nuri bey stared at the overnight case. There must be hundreds of cases exactly the same but it was impossible not to recognise the case which he had had in his hand and on his knee since it was handed to him by Miasma as he left the *yali*. In the local bus, on the ferry boat, in the restaurant in Eminonu, on the bus to Pera and in the airport bus, that case had been with him for the best part of three hours and he knew it was the same one; it was the only certainty in a very uncertain world.

The unaccustomed feeling in his heart was superseded by some practical considerations; it was his absolute duty to remain beside that case with which he had been entrusted, so long as it was in the hands of someone unauthorised rather than those of the young man for whom it had been intended. It was probable that she had stolen the bag during the fracas in the waiting hall.

She ran her free hand through her hair, saying: "Oh, my lord! Oh, my lord!" Any other man would have said: "Can I help you?" but Nuri bey simply stated that he would help her, in English because she would almost certainly be either English or American, probably the latter.

"Where is this?" she asked. English.

"Istanbul."

"Oh, my lord! Istanbul! Oh, well!" Putting the case on the ground beside her she fumbled about in her handbag and brought out a shabby wallet. "Seven pounds, that's all I've got. Can I change that into Turkish money?"

"The bank will be shut now."

Having got the case back into his own hand, Nuri bey felt a lot more comfortable. It was perhaps lighter than he had remembered, but the handle felt the same, in fact, was the same; it was the identical case and he did not intend to let it go.

"I'm in the most awful mess." She shuddered. "I was supposed to be going on to Hong Kong. But I can't now." She was half-crying and, having no pocket handkerchief, she sniffed and wiped her face with her gloveless hand, smudging her eye-black as she did so.

"My boy friend's just shot someone," and, strangely, she giggled a little. "I knew he would, sooner or later. That's what happens if you carry guns; they go off, don't they? I mean, you may not want to . . ." She started to cry now in great uncontrolled sobs, "Oh, my lord, I am in a mess!"

A laden taxi had approached and swung round to stop a few yards from where they stood. The two passengers and the driver were quite unaware of what was happening behind the swing doors. Their baggage was deposited beside them, they paid the driver who was looking towards the exit for other passengers when Nuri bey took a sudden decision, arising from the quick calculation as to the money he had on him.

"Come," he said, indicating to the taxi-driver that he wished to become a passenger and opening the door for her to step inside. And thus, with the driver probably congratulating himself as to the speediness of his re-hire, they were being driven away.

"Oh, very neat indeed," the girl remarked, sniffing. "Anyone would think you were a wide-boy yourself. I do seem to have fallen on my feet." She had brought out a small hand-mirror and was doing things to her face; her hands were trembling perceptibly, he was amazed at her poise.

"Do they hang people in Turkey?"

"Yes," he replied, "they do hang people in Turkey. For murder."

"Oh, my lord! But maybe the chap's not dead. He looked it, though, didn't he?"

"The man on the ground?"

"Maybe he was shamming dead."

Yes, they hanged murderers in Turkey and Nuri bey thought it unnecessary to tell her that they were public hangings.

"He was some kind of bobby," she volunteered.

"A bobby, what is that?"

"A policeman. He'd been watching Tony. I thought there was something wrong. If I could have warned Tony that the man was watching him it might have been all right but they won't let you out of that beastly transit lounge; they wouldn't in Athens or Rome either. Where are we going? I hope you're not kidnapping me, or anything."

Nervous chatter, Nuri bey decided. Reaction.

"But where are you taking me to, really?"

"A hotel," Nuri bey said grimly.

"Oh, my lord, no!"

"You'll be all right. Istanbul isn't a savage place, you know."

"Not a hotel. I couldn't! I'd have to sign the register . . . no, honestly, I can't."

This was the kind of thing one should leave severely alone. No good could come of it. Nuri bey stared unhappily at the fibre case on his knees. For a moment or two the idea of simply stepping out of the taxi and disappearing amongst the crowd in Eminonu Square seemed irresistible. He had the case . . . why bother about the girl? But it was a question that was to go forever unanswered. It was unthinkable that he should leave this young, young girl alone in a strange city in such terrible circumstances. Charity occupies a large place in the mind of every Mohammedan and Nuri bey knew that it was his duty, if not his inclination, to take her to his home.

If his sister had lived in Istanbul rather than in Trebizond, he could have taken her there. Or he could have taken her to the Consulate or to his friend from the British Council who lived in a flat in Pera but under the circumstances it would be like handing her over to the police.

Though he was full of uneasiness and foreboding, Nuri bey felt that he must be doing what was right when he leaned forward and gave his address to the taxi-driver.

There was plenty of cold water from the one tap in the house, and there was enough bread but his larder was that of an ascetic; there was a little goat cheese, a stale egg and one cold section of swordfish which had been grilled on a skewer over charcoal.

His salon had no door, being separated from the hall only by a large open archway. He placed her in the seat of honour, the centre of the stiff upright sofa, told her to relax and went to find food and drink. On a small tray he put everything he had to offer, with the exception of the egg. As he left the kitchen, in the manipulation of the double doors, the tray tipped sideways and he was unable to retrieve it; with a sickening crash out of all proportion to the content, everything went to the ground.

With every muscle tensed, Nuri bey waited for her to rush to his assistance. The sound of the crash seemed to hang over him, echoing and re-echoing faintly till it died away. It took him ten minutes to mop up the water, pick the pieces of glass out of the cheese, remove the wet part of the bread, reassemble the fish and reinstate the small meal as attractively as possible on another tray.

And when he returned, more carefully, to the salon, she was sitting exactly as he had left her except that she had removed her white raincoat. She was wearing a tight dark skirt and a thick white sweater and round her neck was a silk patterned scarf, with the ends of which she constantly fiddled.

"You are a dear! I don't know why you should bother,

honestly I don't! There was some food on the jet but I didn't feel like it. I don't feel like eating, I'm afraid."

"But you must eat," he urged. "To have a good night's sleep you must have food inside you and it is essential to have a good night of sleep before to-morrow when you may have much to worry you."

"My lord! Haven't I got enough to worry me now?"

"Now you must relax. . . ."

"But you don't understand. . . ."

"No, I do not understand," he returned grimly. All he understood was the wickedness of a mother who could allow a young girl to stray so far from her side that she was discovered in these circumstances. It was a state of affairs over which Nuri bey had often sighed, frowned and remained quite bewildered. He frequently saw, in the streets of Istanbul, perhaps arm-in-arm with a young man, very young American or English girls, no more than female children, dressed in fantastically short skirts, or even in tight trousers, with breasts outlined in strange revealing upper garments, and hair flying all over the place; children of the Western world. What kind of monsters of neglect could the mothers of these young girls be?

"I do not understand," he repeated, sitting down in a chair by the low table on which he had placed the tray, "how your mother could allow you . . ."

She began to laugh. "My mother . . ." but her eyes looked sad, Nuri bey thought. "What a funny old-fashioned old thing you are," she said kindly. "What on earth have mothers got to do with anything?"

This was such a strange remark that Nuri bey needed time to think it over. His own mother had died when he was twenty and the simple word mother filled him with sacred feelings.

"Mothers are out," she went on, "I mean, we don't bother with them any more." She put butter on a piece of bread and bit into it. "This bread is rather good."

He was more than shocked, he was completely horrified. Here in his house, eating his food and drinking his water, was sheer heresy and naked unashamed blasphemy. He watched her eating with some enjoyment the rest of the bread. The fish disappeared too, and some of the cheese. When she had finished eating she thanked him prettily and said she felt a good deal better.

"Who are you?" she asked.

Solemnly he told her he was a Turkish philosopher called Nuri Izkirlak, commonly known as Nuri bey. That he lived alone in this house and studied the writings of world philosophers. She said that she was afraid she did not know much about philosophy but her brother did, he was studying it at Oxford. He was the clever one of the two.

"Oxford," he repeated. "Oxford." Since he had left his house not so many hours ago, Oxford had come near, had been very real, and had as suddenly retreated so far from his grasp that it was now an imaginary place, as intangible as the twilight of the gods. And the passport remained in his inner pocket as insignificant as ever.

"Nuri bey," she repeated, "the bey being mister, I suppose? My name is Jenny Bolton and my boy friend's name is Tony Grand. At least I thought that was his name, I'm not sure now. I'm nineteen and I thought Tony was twenty-five but I'm not sure about that either, now. I'm one of those English teenagers I suppose you've heard so much about. Some people think we're the top people, and others think we're an awful bore. I can see you don't think us a bore, Nuri bey, because you're shocked, aren't you? You can't be both bored and shocked at the same time."

He was listening passionately, that is, he was listening with strained attention in order that he should not miss one word or implication that might help him towards understanding.

"We're kind of drunk with being young and important, some of us." She dragged her hands through her hair in the nervous way he had already observed. "Those of us who can't do clever things, do utterly mad things . . . like me. 'I was a teenage-rebel,' har har," she mimicked hollowly. She ran her hands through her hair again. "Oh, lord, how I've aged since that jet left London to-day. Was it only to-day?"

There was a long pause whilst she picked tiny pieces off the remaining goat cheese.

"Tony has a sports car. A sports car and a revolver. And what do you think? He kept an old shirt in the car and when we went out into the country he'd hang the shirt from a branch of a tree and fire at it. That, I might tell you, was after he'd read a book I pinched from my brother, called *Lolita*. I wish I had never lent it to him, even though he said he was only going to read the dirty bits. The chap in that book does it to practice shooting someone he hates and kills in the end. Tony thought it a madly original idea. Actually it's made him a pretty good shot. Oh, my lord!" Now she put her head down into both her hands and her hair straggled forward like a ragged curtain; misery obliterated her.

Nuri bey slipped away to put up an intransigent truckle bed. Of all the rooms in his house, he chose to put up the bed in the tiny turret room. The reason for this, he told himself, was that the other rooms were full of antiques, dusty and unused and entirely unsuitable for a young girl. The turret room was empty and clean.

It was also the room farthest away from his own.

"Jenny," he murmured now and again, "Jenny." Straight out of the *Oxford Book of English Verse* which he had studied at the University, and into his house . . . Jenny!

He clattered down the steep and narrow stair from the turret room and opened his mother's best linen press on the landing. From this he chose a long-haired cream-coloured rug worked into lattice pattern from the hair of Anatolian goats. Returning to the turret room he laid it first on the bed, and then on the floor beside the bed where it gave the room a more comfortable, even luxurious look, in spite of the sheet of brown paper which hung from one drawing-pin over the window and which was all there was in the way of curtains.

Downstairs again in his own room, he picked up the telephone receiver and dialled Miasma's number. It was engaged, as he had half expected; she spent a great deal of time talking on the telephone to her numerous friends and acquaintances. Many of them were so old that they had not been out of their houses for years but their friendship with Miasma was kept fresh and up-to-the-minute by telephone.

In the salon she was sitting as he had left her but when he came in she raised her smudged face and said: "Can I wash?"

Wash, there was a problem. Nuri bey was still confused with regard to the Western habits of washing. A great deal of washing was done daily here but Nuri bey understood that Western washing was of a different order, taking place less frequently but more extensively, at different times and not always, as Mohammed had ordained, in running water. After some quick thinking he remembered an early ewer, used in the Coptic Mass some three hundred years ago and still not leaking. He took this full of water, together with his red plastic washing-up bowl and an enormous lump of scrubbing soap up to the turret room and placed it on a tiny eight-sided mother-of-pearl Moorish table which he brought up for the purpose. Efficiency having taken complete hold of him, he also took from his mother's best linen press, her third best *hamam* towel, a splendid striped affair with a gorgeous fringe.

Finally, with the pride of the host, he showed her up to her room.

"You really are sweet to me," she said, looking round. "I always heard Turks were wild and woolly, but you're a pet."

"Wild and woolly," Nuri bey repeated, puzzled.

"Oh, never mind. It's only my careless talk. Oh, my lord, I'm so worried about Tony I hardly know what I'm saying!" She was carrying what Nuri bey was now thinking of as THE CASE, in capital letters. He watched her put it down.

"You have your night requirements," he murmured formally.

"I've nothing," she returned. "I left my case in the plane, everybody did who was in transit."

Nuri bey stared fixedly at THE CASE.

"Oh, that!" she said, following his thoughts. "It's Tony's. 'Here, take this a minute,' he said."

"He gave it to you in the transit lounge?"

She nodded. "It all happened so quickly I hardly know what *did* happen but it seems to me he passed it to me over the barrier: 'Hold this a minute,' he said. I took it and he walked away. I wasn't watching exactly but suddenly there was a frightful great bang, and several others. Of course, I knew it was Tony's revolver, I've heard the sound often and I turned quickly and saw him putting what I knew was his gun back in his pocket. He vaulted the barrier and shot out through the transit lounge on to the tarmac whilst everybody was standing wondering what on earth had happened. Then I saw the man lying on the ground and everybody started shouting."

Both of them stared down at the small case.

"What do you think?" she asked at last, turning her head and looking straight at Nuri bey, her huge eyes still blotched and puffy.

Nuri bey started back slightly. He was not in the habit of being asked so directly what he thought, and by a young woman.

"I suppose he shouldn't have handed me the case, but, you see, he told me to carry it back into the jet for him. I didn't think anything of it because, you see, he is a Zenobia Airways steward."

Having begged her several times to relax, to exclaim that the information made the situation even more serious and complicated would have been inconsistent and unkind. Nuri bey received this new jolt with no outward manifestation whatever.

It was clear from the way in which she was looking at the case that she was not without brains; it was also clear that she was considering it objectively for the first time. There was something about the way she was suddenly tense and avoiding his eyes that told Nuri bey she had ceased completely to trust him; loyalty to her wretched Tony now included loyalty to the case he had given her and she must already be regretting that she had mentioned it at all.

Both of them now stared down at the little fibre case fascinated as though it had suddenly taken upon itself a life of its own and was emitting sparks or blue smoke.

When she spoke, her voice was thinner and higher and shook slightly. "There's probably a pair of pyjamas in Tony's case, I'll use them, though I shan't need his electric razor." The feeble little joke was a complete failure and she hung her head so that her hair came forward to hide her embarrassment.

"Well, I'll say 'good night.' " She held out her hand, having the idea, apparently, that foreigners shook hands upon every occasion. "And thank you for being so very, very kind."

He took her hand and shook it as he did with all his European friends. "Good night, and try not to worry," he murmured, "too much . . . Jenny." The name stayed on in his mouth like a delicious sweetmeat.

On the way downstairs Nuri bey did what he did every night. He took from his room the heavy carpet-bag, the English travelling luggage of a well-to-do forebear, packed with his most valuable treasures, and carried it down to the hall where he left it behind the hanging Shirvan rug which in winter served as a curtain for the front door. No insurance company would take on Nuri bey's house, built as it was of inflammable old timber with the stove-pipe in the salon rising in the corner behind the white porcelain stove and running round two sides of the room before disappearing through the wooden ceiling. So Nuri bey took this simple precaution in order that he might snatch up at least some of his treasures as he raced for safety in the very likely event of fire.

Tonight, however, there was a slight variation to his usual procedure. After bolting the front door, he locked it and carried the key up to his room, where it spent the night under his pillow.

Chapter 3

HE WAS up at six, washing up under the cold-water tap and thinking over the wording of his report to Miasma. The slightest mishap would send her into a raging torrent of words which, by now, had no effect upon him at all.

Nuri bey was a great collector, not only of objects of art and beauty, but of human beings, and Miasma was one of the prizes of his collection. Though no details had ever been supplied, it was always understood that, in her early youth, by a series of mishaps, Miasma had missed being the *Validé* by inches. The *Sultan Validé,* or the mother of the Sultan, used to be the most important person in the whole great Turkish Empire, but jealousy and ambition for the position ran so high in the harem that any woman who did finally become the *Validé* earned all the honour that was due to her for sheer tenacity of purpose. She would, of necessity, have to be a woman beautiful, nubile and seductive, ruthless, cunning, single of purpose and satanically clever. Miasma had simply not made the grade. When the imperial harem was finally dissolved, she had emerged into the modern world with a few jewels and a yellow, hairless, dead-eyed eunuch as her only prize.

Gibbon called eunuchs "pernicious vermin of the East," but Nuri bey graded Hadji the chauffeur even lower, as a complete nonentity, and did not waste a moment's thought on him.

But Miasma fascinated him. It was said, as has often been said about the favourites of Sultans, that she had been a *hamam* attendant whose beauty had attracted one of the Sultan's agents and that she had been acquired by the harem. The *hamam* attendant's main duty is to rub the bodies of women who come for their bath and, as this rubbing is neither therapeutic nor skilled, the purpose of it is ambiguous. For a long time after being introduced

38

to the household, Nuri bey had believed that the relationship between Miasma and her French companion Valance
had been lesbian. But as he got to know them better, he
realised it was not so; Valance had not, in fact, been as
devoted to Miasma as it had appeared, but had been ad-
dicted to the money that was paid her and to the uncertain
glamour that was attached to the job.

Nuri bey treasured every manifestation of Miasma's
absolute conformity with the attributes of the women in
the Sultan's harem, which, notwithstanding the weight of
years which had passed, was untouched since she had
ceased to be an *ikbal* (the name given to those members
of the harem who actually slept with the Shadow of God
upon Earth).

There, he could say to such friends as were interested,
is the typical *ikbal*. Though she had a tiny mind, she was
clever, quick in the uptake and shrewd. No longer able to
attract men with her body, she kept up with world affairs
in order that she could attract them with her talk and
there was nothing she liked better than to have long
conversations with visiting statesmen of any nationality.
Though she appeared to be a thoroughly emancipated
woman, she was, in fact, not; there was not a trace of
dispassionate masculine outlook in her. Though he might
dislike her very much at times, he was proud to know
her and to have her for his collection.

That there was going to be a row about the errand to
the airport was certain, and he was undecided whether to
go and see her or to telephone the news.

Miasma found nothing important that was of the spirit;
everything that concerned her was trivial, in Nuri bey's
opinion. If she suddenly wanted something, she must have
it, be it a visit to a western film, a piece of jewellery,
a portable radio set, a lottery ticket, "I want it" was the
criterion.

Knowing this, Nuri bey had asked no questions about
the case he was to take to the airport. There had been
many similar trips to the airport, the seaport and the
railway stations over the years, undertaken by Hadji or
Valance. Once, he remembered, there had been an im-

mense fuss about a Pekingese sent to her from Hong Kong which, shortly after its arrival had fallen into the Bosphorus and been drowned. Another time it had been a French cook who, within a few days, had left to go to a friend of Miasma's who had offered him twice the money she was paying. There had been the China tea episode when Miasma had sworn she could drink nothing but tea from China and the customs had got very restive about the large quantities of tea, which appeared too frequently for their liking.

The import restrictions into the new Turkey were extremely strict and she was forever sending one or other of her servants to redeem from the customs parcels of various cosmetics she ordered abroad on which she had to pay large duty.

Thus Nuri bey's light-hearted undertaking of her commission now gave place to some grave misgivings. So far, the mere fact that the young man who met him had been armed with a revolver and had actually fired it at someone within two or three minutes of having spoken to Nuri bey, made him shiver with apprehension. You couldn't lightheartedly do that sort of thing in modern Turkey. A gunshot could easily tip off the start of a revolution. There were spies everywhere, the army was on its toes, ex-primeministers were about to be hanged for apparently ridiculous reasons and all Nuri bey wanted, apart from Oxford, was to be left in peace to pursue his speculative excursions into mysticism.

When the telephone rang in his bedroom above, he jumped so violently that he broke a tea-glass. Unwillingly, he went upstairs to answer it but, when he got there, he decided to let it go on ringing; he did not wish to have his early morning disarranged by the bullying tones he knew would scald his ear when he lifted the receiver. He let the ringing sound chip at his nerves till it stopped.

He tiptoed across the landing to the foot of the stairs up to the turret room. He could hear no sound.

He hated doing housework but, as he had not enough money to pay for a servant and to buy books as well, he chose to spend the money on books, and unwillingly and inefficiently undertook the housework himself. He now found a broom with a few bristles left in it and sprinkled green tea leaves on the salon carpet from the sink drainer in the kitchen. Next he flipped away in a small mist of dust at the worn old rugs. Then he got an equally dilapidated mop and neatly flicked the dust and tea leaves into a mother-of-pearl dust pan. Finally, he took out a feather duster that looked like the remains of a Red Indian's war hat, and touched it here and there about the room. He realigned his furniture exactly and lovingly, tidying the white raincoat by hanging it by the shoulders from a chair back.

Locking the front door carefully behind him, he left an old saucepan on the doorstep for the *sütcü* to fill with milk and went quickly to a shop not far away to buy food and, farther along, a newspaper. Walking back with the bread tucked under his arm, he read the headlines which amounted to the not-unfamiliar lines in an English newspaper: SEARCH FOR ARMED GUNMAN.

It was all there, everything except mention that the armed gunman had been an employee of Zenobia Airways. The identity of the gunman was unknown, it said, but the dead man had been identified as a detective on a brief visit to Turkey, who was one of the chief security officers of the airline. Under cover of darkness, the assassin had escaped from the airport and was believed to be hiding in the city. A short description of his appearance followed and an appeal was made to anyone who saw him to get in touch with the police at once. It was understood that Interpol was assisting the police in their search and that a sharp watch was being kept on all outgoing traffic, in the air, on land and by sea to ensure that the miscreant did not leave the country. An arrest was expected at any moment.

An Englishman or an American in the streets of Istanbul is as distinctive as an ostrich would be in a herd of goats. He wouldn't last twenty-four hours, in Nuri bey's opinion.

Arriving home, he spread the newspaper on the hall table and read it through carefully, making sure that there was no mention of a case or of an English girl. An eye-witness had told the reporters that the murdered man had been having drinks at the bar before the jet arrived. That he had been there from half an hour to an hour was confirmed by the bar attendants. After the arrival of the jet, the transit lounge had filled up with people, the bar had also been more crowded. A portable barrier had been erected between the people in transit and others who wanted to move to and fro in the lounge at will. Nothing more seemed to have been observed by anybody until the shot was fired and after that nobody seemed in a fit condition to take in with any sort of clarity what had happened. A man was lying on the ground and another man, short, thin, dark, young, in black trousers and a sports jacket, had been seen to jump the barrier, run through the crowd and out through the swing doors. Many of the men had started off in pursuit but once he was out on the tarmac he had vanished. A thorough search had been made with all the vehicles with headlights that were available, but it was fruitless. The victim had died in an ambulance on the way to hospital without regaining consciousness.

He ran his hand across his forehead; though no sweater, Nuri bey was certainly sweating now. He was a man of peace and his life was contemplative; he was simply not up to a quickened tempo, to dissembling, to the making of snap decisions, to the low cunning essential to the successful handling of a situation such as the one he had had forced upon him. He was no Knight Errant, nor Scarlet Pimpernel nor Sherlock Holmes; nor had he any wish to be any of these persons. He did not wish for events, for excitement, for novelty, for danger. His excursions into contemplation provided all the excitement he would ever need; his quest was for wisdom, not for ingenuity.

He had a sudden horrifying glimpse of himself driving about all over Istanbul with a tearful Jenny at his side, in a packed *dolmus* (or shared taxi) because he would not be able to afford any other kind of transport, searching, searching for an ostrich amongst a lot of goats. And when they found him, what then? Was Nuri bey to conceal him in his house until such time as they could both be smuggled out of the country, heavily disguised as *hamals,* or human mules?

Weak as a rag, he supported himself against his hall table. It wouldn't do. He must persuade Jenny to go to the police with him and tell them all she knew. And if she failed to do so, as he could well expect, then he would have to go himself and report that he was sheltering under his roof a young English girl who was closely connected with the missing assassin.

He prepared breakfast, laying the low table in the salon, muttering to himself the English phrases with which he would persuade, indeed insist.

As he went to and fro in his preparations, he sounded, and looked, like a man demented but not yet dangerous, and was startled and mortified to discover that she had been observing him for a few seconds before he noticed her standing in the shadow at the bottom of the stairs.

"I say, old dear, what's wrong? Do you always talk to yourself?"

Then there was a search for a looking-glass which Nuri bey knew he had somewhere; it turned up in a box in the woodshed outside and was more red-velvet frame stuck all over with shells than a mirror. He polished it lovingly. "It was with some books I bought. You should be able to get a good reflection; it has reflected many beautiful faces, it came from the old seraglio. Many things were stolen in the looting which took place."

They sat formally together in the salon and ate yoghourt and goat's cheese and bread and, as a special treat, drank Nescafé of which Nuri bey had been given a tin by his English friend at the British Council.

And when they had finished, he read extracts from the newspaper, then fired off some of the rolling phrases which he had been practising. Turkish women do not look directly at men, even now; their eyes slide away and Nuri bey, though he had met many European and American women, had never become used to the direct gaze they would give him. There was something particularly unnerving about Jenny's direct look; clear and unflinching and full of question.

"You don't really mean you're suggesting that we go to the police?"

"I do. If we do not, much worse may happen."

"You can't make me go!"

"I can telephone to them now."

"What would they do to me?"

Nuri bey faltered slightly. "They would question you. You would help them."

"And if I wouldn't answer?"

"They would keep you there till you did."

"Brainwash me?"

He shrugged.

"How could you be such a damn' beast? I thought you were a pet, now I see you're a terrible Turk."

"That is not kind."

"You don't mean it, do you? I can see you don't. I—" she took a great deep breath—"I would rather kill myself, and I mean it. I dare say you've often heard people threaten to do that, but I mean it. My life simply wouldn't be worth going on with if you did that . . . can't you understand?" she pleaded.

"I understand nothing," Nuri bey said firmly. "Nothing at all."

Suddenly she changed mood completely. "Oh, I know I need a good whipping, everyone thinks so and has said so thousands of times. All right, whip me, somebody, I don't want to be the way I am." She began to cry and Nuri bey tactfully kept silent whilst she cried.

"If you are innocent," he said sedately, as she was recovering, "you should willingly go to the police and tell them all you know."

"Innocent!" she cried, "what a goddam awful whiskery, mildewed, beastly, Victorian word." She blew her nose violently. "Innocent!" And if he wanted to know, she was not innocent, neither was she a virgin, she had been sleeping with Tony. She was not a nice young girl. What she did regret was that Tony had not trusted her, had not confided in her. That was what gave her such a shock. She had given herself to Tony and trusted him; why had he not done the same? For Tony's sake, she had left her family, her home, the job she had with a friend of her father's in an antique shop. She had given Tony everything a girl could possibly give a man, including all her post office savings. And she would have given him all her savings certificates, too, if it hadn't needed an assent from her father.

And what was left? As far as she could see . . . nothing. Her family had finished with her for good and ever. She had no money. No job. And, alas, not even her virginity was left to bargain with.

She could not use the rest of her ticket to go to Hong Kong because she did not know anybody in Hong Kong, nor did she want to go. She had simply agreed to go because Tony had said suddenly that it would be fun if they had a honeymoon-kind of trip to the Far East "for a few days."

She had thought, in fact he had told her so, that Tony was a high-powered sales representative who travelled all over the world. He had suggested sending her to the airport in the bus, telling her he would meet her "on the plane" because he had some last-minute business to do. Excited at the fun of this sudden treat, she had taken her ticket from him, packed a few clothes in a canvas grip and joyfully gone to the London air terminal.

She'd met him on the plane all right . . . wearing the striped cotton jacket of the Zenobia Airways stewards. It wasn't that she'd minded a bit that he was a steward, far from it. It was deceiving her she'd hated.

If that had been all!

And there wasn't even a return ticket from Hong Kong to London! She hadn't got the money to return home if she wanted to. She had just this seven pounds which was part of her earnings from temporary typing jobs from an agency in Bond Street. If Nuri bey wanted to send her back home, he would have to do so by train, "Goods," she added with a wisp of a smile, "or it might run to passengers' luggage in advance."

Nuri bey's eyes were brilliant. "What courage!" he breathed.

"There you go again! If there's any label to be stuck on me, it's *baggage*. It's no good, you can't make anything of me, Nuri bey, and you'll never make me go to the police, never. You see, I don't know anything. And my going to the police wouldn't help Tony, not as far as I can see." She toyed thoughtfully with her hair: "I've got myself in an awful mess, haven't I? Just the sort of mess that girls who *go wrong* are expected to get into. It's bad enough having pulled all this down on myself; I'm not going to get my family mixed up in it," she added sulkily, "much as I hate them."

Nuri bey, finger and thumb meeting in a precise point, tapped his pursed lips thoughtfully. He believed something of what she had told him, in fact, most of it, but he could not bring himself to believe that she was found with Miasma's case in her hand at the airport, knowing nothing whatever about it except that her lover had *handed it to her*. That . . . he could not accept.

"And if anybody in Istanbul, a reporter or a member of the British colony got hold of my name connected with this affair, it would be all over the English papers. As it is, I'm going to be reported missing."

"But not till the jet has arrived in Hong Kong, perhaps."

"Let's think." She put her hand into her skirt pocket and brought out a yellow ticket with TRANSIT printed on it. "They gave me this and told me to leave my things on the plane. When everyone got back into their places they would notice I wasn't there. Would they think I had anything to do with the gun episode . . . or not? Do they carefully count the passengers to see everybody is there? Or would they have been so upset by the whole thing that they simply didn't? Tony was one of them, one of the air crew! Oh, isn't it agony?"

Nuri bey at least looked extremely wise and profoundly knowledgeable but as he stared at her enchanting chubby face he was completely bewildered: woman or child? He was unable to decide. Her candour, her completely natural manner, her brash way of talking, her schoolgirl giggles, her intense femininity. . . . She was in a very serious position indeed and he thought that she fully understood; but if, in fact, she did, her manner certainly did not match the situation. She was not his idea, nor surely anybody else's, of a "young girl in distress"; she ought to be taken by the shoulders and shaken into her senses; he should tell her to stop making light of it because she could quite easily not get out of this "scrape," as she called it, *alive*.

The mere fact that she could groan: "Oh, isn't it agony?" showed him that she had not the slightest idea of the meaning of the word "agony."

Nuri bey remained thoughtful for a long time; it was not that he was deciding how to play it because he never played anything, he was always completely himself; but he was deciding, or trying to decide, what was the best thing to do.

What he wanted to say and what he ought to say worried him a lot. Firstly, he very much wanted to say that they should rid themselves of the idea that she loved this young man or owed him any loyalty. He wanted to tell her that in his opinion she was in love with love, with the idea of herself in love; if, in fact, she loved the young man, she would now be in real agony, not simply exclaiming that it was agony.

Secondly, he wanted to say that having disposed of the love side of it, they must do what would be best for her.

And thirdly, they must somehow get in touch with her family and assure them she was safe and on her way back to them.

But overriding all this was the certainty that to propose these things would be to blacken himself in her eyes.

And furthermore, Nuri bey faced the truth, as he always did because his life was spent in the search for truth, that he was now deadly afraid of Miasma. He had always been in awe of her because, though old, her craftiness was something out of the ordinary; now he was suddenly afraid that she was wicked as well as astute; he did not allow himself to formulate, in his own mind, wherein her wickedness lay but he was filled with an unease which stirred the small hairs along his spine and gave him an actual nausea.

To be excessively old and excessively cunning was, at best, an unpleasing combination, but now Nuri bey realised that she had been using him so that his act of simple friendship in going to her house weekly to read the papers to her had surely not been, as he had thought, simply the desire to keep in touch with world affairs.

But the most immediate problem was the case; he must examine the contents . . . at once. And this seemed to him to be the trickiest problem of the lot. If, as was almost certain, Jenny knew that it was the key to the whole affair, she was not going to leave him alone with it until she knew more about him. And if, as was also possible, she was entirely innocent, he did not want to draw her attention to it because, if it contained something of serious significance, it would be a great deal better for her if she did not know.

Or would it?

If she knew, it could have a salutary effect, as would the shaking by the shoulders he had contemplated, making her realise how serious her position was.

"Tony's going to be frantically worried about me," she went on, after a long pause, and Nuri bey hoped she was right. "The thing is, will he know I've had the sense to stay here, or will he think I've flown on? Because if he knows I'm still here in Istanbul he'll find me somehow, he won't rest till he does, I'm sure."

"He'll never find you here in this house," Nuri bey said firmly.

"Then I'll have to go out and find him." There it was, the expected.

"Don't be ridiculous," he snapped. "This is a big city of three-quarters of a million people; you could spend a lifetime looking for him and not find him." He did not, of course, believe this, but he believed that he should put that viewpoint to her. Amongst those three-quarters of a million people, Nuri bey had many, many friends; lawyers, a judge, doctors, members of the police force, brass hats in the Army and the Navy, schoolmasters, priests, *imams,* owners of stalls in the Covered Bazaar and the Spice Market, cargo boat owners, steamboat operators, waiters and restaurant owners, hotel directors, business men, museum attendants, roast chestnut sellers and many more.

From the ferrymen and fishermen at Eyup, at the far end of the Golden Horn, news of a missing young English gunman could, literally, be passed on the drums over that stretch of water and along the whole length of the Bosphorus coast on both sides, and quite some distance along the Marmora coast, too.

He could be out now, putting the news about, were it not that he must not leave Jenny alone with the case until he had inspected the contents.

Chapter 4

AND THEN, as though to underline how unused he was to this kind of thing, when the front-door knocker was banged he went straight to the door and threw it open with the expansive gesture with which he welcomed all comers to his house.

"Good day, Efendim, good day!"

Hadji stood there in his usual cowering and self-effacing manner and, seeing Nuri bey was at home, he went down the steps to the taxi at the gate and helped Miasma down. Nuri bey's smile of welcome faded but he hurried down the steps to help her mount them and it was only when all three had gained the top step and she was pressing forward into the house that he remembered that Jenny must not be seen. There was nothing he could do about it now; furious with himself he followed her into his hall, looking across to where he had left Jenny on the sofa in the salon.

Not only had she gone but she had taken away the remains of their breakfast on the tray.

Miasma began by saying that she had tried to telephone to him earlier and getting no reply she had decided it would be better to come in person; they had things to talk over which could not be discussed on the telephone.

She had been up all night; the delayed shock of Valance's death had prevented her sleeping. The funeral had taken place at an early hour, in fact the *imam* and his attendants had arrived before it was fully daylight. She had found the walk up the hill in the wake of the bier extremely trying; she had been obliged to pause for breath many times. However, it had all been well-timed. As the sun rose Valance's body was lowered to its resting place. And that was that.

She asked Nuri's forgiveness for such an early appearance, unannounced, but with the telephone unanswered . . . it had to be. It was many years since she had crossed the Bosphorus at so early an hour but here she was; they must now discuss the very serious occurrence at the airport last night. He would be thinking that it was a little strange that Miasma had not mentioned that the young man to whom he had to give the case was an Englishman called Tony Grand. But in fact it was not at all surprising.

The whole thing was, really, of no consequence at all, a frivolity, and she pronounced the French word with lightness and a flick of the fingers. A little *locum* for a friend in Hong Kong, Nuri bey had surely often heard Miasma speak of her, a Turkish woman married to a Chinese business man, the same woman who had so generously given her the beautiful Pekingese some years ago; a present of a little Turkish delight for which the native of Turkey longed. To think that the tiny gesture to please an old friend should have developed into this shocking accident had frightened her very much indeed.

"Accident!" he exclaimed.

"The poor young man evidently had a bad record, a guilty conscience, eh?" Seeing himself observed, she went on, he took fright, brought out his revolver and . . .

there it was. An accident. She was quite sure that he had not intended to do anything more than give everyone a nasty fright. It was a great pity, she went on smoothly, that Nuri bey, having put himself out to do something which in the ordinary way would have been entrusted to her companion, Valance, should have become involved. . .

So much talk and all so smooth and comfortable, as though she were talking to a half-witted child; she was insulting him, prattling along about *locum* for a friend in Hong Kong.

Slow to anger, Nuri bey was now convulsed with a wild rage. He was tense from head to foot and his face was grimly set. He held on to the back of a chair, using both hands, which seemed to want to act on their own impulse. With control he left the chair upon the ground and did not raise it above his head to bring it crashing down to the floor.

In a corner by the front door Hadji cowered.

"Yes, my lion," she soothed, not meeting his eyes nor looking into his grave face, but putting one of her small hands, like a dead mouse's tiny claw, on his arm. "I regret very much that you should have become so entangled. . . ."

Her voice tailed out because she had seen the raincoat, hanging over the back of a chair, where Nuri bey had spread it early this morning; the white raincoat which Jenny had worn last night when she left the transit lounge and stood at the exit, looking for a taxi in which to run away from the scene inside.

From then onwards she seemed to have changed into another gear. She seemed easier in her mind, more confident. "And so, Nuri, my lion, we must help this young man as far as is possible."

He collected himself. "It is no business of ours. If he lost his head and used a gun, it cannot possibly have anything to do with us. . . ." But she was staring so fixedly at the raincoat that he closed his mouth over a thousand unsaid things. What did she know about the raincoat? Was it in any way distinctive? Was it any raincoat left by any woman whom Nuri bey might have been entertaining for the night? Or as a guest for a meal the previous day? Or did it proclaim itself an Anglo-Saxon raincoat? Or was it that she recognised it as the raincoat of . . . Jenny?

The Turkish language is soft and sibilant, sounding like a lot of vowels with s and k as the only consonants, the dominant word always seeming to be *yok,* which means no, a very definite and final no.

Yok, Nuri bey now said, *yok, yok,* and again *yok.* He would have nothing more to do with the affair; it was none of his business. He was a well-known and respected citizen of Istanbul; it was quite impossible for him to mix himself in any anti-social business. And if the case was of such trivial importance as Miasma had implied there was no need for her to get any further involved either. They could now leave everything to the airline's security officers and Interpol.

He had not invited her to sit and he now wished to get her out of the house quickly whilst he was still able to keep his anger in control. She had moved across the hall but continued to stand, stroking the shoulders of the raincoat thoughtfully and he realised that he would have to fulfill the requirements of the owner of the house when a caller comes, he must offer something to eat or drink.

Hadji stood in the shadows by the door, a shabby and ludicrous figure. The Turks did themselves a great disservice when they discarded their robes for European dress; the lower classes are quite unable to keep themselves even reasonably tidy and well-groomed; their trousers are too wide and too long and made of such poor material that they soon go into holes so that nearly all Turkish trousers are patched to a greater or lesser degree; braces lose their elasticity, belts get lost or broken and more often than not the trousers are kept up only by the Will of Allah. The final result cannot possibly be called "European dress." As the chauffeur of a well-to-do lady, Hadji was a comic figure. Wearing a cloth cap, he stood with head bowed, hands thrust into each opposing sleeve; his thoughts apparently far from the present scene.

Nuri bey looked at him; in the ordinary way he would

have sent him into the kitchen to prepare coffee or tea but now he went himself, not to make tea, which would take too long, but to bring a dish of sweetmeats to offer his guest.

Jenny was standing at the open back door, holding one of the scraggy and pathetic kittens with which Istanbul is overrun. "Look," she cried as soon as he came in, "look at this poor thing . . . it's dying of starvation."

Nuri bey pressed his finger to his lips, shook his head, frowned and gently pushed her outside, closing the door. "Stay there," he hissed, "for a few minutes more."

He snatched up the dish of sweetmeats and opened the door into the hall only to encounter Hadji now standing immediately on the other side: listening, of course. He looked into his sad, old monkey's eyes and something he saw there caused him to keep the words he had been going to utter, something about the raincoat being the property of the wife of a professor friend who had called yesterday morning on his way through Istanbul, behind the barrier of his teeth.

Instead, he said to Miasma as he offered the sweetmeat: "All the same, I do not understand why you came. To come all this way to discuss what happened last night . . . I don't understand."

She gave her attention to the extremely sticky small piece of shredded wheat, soaked in honey. "I rang only to see if you were in. There are things one cannot discuss on the telephone," she declared. An absurd answer from someone who spent a large part of the day discussing everything and everybody with her friends on the telephone. Furthermore, getting no reply, why did she come knowing he must be out?

"You must accept, my friend, that by misfortune in carrying out a small favour, asked of you by *me*"—she tapped her own shrivelled chest to make sure that there was no mistake as to whom she referred—"you have involved yourself in something of international importance. One thing leads to another; in the strangest way Kismet suddenly has us caught in the web of destiny."

This form of speech sounds less absurd in Turkey

where Kismet, and Destiny and the Will of Allah are everyday words. Having finished the sweetmeat, she brought out a handkerchief from which came an expensive scent and dabbed her sticky lips. "Delicious, my lion." She tucked the handkerchief away in her crocodile handbag. "A tiny clot of blood in the brain of my poor Valance and the heavens can fall about our ears. Old Turkey and new Turkey, the difference is only superficial; underneath the thin coating of Western civilisation we are unchanged."

"But this has nothing to do with us. It was one foreigner wildly shooting another foreigner," Nuri bey almost shouted.

"Nonsense, my friend, it has everything to do with us; you cheat yourself if you think otherwise. I gave you a case with simple innocent contents. . . ."

"Why a shabby used case, Madame? If the contents were so simple why was it not a parcel of boxes of *locum* wrapped in the paper of the shop of Haci Bekir from which they were purchased, I take it?"

"*Because*—because that case is continually used by me to send *locum* to my friend in Hong Kong; she, in her turn, sends me bean shoots, soy sauce, tinned chow chow in thick syrup and other Chinese delicacies, which you, Nuri, have occasionally enjoyed in my house. With our absurd customs restrictions one cannot, as you should know, bring foreign consumer goods into this fiercely nationalist country. That small case has made many trips over the years, through the customs."

"Ah, a simple explanation, Madame. I thank you. Perhaps there is an equally simple explanation about how you come to know Tony Grand, a young steward in Zenobia Airways."

"Yes, you are right, there is an equally simple explanation for that. Tony Grand is a relative of a friend. . . ."

"All these mysterious friends," he exclaimed impatiently.

"You too have friends, many friends, Nuri," she returned, grieved but unruffled, " and if I remember rightly," she went on silkily, "you sent an illustrated Koran to a

friend of yours in Edinburgh by a friend of mine whom
you met in my house."

"That was to a professor friend of *mine* who had been
very kind and had me many times to breakfast at the
Hilton Hotel."

"You see? Do not attribute to the actions of others
a significance which you would never dream of attaching
to your own."

"But this particular person wasn't armed with a loaded
revolver," Nuri bey returned nastily, "and did not shoot
a detective in a crowded waiting lounge and then run for
his life."

The score now standing in his favour, he picked up the
raincoat, smoothed it affectionately and took it across
into the hall where he folded it slowly and carefully and
laid it gently upon the hall table.

"The raincoat of another friend, I suppose," she called
sharply.

"Certainly," he replied smoothly, "I return it to her this
evening."

She followed him and he felt considerably heartened
because she was now pulling on her long black gloves,
clearly on her way.

"There is no mystery, my lion. It is all perfectly simple."

"Everything is far from simple, Madame."

"But look, my friend, Valance was to perform a simple
task, one of many such small commissions she did for
me. She died suddenly, the poor soul, and I, having
made the arrangements, ask you to oblige me by doing
this small thing for me. May I remind you that the
body of my poor Valance was resting in my house overnight until her burial to-day at dawn; would you have
wished for me to be alone with the corpse whilst I sent
Hadji on this trivial errand? What could be more natural
than that I should ask you to do it for me?"

Nuri bey thought that it would have been a good deal
more natural to have forgotten the present of *locum* for
the friend in Hong Kong, under the circumstances.

As he did not reply she gave him a really dirty look

and tapped her fingers impatiently upon the green-satin-covered table top. "Why will you not tell me in detail what passed at the airport last night?"

"There is barely anything to tell. The young man approached me. . . ."

"What did you say to him?"

"I did exactly as you instructed me, Madame. In fact, he asked me first if I had come from Madame Miasma, and then he asked if 'the old woman' was ill. I asked which old woman. He said 'The French companion.' "

"What did you say, Nuri?"

"I was not sure if I should say she was ill or what I should say. But remembering your instructions I said nothing. The young man said *'Just one of those things'* in English. Up to then we had spoken English. This was an idiom I did not quite understand. However, he thanked me and took the case. He walked away into the waiting lounge, and that was the last I saw of him."

"From my standpoint the affair is innocent, simple, but in view of what actually happened . . . why are you keeping back information that might help us?"

"Help you in what way?"

"To understand what happened last night there, at the airport, and why."

"If it is all so simple and innocent we don't need to know. The man who was to carry out your tiny commission was a gunman, perhaps a dangerous lunatic. A detective has been killed. Your hand case has been lost."

He felt suddenly as though he were bullying. She was old and looked frail, though he knew she was not. The early start, the unaccustomed excitement were making their mark; she looked grey and pinched.

"I would like it back," she murmured mildly.

"If I had it, you should have it back," he said, almost gently now. "If I had it."

She gave his face a long searching look, which was a very unusual thing for her. "I do not understand you, Nuri bey." She turned away. "Come, Hadji," she said.

He stood at his door, watching them going down the steps to the waiting taxi, all his anger gone.

In the kitchen, pinned to the table with a sharp-pointed french cooking knife which Nuri bey used for chopping onions, was an envelope on the back of which was written in lipstick.

GONE OUT BACK SOON. J.

It was a used envelope and Nuri bey turned it round, thinking instantly that he would now have her English address and would therefore be able to communicate with her parents. But reading the address made him, somehow, less hopeful: Miss Jenny Bolton, The Three Diamonds Hotel, Greek Street, London, W.I. It sounded distinctly transitory and not very wholesome.

From what he knew of the English, which was a great deal because he made a study of that nation one of his minor interests, her parents would have an address something like: The Old Mill House, Wealdney, nr. Oxford. Class distinctions in that so-called classless country were less numerous than those of India, but at least as distinct and Nuri bey guessed that she came from an upper class, though not top class. He knew that a young woman in "The Old Mill House" class ought not to have "The Three Diamonds Hotel" in Soho as her permanent address.

The envelope bore an Italian stamp and was posted in Rome. It was probably from Tony Grand for whom Nuri bey felt an increasing dislike which could hardly be called unreasonable. If he could do anything which would help the authorities to take that young man into captivity, he would unhesitatingly do so. And with that aim in view he bounded out of the kitchen and up the stairs to the look-out room.

It was an ungentlemanly thing, he knew, to search a young lady's bedroom, but in a mood in which he would have been breathing fire if he could, he ripped the clothes off the truckle bed, smelling faintly of something very pleasant, snatched up the mattress, turned the bed upside down and shook it. He shook it because there was nothing else he could do; he shook it in anger, he shook it as he would like to shake Miss Bolton, he shook it until he was breathless. Shaking an old-fashioned truckle bed is a risky business, and what one would expect to happen happened. The skin of a finger of his left hand was trapped and he uttered a cry of mingled pain and rage. There are no really satisfactory oaths in Turkish but he let off all there were.

He tore downstairs, placed himself in the salon and reviewed the geography of the house: the hall was wide and square, the archway to the salon being on the right of the front door and the double doors into the kitchen beyond. At the end of the hall a hideous stained-glass window would show the patch of ground behind the house, if one could see through it. Beside this the stairs rose to the first floor.

He could see now exactly what had happened. From the kitchen she could easily slip upstairs unobserved and down again with the case and out by the back door, which Nuri bey hardly ever used and which was usually bolted inside. She had done this when he was plying Madame with sweetmeats, silently and swiftly.

Hadji, crushed in a corner beside the front door, might have noticed her, but one wondered if such a dim shadowy creature ever noticed anything.

To be outwitted by a woman is defeat indeed; he stood and let the blood from his injured finger drip on to his precious green-satin table cloth, defeated beyond defeat.

He never expected to see her again. In fact, he hoped he would not see her again; his feelings about her were so mixed that he felt he would be quite at a loss as to how to treat her. He no longer wanted her in his house, if, indeed, he ever had. He would rather house an unexploded bomb. Though she had certainly been in some distress at the airport, she had recovered with remarkable speed; he believed now that he was a great deal more upset than she. He believed now that she was enjoying herself and he was perfectly prepared to believe that the whole thing was a put-up job, planned to the second and himself a pawn, the man who happened to be on the spot at the time. At least saving her taxi fare into Istanbul, he thought, bitterly, because he could not afford to take private taxis for any distance.

He wrapped a handkerchief clumsily round his wounded finger and went into his study, the room opposite the salon, on the other side of the front door. As a hurt animal retires to its den to lick its injuries, Nuri bey closed the door and went to his bookshelves which lined the walls. He could be led blindfold to his study and pick out the book he required. Unerringly he brought out the book which he needed for his comfort; as soon as he had it between his fingers, peace flooded his soul and he knew security again. He knew the russet-apple colour of the binding and the feel of the smooth calf as a prelude to the calm wisdom of the Indian mystic between the covers. And even if he had not been able to hold it, he would have recognised the book as soon as it was opened by the faint smell; not as delightful, he thought, as the smell of a young lady's bed, recently vacated, but much, much more familiar, and therefore safer.

In a formal upright chair, his long legs elegantly crossed, he read on, assimilating an enormous amount of unpractical wisdom. He read on, through the day, past the time of the midday meal, on into the late afternoon until his face was smooth again and his eyes once more upon the stars.

He had not rebolted the back door, perhaps deliberately, and perhaps his ears had been alert for a sound all the time; the wise can be strangely sentimental. He neither moved nor allowed his eyes to raise themselves from the printed page when he heard the door bang.

She was back, that was what mattered, he could hardly be bothered to look up from the book when she burst in: "This is where you are? Oh, gosh! I'm absolutely worn out!"

She flounced herself down into a chair and kicked off her shoes. "Look what I've bought." She held up a pair of French-type espadrilles. "I had an awful job finding some. I couldn't teeter about the quite awful streets in these silly shoes, so I went round and round, and where do you think I found these? In the Spice Market! An absolute pet of an old man picked them out of a pile; they're second-hand . . . do you think I'll get foot rot or something?"

Nuri bey had not got up when she came in; he looked at her, finger and thumb pointed, tapping his lips, thoughtfully. He was packed with wisdom now and felt he could deal with any situation.

"I love finding my own way about a foreign town; when I asked one man where a bank was where I could change some money, he couldn't speak English, and asked another, and he couldn't speak English either. But we lined up and went along till we found someone who could and he said, 'Come along, I'll show you,' and so he and I and the first two men I'd asked all marched along in single file, up and down filthy little alleys, up and down steps, and past stalls until we came out into a street that looks a bit more decent than some, and there was a bank. And we all bowed to each other and said fearfully polite things and they called me 'Efendim' or something . . . I was quite sorry when they went. But it's not like Italy, is it? I mean they don't pick you up and stick and stick until you want to kick them."

"Indeed," Nuri bey said.

"I love the Turks," she went on enthusiastically, "they're so kind and considerate. I had to go and look inside a mosque; several men hurried up to tell me to take off my shoes, which of course I did. I say, aren't the mosques marvellous inside! All those wonderful carpets! It looks as though several huge tanks of paint in different shades of red and orange had been upset all over the floor; the red kind of *flows,* doesn't it, all round the pillars and all over the huge, huge floor . . . are you cross with me, Nuri bey? It was rather rude, but you were having such a session with that old lady, I thought I'd hop it and go exploring on my own."

He said nothing.

"You are cross! Please don't be!" She jumped from her chair and came, barefoot, across to him, bending over and kissing him warmly on his smooth, cool cheek.

She sat down on the floor, shining up into his face: "And the kittens, Nuri bey! Staggering about *dying*. I was going to bring one home, back here I mean, and had it under my arm, but I saw hundreds of others, wandering about the forecourts of the mosque; I put it down when I saw one in worse condition but, do you know, it died as I carried it. I found I was carrying a dead kitten! And they are mostly tiny kittens, not cats, and they are so sweet, their eyes are absolutely pathetic; don't they ever grow to cats?"

There was a pause. "Nuri bey, do say something. I'm afraid you're really cross. Don't you trust me? You're thinking about the case, aren't you? Do you think I've been seeing Tony, giving it him by pre-arranged plan?"

She leaned forward, peering into his face, her hair falling forward and she pushing it back impatiently. "Because I haven't, I promise you I haven't."

He might have said a great deal but the kiss had knocked the punch out of him, he was winded, out for the count.

"You don't believe me, do you? Well, I think last night took all my wish for adventure away, at least, for the moment. I've done something safe . . . the sort of thing my family would do. They would call it 'playing for safety,' it's something which I vowed I'd never do. And now I have. I chucked the beastly thing in the river."

"River?"

"Over the bridge; where the river runs out into the Bosphorus."

"Over Galata Bridge?"

"I suppose so."

"The river was not a river, it is the Golden Horn."

"That's a very glamorous name for it; it looks like the Manchester Ship Canal. Anyway, it sank, and several people shouted at me; I didn't understand, I made sure it sank, it was quite heavy, and I left the scene of the crime, as they say, pretty hurriedly."

"Perhaps it is as well," Nuri bey said heavily, "a great many things, people and things, which cause trouble, end up in the Golden Horn . . . or the Bosphorus."

"And after I'd done the dirty deed I went across some rough ground, through some filthy puddles and into a sort of slum where there was a shop selling Turkish Delight! I pointed and he gave me a box, I held out some money and he took it and gave me change; they're very honest, aren't they? The shop is called Haci Bekir and I gather it's *the* place for *locum*. Anyway, it's heavenly! Much, much nicer than English 'Turkish Delight.' It's stiffer and lasts longer and it's got delicious fresh nuts in it. I'm afraid I ate the lot; it was about lunch-time. And after that I went into a café over the bridge, near the Spice Market, and had some tiny glasses of tea. There were nothing but men in the café and they did stare, but not to worry, everyone was marvellously civil."

Nuri bey was coming to life, the wisdom was receding and a delightful warmth was creeping over him.

"Oh, what have you done to your finger, old dear?"

He looked down at the blood-stained handkerchief; the wound no longer hurt and he had forgotten about it. She unwrapped it, made sympathetic noises.

Later, in the kitchen where she had held his finger under the tap, they found some clean cloth, tore it into strips and rewound the injury.

"Don't go upstairs," Nuri bey said, "there is the mirror there, in the salon, where you can tidy yourself. We are going out. I shall take you to supper in a little restaurant near the Tulip Mosque, and we will eat a dish called 'The *Imam* Fainted'!"

Chapter 5

THE RESTAURANT to which he took her could hardly be recognised as such; it was a mere hole in the wall and, at first glance, looked like a den of thieves, full, as it was, of men with faces like Ali Babas' talking together in a manner that they might have used when planning a particularly bloody revolution, but were, in fact, merely gossiping as mildly as old wives at the well.

Nuri bey ordered *raki,* a strong spirit, gentler but with a more insidious and lasting effect than the Scandinavian schnapps which it resembles.

"And now you will tell me about Oxford, please," he demanded and she obliged in the way he would have wished. Gently prompted, she talked about the public-house clinging to the tiny scrap of medieval turf in the quiet heart of the city, of the Best Bookshop in the World, of the hot-dog stall which came to roost most evenings at ten o'clock outside the Taylorian, of the sobriety of the Martyrs' Memorial.

And in return he told her about his father who had been one of the last of the Dancing Dervishes, a member of an esoteric Moslem fraternity called Mevleir who would dance themselves into frenzies and ended up in a queer trance-like state "more metaphysical than physical."

He told her about the old woman who had come to visit him that morning, Madame Miasma, and how she had very nearly become the *Sultan Validé.* How she lived in a *yali* on the Bosphorus and how he went to read the newspapers to her each week.

"Who was the old man she had with her?"

"That," was his delighted answer, "was her chauffeur, one Hadji who was in her time a servant and attendant in the Sultan's harem . . . a eunuch, in fact."

They sat in a small yard at the far end from the entrance; there was room in it for four tables, it was lit by oil-lamps hanging on the whitewashed walls. Several small starving cats wandered about; the waiter brought earthenware dishes containing a delicious sizzling mixture with chicken and cheese and aubergines and onions. And afterwards they ate a kind of rum baba, very sickly and bad for the figure.

"I'm having a lovely time," she said, "I oughtn't to, ought I, with poor Tony on the run somewhere? I should be frantically worried; in fact, I am, though I don't look it." She sipped her strong sweet coffee appreciatively. "Fiddling while Rome burns, and all that. But what can I do?"

"Do you speak French? French is more popular than English here; we do not find English easy."

"You speak it perfectly, though rather carefully as though you had learned it from a book. Yes, I can speak French." She smiled. "That was one of the things the family have against me. My sister Daphne went to a finishing place in Paris, madly expensive, and had a ghastly time. She never went out except on a lead."

"I beg your pardon?"

"I mean metaphorically speaking. She loathed it. So when my turn came, I said I wasn't going, and I arranged to go to a French family in Touraine and I didn't speak a single word of English for six months . . . the result is that I can speak good French, but the family darkly say it was that that started it all."

"Started what?"

"Started me going off the rails."

"I see." Nuri bey was on her family's side but wisely refrained from saying so.

She looked round at the other customers. "Oh, my lord, I wouldn't dare to come in here on my own! I'd be scared out of my wits."

"Some are students in the university which is nearby. I come often; I spend much time at the second-hand book shops. The university library, too, is just up the road. If you are safe anywhere, you would be safe here in Istanbul," he said sternly, "Moslems are on the whole peace-loving people. They do not stick a knife in a back without very good reason; they do not have drunken brawls in cafés because Moslems are not alcohol consumers."

"That does sound pompous," she returned, "and I must say for a country of teetotalers, you've got a fine national drink . . . here's to *raki*!"

Walking back across Galata Bridge, she stopped to look. The moon was up, making a wide highway across the water. The lighted ferry boats caused great stains across the night sky with clouds of filthy black smoke from the poor quality fuel, their headlamps made fan-like sweeps of light in front of them, warning fishing-boats of their approach. There was much activity and noise.

"You couldn't call it beautiful exactly," she said, "but it is certainly fascinating!" and then she suddenly seized Nuri bey's arm and squeezed it. "Thank you for being so kind; it has been a wonderful evening. What can I do for you?"

She kept her arm in his as they walked on and Nuri bey went to some trouble to conceal his extreme pleasure. "You can, in fact, do something for me, you can read to me."

"Aloud?"

"Why not?"

"No reason why not . . . I'd like to. Of course I will."

As they walked on, up the long and tedious hill to Taxim Square she said: "The streets crowded with seething masses of people and I may have passed Tony for all I know. I'm sure he's here, Nuri bey. He must be. Big cities are much the best places to hide. If he'd made any attempt to leave the country he would have been caught, he wouldn't dare. Poor Tony, perhaps this will cure him of boredom."

"Boredom?"

"Yes, he's bored, that's what is wrong. Not wicked, merely bored."

"Boredom is a state of mind," Nuri bey said, "I do not understand how anyone can be bored."

"You're lucky. Lots of young people are bored, I suppose because they have never been taught how not to be, and you should remember that when you start thinking how wicked some of them, us, are. Anyway, Tony won't be bored now!"

"Are you going to marry Tony . . . or, I should say, were you?"

"Well, that's a moot point."

"What is that, moot point?"

"At first I didn't think I wanted to settle down and get married and start a life of eternal nappy-washing. But now I'm beginning to think there is something to be said for it, for being settled, I mean." They walked on, still arm in arm. "And I'm kind of used to Tony. I thought I knew him very well."

"No, you do not know him very well. He has deceived you completely."

She sighed. "Don't let's talk about it, only you started it, asking me if I want to marry Tony."

As they approached his house Nuri bey began to worry over what he was going to do about the torn-apart bed in the turret room. Maybe if he left it, she would merely think it was a particularly thorough bed-airing.

"It's not too late to read to you now for a bit, if you'd like."

Yes, he would like it very much. The house was in darkness and there was no street lighting near enough to be of any use. The big plane trees growing lavishly out of the hard flat earth-patch that was his garden, were coming into leaf; moonlight lit the way up the front steps. He unlocked the front door and they went inside.

"You really feel you could read now? It is nearly midnight!"

She nodded. "Yes, after that glorious meal and the lovely drink I'm not a bit tired."

"Very well." His face alight with pleasurable anticipation, Nuri bey went into his study.

"My library," he said proudly.

"Whilst you are deciding what you want me to read, may I go and see if that kitten is still outside, round the back?"

"Of course, the back door is bolted but you know how to undo it. There is a little yoghourt left in the big jug on the table, you can give the wretched animal some if you like."

When she had gone through the doors into the kitchen, Nuri bey dashed upstairs, two at a time and hurriedly restored order to the chaos in the turret room, remade the bed and slipped downstairs; it took him about four minutes. He went into the study; what would he choose for this treat? Something by Sir Thomas More, perhaps? Or a letter of Saint Augustine? Or a page from this book by Bertrand Russell? St. Francis's Canticle of the Sun? Like a connoisseur walking round his wine cellar in happy anticipation, Nuri bey went from book to book: this? or this? or this? At last he decided: Milton's *Paradise Lost*. He smoothed it between his hands, opened it and smelled the inside. Then he sat down in his upright chair, crossed his long legs and dipped into it at random, read a few words and rolled them about in his mind like the same connoisseur tasting the wine. And time passed, as time will, and presently Nuri bey wondered why she did not come. He rose and went into the kitchen. The light was on, the door wide open.

"Jenny," he stood on the back doorstep and called: "Jenny!"

The small dirt track that was his back garden or yard could only be approached from the front through a small rickety wooden gate in the fence that divided front from back.

A black and white kitten, its stomach meeting in the middle so that it looked as though a giant thumb had pressed its sides together and they had stuck, staggered up out of the tortuous shadow of the tree branches which the moon drew on the hard earth. It opened its mouth very wide so that all its face became a great open mouth, like a lion, and from it came the smallest sound, intended for a miaow but the frailest cry imaginable. Nuri bey kicked it aside slightly because in Istanbul no one takes any more notice of a starving kitten than of a fallen leaf.

He stood in his domain, realising she was not there. He pushed the gate between the front and the back; it was hanging from a rusty hinge and would only just swing open and it did so with some small effort.

Not believing what he was being forced to believe, he tore upstairs again to the look-out room. It was as he left it. There was not a trace of her. She had had her handbag with her all evening and he had made her take the white raincoat, carrying it himself over his arm, because the nights became cold. She had worn it walking back, and when she had left him to go out to the kitten in the yard.

Not a trace. It was as though she had never been.

Had she, in fact, ever been?

Leaving the back door yawning open to the chilly night air he returned to the study. The kitten entered the kitchen and walked round, weaving in and out between the table legs, and round and round. And Nuri bey sat stiffly in his upright arm-chair, his legs crossed, *Paradise Lost* upon his knee, opened where he had left it, his eyes fixed on the page, but reading not a word.

He was listening for the bang of the back door as she came in.

Hours later he was still sitting, stiff, cold, taut, upright, mentally feeling himself all over to find out how much he was hurt; and he was hurt very badly indeed.

Chapter 6

IT IS not easy to realise, in Istanbul, that one is in Europe (the scrag-end of Europe somebody has called it). Nor is it correct to say that one feels oneself to be in the East or Near East. Neither Eastern nor Western, it has a strange exotic flavour of its own, at times deadly dull and at other times causing such a penetrating wave of emotion that those who feel it never forget it nor do they get quite the same thrill anywhere else. It is as though one suddenly gets on to the beam and feels the vibrations of the atmosphere still oscillating from the terrible and fabulous events which have taken place on those few square miles inside the great Roman walls.

Jenny, the English girl who liked to think of herself as a beatnik (i.e. one who is non-emotional, non-intellectual, non-social, amoral and likes it . . .) and who was, in fact, nothing of the sort, went down the few steps from Nuri bey's back door and stood in the back yard making small sounds to attract the kitten. She was not an imaginative girl but perhaps the *raki* she had drunk increased her awareness; she was suddenly seized in the grip of a cold fright. No traffic passed in the quiet by-road, no light shone from any of the houses in the immediate vicinity, only the moon shed a particularly brilliant radiance and made more defined the shadows on the ground.

This was how she later described her experience to Nuri bey.

There was a sharp hissing sound such as unfortunate people who were not in the know, at one time used to summon waitresses; a sound made frequently in Spain by men when they think they have escaped a woman's notice. She heard it at once and as it was repeated several times she stood literally shivering with fright.

"S-s-s-s!" It was as terrifying as a snake hissing from the grass in its implication of danger. One cannot really look into a snake's eyes because they are often so widely separated that one only looks into one at a time; Jenny found she was looking at the fence through which a pair of close-together eyes were staring at her. Now that it had achieved its aim the hissing stopped and became: "Toh . . . nee, Mademoiselle, Toh . . . nee!"

His cloth cap having prevented him pressing face to fence, Hadji now replaced it, pushed open the rickety gate and came into the yard. He indicated by a strange flapping in his own direction of the finger-half of both hands, that he wished her to come with him. "Toh . . . nee, Toh . . . nee!" he went on as though that were the particular noise made by the animal that was he.

Jenny pulled herself together remarkably quickly. *"Je rentre dans la maison . . . un moment,"* she tried to excuse herself.

"Mais non, Mademoiselle, viens avec moi!" and a long thin hand took her not firmly but quite gently by the wrist. *"Il ne faut pas rentrez. . . ."*

"Nuri bey . . . "

"Non, non, venez vite! Plus tard, plus tard . . .!"

Later when trying to explain her actions, Jenny said she thought that Tony was immediately outside, waiting in the road, and dare not approach the house. The whole

thing appeared to her then so immediate that there was
no moment of decision—shall I or shall I not go? Tony
was there and wanted to see her: she went.

Tony was not immediately outside but apparently in
a car which was parked in deep shadow some little way
up the road, an anonymous car, hired as it turned out
later, and driven by a hired chauffeur under the direction
of Hadji who knew his Istanbul to the last block of
reinforced concrete.

Once out in the road and hurrying towards the car,
she remembered Nuri bey, waiting for her with the chosen
book in his study, but knowing that she would return
immediately to tell him, at least, that she was going out,
she said nothing and, full of curiosity, allowed herself
to be guided, still held by the wrist, to the waiting car.

Only when Madame Miasma leaned from the car and
started talking in rapid French did she hesitate, saying
that she had left Nuri bey's door wide open, and she must
return to him for a few moments.

But no, Madame said, Nuri bey must not know, he
would insist on coming too and Tony's life was in danger.
They must do nothing that would attract the attention of
any more people than was necessary. She must come;
Madame would immediately telephone to Nuri bey to
explain the sudden absence.

Afterwards she remembered that Hadji had really put
a hand on her behind and literally pushed her into the
car; she often had plenty of time to wonder why she had
not turned and kicked him where it would hurt most. As it
was, she yielded to the excitement and immediacy of the
moment and sat in the car beside Madame, Hadji taking
a place in the front beside the driver and the car hurtling
off down the road, past Nuri bey's house, out into the
main road and away.

A torrent, a flood, a volcano of Turkish flowed over
Jenny.

The girl *and* the case, Madame had evidently told
Hadji, and now here was the girl and no case. What was
the good of the girl without the case? She could go and
throw herself into the Golden Horn for all Madame cared

about her, but the case! Once more Hadji had proven himself an inadequate, stupid, impotent, idiotic, unimaginative, careless, lazy, incompetent, verminous, vicious, weak, infidel; a faithless, untrustworthy, disloyal, incompetent mongrel; a contemptible, abject, rascally, inglorious half-wit.

The chauffeur driving the hired car drew his head into his body, so that he had no neck which would be seared by the bitter wind which blew about him.

Turning to Jenny, with a widening of her lips which can only be described as a rictus, Madame said:

"Eh, alors, ma petite, où est ta valise?" and then impatiently, as Jenny appeared not to comprehend, *"Le sac à main, ma fille, la valise!"*

"Oh, that! Madame, please, where are we going?"

Madame pushed her face so close to Jenny's that Jenny could no longer focus; she smelt overpoweringly of her expensive scent, the merest whiff of which, Jenny said later, would turn her faint and sick ever afterwards.

"Madame, where is Tony?"

"Mademoiselle, where is the case?"

"What can that possibly have to do with you?" Jenny asked to gain time.

"It has everything to do with me. Tony was the messenger who was to take the case to my friend in Hong Kong. I gave the case to Nuri bey to take to the airport. . . ."

"Nuri bey!"

"Nuri bey, whom I have known for many years, an old and trusted friend."

"Nuri bey," Jenny repeated, almost ready to burst into tears.

"Ne dites pas, Nuri bey, Nuri bey, comme ça, it has no significance whatever. He went to the airport for me because my maid Valance died and was buried early today. Valance would have gone . . ." Madame's face, illuminated by the weird quality of the street lighting, became suddenly quite hideous, falling into a mould into which it must have fallen many a time when she was alone, a pattern of face such as no one should ever show to anyone else; a face of hate.

Jenny gasped. The taxi-driver turned round disregarding oncoming traffic: "Where to go?" Madame told him and it seemed they were quite near, he turned off suddenly and pulled up outside the new building with a large waiting hall for the Bosphorus ferries.

From what was obviously habit, Hadji slipped into place at Madame's side and helped her up the stairs and into the now empty waiting hall.

"You are taking me to Tony?"

"No, I shall not take you to Tony until I have the case."

"Then you got me away from Nuri bey on false pretences!" Jenny said in French. "Tony knew you before; he went to your house from the airport and asked you to take him in. That's it, isn't it?"

"Where is the case?"

"He's at your house, isn't he? And as your house is on the Bosphorus, as Nuri bey told me, you can arrange for him to slip away, perhaps by fishing-boat. So, you are with us, is it not? It must be so. You are taking me to him so that I can slip away with him, because Tony wouldn't let me be here alone; he wouldn't go away leaving me here to . . ." She hesitated, trying to think of the French for "hold the baby" but giving it up and merely saying in English: "I ought to have known Tony wouldn't let me down."

"You are partly right; I see you are not without brains, but you have made a mistake if you think I must do anything for you. I do not admire either of you two young people, and you particularly, my girl, mean nothing to me. Tony Grand means something to me because he has . . . let us say, helped me many, many times. I shall continue to help him but you I can destroy completely if you do not return to me the case."

"How?"

"By taking you to the police and saying that you are the girl of Tony Grand."

Though she winced, Jenny kept her head: "You would not dare do that; they might ask you what was in the case."

"You know, then, what was in the case?"

"Locum, mostly," Jenny said smoothly, admiring her own reply. "I must say . . . that there is rather a bit of fuss being made about four boxes of Turkish Delight, isn't there?"

Hadji had not sat when they sat but stood before them, looking from one to the other, clearly understanding the French they spoke.

It was probably the *raki,* having an enduring effect, which made Jenny think she was successfully playing the part of beautiful female accomplice. "Hurry up, Madame," she said impatiently, "it is becoming late. I need to sleep."

"Sleep! You shall not sleep until you have told me where the case is and promised that you will return my property to me at once."

"Oh, I see," Jenny murmured in English, "brainwashing!"

"What was that?"

"Madame, I cannot return the case to you. . . ."

"Why not?"

She had an idea. "Why not send Hadji to Nuri bey's house for it?"

Madame took Jenny's hands in hers and shook them emphatically as though to be sure of getting something into her head. She loathed the touch and tried to release her fingers. *"Laissez, laissez!"* she cried, unnerved.

"Whilst you were out with Nuri bey this evening, Hadji climbed into the house through an unlocked window. He may believe his house is locked up but he is too un-practical a man to secure it properly; besides, Nuri bey has no enemies, no one would rob him. I sent Hadji into his house to recover *my* property, *mine,* understand?"

"And he did not find it?"

"No, because you have hidden it somewhere in that house. Oh, I know, you cannot fool me!"

"I shall tell Nuri bey," Jenny returned indignantly, "you had no right to break into his house!"

"And you have no right to retain *my* property. Hadji waited for you outside until you both came home, he intended to enter again when Nuri bey was asleep, to wake you and to ask you to let him have the case. It would have been the better way, *my* way, but the fool chose his way. So now you must tell me exactly where he can find it; you shall not return to Nuri bey until I have it." And, as an afterthought she added, almost absently, "Nor shall you see Tony, either."

Jenny looked wildly round; this was ridiculous. She could easily push the two old people aside and run for it. But it was quite certain that if she took the contemplated action she would end up in the police station and, as Nuri bey had told her at some length, Turkish police stations are not like English; it is very unpleasant indeed to be locked up in Turkey.

"Madame," she said at last, as though preparing to be reasonable, as, indeed, she was. "I cannot return your property to you. I did not know it was yours. I only knew that I did not want to have it any longer. I threw in into the water, over the bridge."

The old woman shook her head. "Do not try," she begged, "to fool me."

"It is quite true, I swear it."

The old woman went on shaking her head so that Jenny wildly wanted to hit her. "You wouldn't do that with my valise. It was worth too much."

"Worth too much!" It was as though Jenny's heart seemed to contract she said afterwards, for here, in so many words, was the thought that had haunted her. Tony shot and killed not for fun, not because he was trigger-happy, as she had told herself, but because that for which he was shooting was *worth too much!* And she threw the case over the bridge into the Golden Horn not because it was worth so little but because it was *worth so much!*

The lighting in the waiting hall was ghastly at any time but now Jenny's face was almost pea-green from the shock she had given herself.

"Very well," Madame said, "if you will not tell me . . ."

"I have told you," Jenny almost shrieked.

"If you will not tell me truthfully I shall be compelled to show you what will happen to your Tony if you do not."

"Happen to him . . ."

"Do you love your young Tony?" Madame leaned forward and leered into her face, Jenny shrinking back as far as she could go and not answering because fear was catching at her throat.

Madame turned to Hadji and gave a long speech which seemed to be some kind of instructions. Hadji muttered a few assents and presently went, slipping away down the stairs like the inconspicuous shadow that he was.

Madame leaned back, tucking her hands into the wide mink-edged sleeves of her black satin coat. "It is fortunate," she observed, "that I am not too tired, though I have had a very tiring day. I can go without sleep like a camel can go without water. We shall be here for the few hours that remain of this short night, so make yourself comfortable, Mademoiselle." She was fumbling with something which turned out to be a small revolver.

"*Regardez,* is it not pretty?" She turned it over so that she could admire the mother-of-pearl handle.

"This," Madame said helpfully, "is the safety-catch, which is on now. I find it easy to use. If you attempt to run away, my small girl, I will shoot you in the back. *I* shall not sleep, but you may . . . there is nothing else you can do."

Jenny thrust her hands into the pockets of her white raincoat. All this was frustrating and rather nasty but what was she worried about? It was authentic adventure in that it had the real element of danger in it. When friends returned from holidays abroad and told travellers' tales of being held up by bandits near the frontier, it all sounded heroic and fine and Britain-keeping-a-stiff-upper-lip; but all along you knew that they knew that they were not in any real danger; that their adventure had not the rancid smell of death. And when she read in the newspapers that a couple of undergraduates with a girl friend had been imprisoned for suspected espionage in a Communist country, she was filled with envy. So why worry? There were implications that something big was behind all this: she might be involved in an international incident and when she got back home the newspapers would be falling over themselves to get her story, offering vast sums of money.

She looked down at the bent old woman crushed into the wooden seat beside her, blinking the lashless lids of her eyes like a thoughtful tortoise. It was Madame Miasma who made her sick, who was spoiling this adventure for her; without her the adventure would be fun, with her there was something sickening and terrifying about it. It was the combination of old age with extreme cunning and greed, that she found so repellent. It was the mixture of old age with hate which turned people into witches, and if ever there was a witch to the life it was Miasma.

"Yes, what is it?"

"You promised to telephone to Nuri bey!"

"Hadji has gone to do that."

Liar, Jenny thought. She looked at her clothes, black satin coat with a mink collar, black lace mantilla over her blue hair, rings on her fingers to the number of seven in all, a three-strand necklace of pearls round her neck.

"Why are you staring at me?" she snapped suddenly.

"I was comparing you with my great-grandmother," Jenny answered shakily. "I am surprised that you can be bothered with all this plotting and planning and arranging . . . at your age!"

"Why at my age?"

"So near death, you ought to be waiting peacefully, with folded hands, not clutching a revolver ready to shoot me in the back. I mean, it's absolutely laughable; my great-grandmother will never believe me when I tell her."

"Tell her! You will be lucky if you ever see her again."

"There you go!"

There was another long silence during which she was evidently thinking over what Jenny had said. "There is yet another difference between your great-grandmother and me, my child. Your great-grandmother was always looked after."

Jenny considered. "Yes," she conceded finally, "I suppose that is so."

"And I—I have had to fight every inch of the way."

"What way?"

"The way into society, into the good life." *La vie belle,* she called it. "I was born nothing, simply another girl wanted by no one."

"Like the kittens here in Istanbul!"

"Exactement! Like the little cats. But much, much worse, I was ugly. If you are beautiful, everything will come your way, everything. If you are ugly and born as I was, you have to fight for your woman's rights inch by inch."

"Not always," Jenny put in uncomfortably, wondering about her own looks, "if you are reasonably pleasant, things aren't too bad!"

"Pleasant!" Miasma exclaimed with an excoriating sneer. *"Voyons!* A woman must have either money or looks."

"I have neither."

"Exactement," she agreed nastily. "That is no doubt why you are in the position in which you now find yourself. And as for death, which you said I am so near . . . who knows who is the nearer to death . . . you, or me?"

Jenny felt cold and unhappy. "I suppose you think that if I had been beautiful, or an heiress, Tony wouldn't have . . . abandoned me, like this."

"Yes, that is so."

"So you think Tony was never more than mildly attracted by me and that, when the point came, he used me as a stooge?"

"I do not know what a stooge is."

"He made use of me, if you like."

"Yes, I think so."

"You think that is why he asked me to go to Hong Kong with him? Just so that, if necessary, he could make me carry the case back on to the plane for him?"

"Certainly. He must have been warned that the security regulations were being tightened and that a more careful watch was being kept on the crews. Or maybe he knew the detective who was waiting in the lounge bar."

"I see. Then you don't think he loves me at all."

She replied with a shrug. "Go to sleep, my girl," she said, "you have a long day in front of you, you will need rest."

"The day won't be one second longer than any other day!" Jenny snapped back irritably.

"Perhaps not," Miasma returned smoothly, "perhaps I should have said, trying day."

Jenny stared out moodily at the black, heaving Bosphorus. Tony . . . Tony . . . Tony . . . she thought of him dispassionately: short and slim and dark, his face tanned; his dissolute looks, fascinating to some women; the hare-lip with which he had been born, well operated on, the final effect being to give his mouth a hitched look so that he always seemed to be very slightly jeering; his nasal voice with the faint American accent fashionable now amongst some young people. Not a man's man, not wholly a woman's man but possibly Jenny's man.

He liked the things money bought, Paris, Jaguar cars, chukka boots, plushy restaurants, luxury flatlets, cosmopolitan hotels, and, Jenny painfully had to admit, women to match. How could she ever have thought she could live up to him?

She stirred uneasily; she hated being awake between midnight and dawn; it was a time of truth, or was it simply truth without the necessary dressing of optimism?

Miasma looked at the small diamond watch on her wrist. "Half-past three," she said, "Hadji should be back and then we go."

"To Tony?"

No answer.

"Why all this stupid mystery? Why can't you tell me your plans?"

Madame answered gently, softly, yet firmly. "I want to know where the case is. Tell me that and you may go back to Nuri bey or wherever you want to go. Now."

For a few moments Jenny contemplated making-up something to give herself time. She could invent somewhere that she could have hidden the case but that hiding-place could only be in Nuri bey's house and, as far as she could see, would involve Nuri bey much further and only give her a few hours' respite. "You don't mean *now*," she argued, "because you would have to confirm that the case was where I said."

Madame conceded that point and added: "It seems to me you have that stupid tenacity of all your countrymen. In spite of danger, against all advice, common sense and wisdom, you will stick to your own stupid ideas."

"You are absolutely wrong this particular time. I have told you, and I feel it is you who are stupid, Madame, because you refuse to believe me. I really threw it into the Golden Horn; you don't happen to want to believe I did, so you don't believe it and you're putting yourself to all sorts of trouble unnecessarily because you'll never see that case again in this life, you won't."

What happened next had a curious dreamlike quality. Sitting beside Madame, her head had begun to nod in sleep when Hadji suddenly appeared: "Come!"

Madame made a movement as though to take her arm but Jenny walked stiffly beside her, slightly aloof. It was still fairly dark but there was a lot going on at the water side. A fog hung over the Bosphorus so that it was not possible to see anything to the East but as they embarked into a *dolmus* rowing-boat, with two other people waiting to be rowed across, Jenny could see by the lights from the street that the Galata Bridge which should have stretched above them, was no longer there, the span having swung round to admit larger ships into the Golden Horn. The breath of the people in the boat blew out into the chill morning air in balloons, a fog horn sounded its forlorn moan, an occasional disembodied cry wavered through the mist to be neutralised by the bustling sound of an engine from a passing ferry boat. Jenny did not even ask where they were going; she was beyond caring.

On the Stamboul side they took a waiting taxi and drove sharply uphill. The large dusty open space used as a football ground in front of the Sultan Ahmed Mosque was crowded with people and floodlit.

"They are waiting to watch a hanging," Madame said dispassionately.

"A what?"

"A murderer is to be hanged," she explained, climbing energetically out of the taxi and handing Hadji the money to pay the driver. "These people have been waiting all night."

"Do you mean a public hanging?"

The old woman moved along until she was in a satisfactory position for seeing; Jenny, taller than the crowd, looked over their heads. She stared, stupefied, at the scaffold, consisting of three long poles arranged in tripod form, like the sticks from which hang the traditional witch's cauldron, the floodlighting beams meeting at this point.

"The *idam sehpasi*," Madame pointed out, "or the three feet for the condemnation to death. Look, standing in that circle round are the soldiers who have been there all night, and policemen to keep order." There were also boys with trays and baskets selling mineral water, tea, large wafer biscuits, roast chestnuts and shouting their wares: *"Gazos! . . . gazos! . . . gazos! . . . simit! . . . simit! . . . simit! . . . çay!"* and water sellers with their enormous metal canisters strapped to their backs crying: *"Souk! soo . . . souk!"*

Relaxed and with the air of one on an outing, Madame bought small glasses of tea for the three of them. "Why have you brought me here?" Jenny asked across the glass of tea which she sipped gratefully.

"It is necessary that you should take life seriously, my child."

"You won't frighten me," she returned defiantly. "I'm not completely idiotic, you know. They wouldn't do this to me, whatever I'd done. I'd be taken home and hanged in a civilised manner."

"But not Tony," Madame returned smoothly, "and we hang also accessories."

"Let's go," Jenny suggested, "I do not desire . . ." but her words faded out. They were now part of the crowd which was pressing in as a small red car drove through, along a lane lined with policemen, followed by three official cars.

"There is the *imam*," Madame pointed, "on this occasion he may wear clothes of office." He was distinguishable by the fez he wore with a black scarf over it and a simple black surplice. He was talking earnestly with the prisoner, a poor little example of humanity, obviously shivering in the chill air, his legs emerging thinly from his shapeless white shirt, his feet in Arab-like shoes, with the heels trodden flat at the back. The *imam* lighted a cigarette and put it between the prisoner's lips. An uncouth gipsy-like character now climbed the ladder to the platform and busied himself with the rope. Something was not working satisfactorily, there was a squeak as from a not well-oiled wheel which sounded clearly above the hum of the crowd like a wet finger on the rim of a glass.

The fog horn moaned greyly.

Jenny now found that both Madame and Hadji were holding her by the wrists, exerting a surprisingly firm hold. "Let go, I hate being touched!"

"You hate being touched," Madame sneered. "You will hate even more what you are going to see. Last month a murderer and his two accomplices were hanged; to be an accessory to murder is as dangerous as to be a murderer here. Now, look, if you could read Turkish you would read on the placard which they have pinned to the prisoner's chest what his crime is and what the verdict was."

The cigarette finished, the prisoner was pushed up the ladder by many helpful hands. The human beings on the scaffold now stood out sharply against the lightening sky beyond. It was like a black curtain for a ballet with the great tripod astride the two figures and Jenny was no more moved than she would be watching a ballet, because of the unreality of it all. Like the Book of Revelations, the scene was overstated and become melodramatic. She was now watching so absorbedly that her mouth was slightly open and she made no attempt to free herself.

The hangman's movements were economical and un-fussy. In his ordinary well-worn European-style suit he looked like a busy draper or any other kind of shopkeeper performing familiar movements amongst his stock. He slipped the noose over the prisoner's head, pulling the knot round to the back and tightening it against the back of the neck whilst adjusting it in front well beneath the chin. He then helped him up on to the stool, pulling the spare rope taut and tying it firmly against one of the supports. There was absolute silence now in the square but once more the fog horn sounded. Light was rushing up out of the east, but the deed would be done before dawn.

When everything was to his satisfaction, the hangman kicked the stool vigorously, it toppled over and the prisoner gave several involuntary jerks; there was no sound, though those very near might hear the last exhala-tion of the life's breath in a long final sigh.

Jenny looked up at the huge mosque with its six needle-thin minarets piercing the lightened sky like spears challenging the rapidly approaching dawn.

The gipsy hangman peered into the face of his victim, then nipped down the ladder and across to one of the official cars where he would receive prompt payment for his services to the State.

Hadji went for another taxi as the soldiers re-formed and marched away. The crowd began slowly to disperse. Jenny stood quite still, as though mindless. Miasma walked impatiently to and fro to keep warm, her hands thrust into her mink-edged sleeves.

Now that it was fully daylight, the flood-lighting was superfluous and it was turned off. The street lighting was extinguished too. It was time for the first prayer of the day. The *muezzin* came out, high up on one of the minarets, and leaned over the balustrading, shouting his exhortation with hands cupped to his mouth:

"Allahu akbar! Lā ilāha illā 'llāh!"

Many of the Faithful fell to their knees, touching the ground with their foreheads at the start of their orisons.

More often than not, a Tannoy loud speaker is used

to broadcast the call to prayer, but from the Sultan Ahmed Camii the *muezzin* himself calls and sometimes there are two. His thin high voice sounded across the square with an unearthly delicacy, so that it might have been an assurance of immortality.

Hadji had secured a taxi but a full ten minutes had to pass whilst he prayed, performing with ease and even some grace the movements of kneeling, standing, prostrating himself and again kneeling, with lips moving and eyes closed. Finally, in one movement, surprisingly supple for a small stout man, he leaped from prayer into the holding open of the taxi door for the ladies to enter.

In manœuvring the taxi into reverse, it was necessary to go much closer to the scaffold, and Jenny, strained face close to the window, saw what was now beyond bearing.

All the drama had gone out of the scene, it became quite hideously real. In full cold daylight the lonely figure hung, still swinging perceptibly.

Jenny was not one to have hysterics but, after a day of considerable tension, she had passed a night in which she had neither slept nor lain down. What she now saw was so bitterly sharp that it suddenly became intolerable. She shrieked in protest. She must do something about it and there was nothing she could do but scream, and this she did with everything she could put into it.

The taxi-driver was concerned. It was not possible to drive a screaming girl, in hysterics, through the early-morning streets. He drove to a drinking fountain he knew of and Hadji filled his cap with water and threw it in Jenny's face whilst Madame slapped her cheeks. Almost immediately a small crowd began to collect. As they drove off the screams became loud, abandoned sobbing.

"We must take her home by the first ferry," Madame said anxiously, the noise was unnerving. "There is only one thing left for me to do!" And, though Hadji protested violently, she put on her glasses and brought a pocket syringe-container out of her handbag and with shaking fingers hurriedly put the syringe together. She fumbled at Jenny's sleeve, pulling it up and rubbing spirit on the skin of the forearm, then, as they wobbled and bumped through the streets of old Stamboul, she filled the syringe with a solution from a small white tablet, looking at it carefully at eye-level for bubbles of air, and with a practised ease plunged the needle through the thin skin of the young forearm.

And that was what Jenny told Nuri bey.

Chapter 7

THOUGH IT might seem that Madame Miasma had nothing much to do, her days were, in fact, filled almost completely by three main occupations, that of *la toilette,* which took up most of the morning, talking on the telephone, and twittering to her birds. No major washing of the body being done in Turkish houses, she went on Thursday and often twice a week to one of the big *hamams* in Istanbul, which excursion took up the major part of a whole day. There would be visits to the mosque and a certain amount of time spent in her garden where she would keep a severe eye on Hadji, never an enthusiastic gardener.

This morning Miasma had a great deal to occupy her mind as she fulfilled automatically the actions which had become her habit over the years. She had no breakfast because there was no Valance to bring it to her and as she had not entered her kitchen for years, it did not occur to her to go and get her meal for herself. Hadji prayed and after he had prayed he went into the garden where he was doing a more than usually complicated operation with the basalt rockery, beside the steps.

Though Miasma's mind retained the sharpness of a razor which can cut a hair in mid air, the last forty-eight hours had tried it almost to its full capacity and now she was worried that there was something, some small detail which she might have missed and which could, forgotten, bring the whole complicated and expensive edifice that she had built up, crashing down to destroy her.

She had missed three nights' sleep, she had eaten frugally and now it was essential that she eat something more substantial. As she went through the bird room on the way into the garden, she could not resist stopping to greet some of her favourites. Turks treat their birds with the respect that Westerners do their animals. In a country where the cats are never fed and are left to stagger about the streets dying on their paws, the sellers of food for the pigeons take their place outside the mosques with their small bags of corn, hopefully, at six o'clock in the morning.

She was considerably downcast by the condition of the cages, which had not been cleaned since Valance died two days ago. Hadji must clean them out; he must also repair the rockery and get her some food. He must attend to the motor car, swab the marble floor of the house throughout and do the shopping. Hadji was an old man, almost as old as Madame herself; what if things became too much for him?

A lifetime of activity, of scheming, planning, devising, deciding, organising and conspiring, had become a habit deeply engrained; there was no rest for her who, had she been an Englishwoman, would have been nodding in the ingle of some expensive home for old ladies.

She stumped out on to the marble pavement at the top of the steps beside which Hadji was toiling like the calamity-prone under-privileged character he was. Basalt is rock that was once lava and flowed beneath the sea; the large piece that Hadji was carrying was a bright brown with a faint sparkle from tiny crystals embedded in its surface. Within a few feet of the eastern shore of the Bosphorus, facing north-west, would seem a poor place for a rockery. This particular rockery, however, was distinctly similar to those seen in the tiny villa gardens, sunless and sour, of industrial Lancashire; no flowers grew in it but ferns which uncurled obscenely, and leaves both gloomy and sickly, like those of London Pride and Periwinkle, pathetic plants, doomed to grow in soot and sulphur. For some moments she stood watching him in silence, her hands tucked into her wide sleeves.

Hadji placed the rock in an empty socket of earth, then took it out and replaced it at an angle which fitted the hole better.

"That will do," Miasma said irritably, "at this time of the year the plants will soon grow over it."

Hadji wiped his hands on his trousers. He wished his lady to know that Allah had been speaking with him.

Madame replied that he no doubt wished to tell her what Allah had had to say this time, though, in fact, she was not very interested. Hadji now burst out into a small lecture. Those, he said, who were dead were dead.

Madame agreed.

The dead were now gathered into Allah's bosom. He said a number of deeply profound things about Kismet with certain quotations from the Koran and Madame waited patiently because she knew from experience that it was no good trying to get Hadji to edit and curtail his observations in any way.

Now Allah had seen fit to deliver this young girl into their hands but had distinctly warned Hadji in no uncertain terms that though they might keep her safe and well, they must not harm her in any way. Above all, and Allah had been very clear on this point, they must not lead her footsteps into the ways of evil. But the ways of evil, as Madame and her humble servant Hadji well knew, had been already entered. He stood quite still, immobilised by the importance of what he had to say, one finger raised as he might imagine Allah raised His finger, and denounced the small white pellets soluble in water deriving from the opium plant, invention of the Western devils, which did nothing but destroy.

Madame argued that this was nonsense. No greater benefit to mankind had been invented than the small white pellets, soluble in water, which derived from the opium plant. Allah's infinite mercy lay in allowing men to evolve the white pellet, derivative of the opium plant, soluble in water, so that it might be injected under the skin of those who suffered beyond bearing, and smooth away their pain.

So, up to a point, Hadji agreed. When this small white

pellet was given in hospital, under the protection of the doctor, it could bring infinite mercy. But in the hands of one who was not a doctor, plunged regardless into any arm on the spur of the moment, it brought only woe of the most fierce and fatal kind.

Valance and he had discussed this problem many a time and Hadji well knew how Valance had felt on the subject. They had never understood fully why Madame treasured her new syringe so much and upon whom she had intended to use it. And now that Valance was no longer with them, Hadji felt it to be his duty, in conjunction with Allah, to make the very strongest protest against the use of the syringe.

An invention of the devil, he said, and so long as Madame was needle-happy (though he did not use those exact words), no luck could come to them. He begged her in the name of Allah, coupled with the name of her old friend Valance, to throw it into the Bosphorus, "into which all evil things, in the course of time . . . go."

For many years, probably daily, Hadji had stated that he was the humble servant of Miasma. It was not strictly true; the relationship of Miasma, Valance and Hadji was that of three incomplete people who found wholeness only in each other and together. Now that one of the trio was gone, both of those left assumed a greater importance to one another than ever before. Therefore, though she might state the contrary, Madame listened acutely to all that Hadji had to say, even though his words were extremely distasteful; he was the only person on earth who knew her as she was.

And now, because he was not succeeding in convincing her, Hadji went further and had even more painful things to say. As a girl of eighteen, he said, Madame had had nothing, Hadji and Madame well knew how much nothing she had had, there would be no need to recapitulate. And now Madame had everything, or everything anyone on this earth could want. How had that been attained? By the use of her wits and by the use of power. Allah did not wish that power should be in the hands of his people but there were times when it had to be in order that the human being should survive. Allah arranged as old age came on that the power they might wield would fade, and that was as it should be. Madame's power had faded but, unwilling to accept the Will of Allah, she had taken this devilish device into her possession as an instrument of power. With it she might feel herself to be as Allah, *All Powerful,* and that was wicked and not to be.

With a last gesture of appeal, Hadji held out his hand: "Give me the syringe and the rest of the white pellets," he begged, "for the love of Allah, that *I* may throw it into the Bosphorus and bring to us both a lasting peace."

But Madame only smiled grimly and said that Hadji was a superstitious cowardly eunuch; such wisdom as came from him, came from one who had never known the strength and the pleasure of being a man; born between nothing and an East Wind, he was of no account and what Allah had said to him was for his own use and not to be considered by those who were whole persons. Advice from Allah to Hadji was strictly personal. And furthermore, Hadji was not the only one to whom Allah gave advice. Miasma, too, came in for her share of the divine wisdom. She knew, without a doubt, Allah's wishes with regard to the syringe and the white pellets and they were that she must retain both, and not throw them into the Bosphorus, because she might have occasion to soothe the agony of mind of many an unhappy person. This young girl, for instance, was frantic with worry and tortured with doubt; it was a humane and gracious act that she should relieve her of her misfortunes for at least a short time.

And now, perhaps, Hadji would rustle out of it, get her something to eat, clean out the bird-cages, go out and buy some food and remove from her sight the fork and spade with which he had been disfiguring the rockery.

Alas, all would not be well, Hadji declared. Madame turned her back and went into the bird room, but Hadji shouted that they would be punished, good fortune would recede, ill luck would take its place and all would be fled save gall.

Chapter 8

THERE HAD been no guest staying in the *yali* for many years. The guest rooms were barely furnished and now used as a repository for unwanted pieces of furniture. Overstuffed being the operative word regarding Turkish furnishings (it can in fact be used in reference to most things Turkish: women, taxis, rissoles wrapped in vine leaves and much else besides), the guest rooms were scattered with pieces of furniture from the bird room, which had to be cleared to make room for the ever-increasing feathered population. Standing about the rooms in a state of unutterable gloom, were overstuffed navy-blue cubes, like the European *pouffes* so long now unfashionable, with a pattern of acid yellow and ox-blood red on the top; court cupboards apparently made entirely of black cotton reels, iron-grey prints of historic scenes with fretwork frames, a *bonheur du jour* made of mother-of-pearl which could have been elegant but suffered from thick ankles which would shame an ordinary kitchen table. Limp curtains of real Nottingham lace hung damply from the windows, looking out over the Bosphorus in the same way that similarly-curtained windows looked across the road at their prototypes in St. Annes-on-Sea in the year nineteen hundred and ten.

Valance had always declared that the Bosphorus gave her the shivers (*ça me donne les frisons*); she had demanded and been granted the second-best room, adjoining Madame's but overlooking the entrance yard and the main road. And over the years she had gradually Europeanised her room, bringing from her home in France things which she considered civilised and suitable; a chest of drawers of Spanish chestnut wood, a dressing-table to match, views of Montmartre and the Lake of Geneva, an Empire work-box on elegant brass feet, a round table covered with Valenciennes lace and a collection of photographs. But best of all was her splendid Provençal bed, four feet wide, the head and foot a shining scroll of conker-coloured amboyna, a feather mattress and a heavy lace bedspread lined with pink satin. She would refer to it in a voice of such adoration that anyone who did not know might think she was referring to some beloved called *Mon Lit. Je vais à mon lit* (I go to my bed) she would say when things became too much for her, and that would be that.

As there had been nowhere else to put Jenny when she arrived at an early hour in the morning, Hadji had taken her upstairs to Valance's room and she had fallen at once into a sound sleep on *mon lit*.

If Madame had not felt suddenly tired, she would herself have taken her guest to the room she was to occupy. She did not often go into Valance's room and she cared so little about her guest's comfort that she snapped at Hadji to take her to Valance's room.

And Hadji, who had never set foot in Valance's room, simply opened the door and indicated to Jenny that she was to go to sleep in there. Finding the sheets had not been changed since the last occupant left, Jenny had curled up under the bedspread, a thing which must have caused Valance to turn restlessly in her newly-occupied grave.

Jenny now opened her eyes after her eight hours' sleep and wondered if indeed she were sucking a piece of sponge. Investigation proved it to be merely her tongue. She got up unsteadily, she felt dizzy, sick, and had a headache, almost as though she had a hang-over. She staggered to the looking-glass over Valance's dressing-table and observed herself with horror. She looked ghastly. Then she felt so faint that she sat down hurriedly and put her head between her knees. It was no good, she realised, trying to kid herself that she had had a bad dream. It was much too real for a dream; she remembered every horrifying detail, including her own unusual behaviour and the way in which Madame had dealt with it. She remembered the feeling of exultation she had felt as they waited for the first ferry boat, with Madame and Hadji holding her on either side. She remembered the boat trip to Asia Minor with the small ferry boat aiming wide of the quay and swinging round with the tremendous current. She remembered her hysterical laughter at the sight of the De Dion Bouton parked near the ferry port. "A motor car, not a mere car!" she had giggled. She remembered Hadji, an absurd figure in his cloth cap, as chauffeur. If she had been drunk, she would have remembered very little and felt a great misery and shame but now she felt that she had had a marvellous experience; there had been some special heightened delight about it and Jenny was not so stupid as not to have an idea as to what it was.

She sat up briskly. She must get to hell out of it, as Tony would say. Furthermore, the trick of showing her that disgusting hanging hadn't worked; she didn't believe for one moment that an Englishman would be hanged in a foreign country for a crime committed against one of his own countrymen in that country. He would be— what was it called?—extradited. Anyway, the British Government would certainly never leave him to the untender mercies of these savages. Good heavens, it might cause a war in the Near East if that sort of thing could happen to Tony! Though still far from well, she began to feel better. She sat at Valance's dressing-table, used her brush and comb and did her hair up into a French twist at the back. Like that she looked older and more intelligent. Her eyes were puffy and her lips lily-pale and swollen. Her skirt was still hanging where she remembered putting it, carefully over the high foot of *mon lit* with her white sweater folded on top. She pulled them on, brushing the skirt with Valance's clothes-brush, then looked round the room for signs of washing facilities. There was a jug and basin but no water in which she could swill her face. She moved across to the lace-covered round table upon which stood Valance's photographs. There, amongst the stiff-looking men holding themselves erect with one hand on the back of a chair to prop themselves up, smugly smiling matrons with fronts like pouter pigeons against backgrounds of palms in flowered-pots . . . was Tony, a slightly younger Tony with his twisted smile, wearing a dark blazer with brass buttons. The shock was so severe that her legs began to tremble.

She picked up the photograph and moved across to the window to allow such light as penetrated the greening trees to show it up better. There was no doubt at all that it was Tony. It was in an elaborate frame of twisted metal, a frame which had obviously contained another photograph. She opened it and found that at the back of Tony's photograph was another of a wedding group, taken years ago—a stout, dark-haired young man in soldier's uniform with a small, dark girl simpering from his arm. Tony's parents? Grandparents? Or nothing to do with Tony?

She went across to the door and opened it slowly, trying to make no sound. She stood listening. Above the bird-twittering she heard the distant sound of voices, those of Madame Miasma and the servant, talking in their mumbling Turkish. Quickly she flitted across the landing and opened the first door she saw, looking inside and observing the sullen discarded furniture, smelling the unused smell. She peered into three similar rooms and then, across the landing, into Madame's room. She crept across to the windows, one of which stood wide open on to the balcony which hung out over the Bosphorus. Below she heard their voices and peeping down she saw Hadji standing beside some gardening work he was doing, holding a fork and pointing a finger towards the sky with his other hand. He appeared to be giving Madame some kind of lecture.

The room was pungent and stuffy and reeking of her special scent. The enormous Victorian dressing-table with the lace doilies, was untidy and covered with a film of expensive powder. There was a beautiful mother-of-pearl brush set, inlaid with gilt or gold, initialled M. But there were no photographs, of Tony or anyone else.

She reasoned thus: one thing was now clear; instead of running back to Nuri bey, who would be bewildered by the way she had disappeared, so ungracious was it, she must at least stay here until she knew what was happening to Tony. If it was now obvious that he did not care what happened to her, she owed it to herself to show that she cared, or had cared, about him, and she was not going to brush him off like a tiresome fly now that he was in trouble. Tony had deceived her utterly, posing as something he was not but until she had had a sincere talk and charged him with the deception, she must remain loyal.

He had never talked much about his family or early life, murmuring casually that his father was killed in the war and his mother married to an American and living in the U.S.A., and that he had always had to "fend for himself," and that was all she knew.

Her head was aching severely with the necessity of making the decision, should she charge Madame with knowing a lot more about Tony than she would admit or should she put the photograph face-downwards in a drawer and say nothing about it? She had a strange feeling of excitement now because she felt sure Tony was near, probably in the house. She still thought he was hiding and it was possible that Hadji and Madame had brought her here to be near Tony and to smuggle them both out of the country quickly.

Whether she would go with Tony or not would have to be decided; what, at the moment, she would prefer to do would be to stay and explore Istanbul in the fascinating company of Nuri bey.

Leaving the decision to circumstance, she went downstairs into the marble-flagged hall and into the bird room. Madame came in through the french window to meet her, inquiring, like a gracious hostess, whether she had slept well and Jenny answering like the perfect guest, that she had slept well. Whose room had she occupied, she asked. The room of Valance, Madame's French companion, who, she would remember, had died suddenly two days ago from a stroke.

"Two days ago! Everything seems to be happening at once, doesn't it?" Jenny exclaimed in a voice that rang out like a bell.

Madame apologised that her domestic arrangements were not running smoothly as the result of Valance's death. The shopping, for instance, was not done and there was little to eat in the house. However, presently Hadji would bring something; in the meantime perhaps Mademoiselle would like to look at her pretty birds.

"Let's not fool around," Jenny suggested. "You brought me here for a reason and that reason has something to do with Tony Grand. You're scared of something and you want me under your eye. Is that it, Madame? And you know that silly trick of softening me up by showing me that beastly hanging early this morning hasn't helped one bit. It's just made me pretty disgusted with your barbaric country and given me a beast of a headache. I don't suppose your servant told Nuri bey what we were up to when he rang him, if he rang him, did he? I thought not. It was a beastly trick; a sort of vile inhuman trick no normal person could think up. I don't know what Nuri bey will say when he knows, but he'll be pretty disgusted, I do know that!"

"*Ecoute, mon enfant*," Madame said firmly, "I have nothing against you, you have been used like one of the small men in a game of chess. The game is much more important than you but the fact that you exist will make the game go one way," she gesticulated with her hands, "or the other. And until I know which way you must remain here with me."

"You'd keep me a prisoner? That is virtually abduction and I am sure it's a crime here as well as at home. You can't do it!"

"You are in a very weak position, my child. As I understand it, there is nobody who knows where you are. You have left your home and your family and have travelled far on your own. There is no one anywhere who will miss you. Nobody knows when you come in, when you go out, if you are well fed or if you are starved, what you are wearing or what you are not wearing, if you have money or no money. . . ."

"I've still got my passport . . . I'm still a British subject! The consul . . ."

". . . or even that you are here. You have told me yourself that you have shaken off your family; it may be months, or even years, before they realise that you have disappeared."

"No—no—it's not like that!"

"Not a soul to care where you are or how you are. *L'enfant de personne!*"

Nobody's baby.

"Tony . . ." but as she said it, Jenny's spirits fell even lower. How much did Tony care?

"Nobody anywhere knows where you are at this moment. Nobody . . ."

"When the jet got to Hong Kong they would realise I was missing. . . ."

She thrust her face so close that Jenny backed hurriedly, but she followed, gripping Jenny's hands. "Missing . . . you had your ticket! Do realise, my child, that though you may be their most urgent concern whilst you are airborne, once you have walked down these steps out of the plane they do not care in the very least what happens to you. You will be simply a passenger who missed the plane, and that will be that. It's no good, you are a nobody, wanted by no one, and even if your family love you and are mourning for you in their hearts, there is nothing they will do about it because you have chosen your own path."

"There's Nuri bey!" Jenny cried.

"Nuri bey! Nuri bey! That dreamer of dreams. You ran from his house and he will sit sadly musing."

Something like panic was rising in Jenny's aching head. "Oh, no! You're wrong," she almost shrieked. Miasma had to be wrong somewhere, she could not be allowed always to be right. "You're wrong. I gave him the case; he's got it in his house and if I don't turn up for it he'll know something has happened to me. He'll go to our consul and report that I am missing."

Madame's hand flew to her mouth, of which she traced the outline thoughtfully with her ringed forefinger. "I see, then you were lying to me all the time, as I knew you were, when you said you threw the case into the Golden Horn. Five thousand dollars into the Golden Horn. I knew it was not so!"

"So you see," Jenny gabbled, "you can't keep me prisoner, or dope me, or kill me . . . or anything. Nuri bey will do something."

"Nuri bey will do nothing, he is not one who does. It is I who do. I have done all my life and I will do again. Relax, my little one, come and look at my pretty birds. . . ."

To give herself time to think, as she later told Nuri bey, Jenny obediently lined herself up beside Madame, a young guest courteously giving her attention to her hostess in spite of her shocking headache.

They stood by cage after cage whilst the particular beauties of the inhabitants were pointed out to her: Hartz mountain rollers, silent love-birds, misty mauve budgerigars, smart little black and yellow creatures which Madame's friends had sent from Hong Kong, a nightingale.

"You see, my dear, there are almost no birds in our city; pigeons and sparrows, and an occasional nightingale out here on the Bosphorus, that is all; we treasure our caged birds very greatly. . . ."

It was a crazy room alive with eternal twittering, rendered fantastic by the strange reflected light from the everlasting flowing water outside playing on the faded murals.

I can't think . . . I can't think, was all that Jenny could formulate in her mind. Her absolute isolation, which had been so clearly underlined by Madame's words, was frightening, by far the most frightening aspect of the situation in which she found herself. Apart from all the immediate worries, what terms was she now supposed to be on with Tony and how would they feel towards each other when they met? Tony the boy friend was now Tony the crook, Tony the con-man, Tony the seducer, Tony who had let her down more completely, surely, than any man had ever let any girl down. Jenny now understood that corny old phrase, "Her heart was sore"; quite literally the place in her chest about where her heart must be, was sore, and when she thought of the way Tony had behaved she received a physical pain which made her wince.

Noticing her lack of interest, Madame told her to sit down, she was in need of food. She would go at once and send Hadji out for yoghourt; Jenny sank limply on to the love seat, watching Madame as she hobbled off vigorously. The kitchen had the same den-of-thieves aspect that marks Turkish kitchens. Hadji was dejectedly washing up some yoghourt dishes which had to be taken to the shop in exchange for freshly-filled ones.

"Listen," she hissed. "She is clearly unnerved; she has confessed to leaving the valise with Nuri bey and you must try again and retrieve it somehow. . . ." She held up her hand in protest at the flow of words which came from him. "I cannot hold her here long; she is a young girl of energy and some brains; as soon as she is satisfied that her lover is not here, she will go, she will return to Nuri bey and if she does so before you have found the case, there will be no hope for either of us. No hope, do you understand? We might even be hanged side by side, you and I, Hadji, like the vagabond we saw this morning."

Hadji had said what he had said: there was a lot more to say but he was not going to say it. He dropped the shallow earthenware dishes into a gaudy plastic shopping bag and put on his cap.

"Make same tea, Hadji, quickly. Into her draught of tea I shall put . . ."

"*Yok . . . yok . . . yok!*" Hadji made it clear that there was to be no more messing about with Kismet—or dope.

Madame fumbled in her handbag; huge and capacious, it contained, it would seem, everything that anyone could possibly want under any sort of circumstance. This time she brought out a small bottle of pink tablets. "I shall use only two of the tablets that Dr. MacPherson prescribed to me for sleeplessness," she said smoothly. "Two of them will send her to sleep for the rest of the day, and the night as well. When she wakes to-morrow morning, you will have retrieved the case from Nuri bey, and she will be allowed to leave here and return to Nuri bey or go to the devil. We shall be safe. When we return to-night I shall ring Nuri bey to say I have kept her here because you found her wandering out of his house late at night and she begged us to protect her. I shall explain that the young thing is a little out of her mind, hysterical. You see, Hadji, I am reasonable. You thought I had brought her here to punish her, didn't you? You are wrong. My heart is full of benevolence; I wish only, as you do, to carry out the Will of Allah. But, as we both know, Allah helps those who help themselves. It is *not* the Will of Allah that you and I should hang side by side on the football ground before the Sultan Ahmed Camii, and I am carrying out his wish that we should help ourselves to the best of my ability. Make the tea quickly. . . ."

Chapter 9

THE FIRST half-hour after sunrise is a silent battle for supremacy between the newly arisen sun and the fog which lies lightly along the Bosphorus and the Golden Horn. The sun always wins and comes up brazen and warm and the fog sinks reluctantly away defeated. It was just about this time that Nuri bey stirred in the chair in which he had sat, unsleeping, the whole night. During that time he had received psychic admonition: it was now his intention to do what he should have done before, to go to the police, but first he cleaned his house, tidied his kitchen a little, ate his midday meal, changed his suit.

Then he locked his front door after him, as usual, boarded a tram and went to see his friend, a brass hat in the police force, whom he found finishing his midday meal in his favourite restaurant.

"Tell me," he said, "what is the position now with regard to smuggling?"

It was very bad indeed. More smuggling was going on at the present time than ever before and smuggling by air was at present the most profitable form of carrying contraband goods. So many people flew over so many thousand miles so frequently that small amounts could be carried which, in a short time, could accumulate into vast quantities. A constant stream of gold, diamonds and the raw material of narcotics passed through the sky over their heads daily. The price of gold in India had been raised so high, being now almost twice its value in the open market, that the smuggling of gold into India was extremely profitable and worth any amount of careful organisation. Airline stewards had been found wearing waistcoats with special pockets for carrying gold and had been discovered with as much as fourteen pounds of gold on them at one time. In the first quarter of the previous year it was estimated that over a million and a half pounds sterling of gold had been smuggled into India.

As for diamonds, oil kings in the Persian gulf had sent fortunes in the form of diamonds to safety in banks in the United States. On the North Atlantic run one air steward had been caught with five thousands pounds' worth of stones on him on one occasion. "It is a great temptation, my friend, to these ill-paid young men. They arrive in New York with their small packet, hand their commission to someone from whom they receive in exchange an envelope of dollars! I have no doubt their conscience is clear because if they do not do it, someone else will!"

Nuri bey tapped his mouth with pointed finger and thumb.

"And what about narcotics?"

"Drug traffic. Ah, my friend, there you have something which many of these young smugglers will not handle. They are conscientious objectors. They will carry all the gold and diamonds in the world but they will not touch opium. They know, some of them have seen for themselves, the harm which opium does to many young people like themselves."

"But there is a very considerable drug traffic, I gather."

"The biggest and most profitable of the lot, my friend. Opium grown here, in Burma, Persia and India is converted into heroin and sold on the illicit market in Hong

Kong. One ounce, Nuri my friend, one single ounce reaching the United States, diluted with lactose, can produce five thousand shots for which an addict will pay at the rate of three dollars a shot. Furthermore, the conversion to heroin of a small amount of raw opium can take place in an ordinary outhouse, no need for large factories, it can be done secretly and all trace of the operation removed easily."

The policeman then observed sadly that in time somebody could always be found who would do anything for money. But recently, he added more cheerfully, air security personnel both in the United States and England, had been greatly increased and, given time, he felt sure, this crime of carrying disaster to the young people of both countries would be overcome.

"And what about the young man Grand, who shot and killed the security officer at the airport only the night before last?" Nuri bey asked.

The police officer said that he understood he was a young man with a bad record; Scotland Yard were flying out two detectives to make further investigations but in the opinion of the Istanbul police, between themselves, this young man had friends in the city who were at present hiding him.

"And what will happen when he is found?"

"He will be extradited, of course. No longer any concern of ours."

"And the people who have kept him hidden?"

"Ah, my friend. We shall deal with them ourselves, and very severely indeed."

Something in Nuri bey cringed and curled up painfully. His friend fixed him with a piercing look. "Come, Nuri, my friend, if you know something, get it out. In the name of humanity, get it out, man. When I was in the States I was shown a group of drug addicts waiting outside a druggist's for their daily supply. It was something I can never forget. Anyone who aids and abets in the continuation of the taking of drugs by young people is a criminal, make no mistake, and he deserves the worst punishment that can be handed out to him."

Nuri bey then admitted that, in fact, he *knew* nothing but he had grave suspicions.

In that case, his friend returned promptly, he owed it to humanity to make known his suspicions; if they proved to be groundless no harm would follow—if not, justice would be done.

"I must be a little more certain," Nuri bey said. "My suspicions are so fantastic that I must have a little more time to make quite sure that I am not wrong. Otherwise I could cause great harm and suffering."

His friend told him, in Turkish words, the equivalent of: well, step on it, old man, we don't want to look fools in the eyes of these foreigners; if we can have the accomplices lined up by the time the English detectives arrive, it will be very fine.

Nuri bey hurried away bewildered, like a long pair of scissors, and took refuge under the enormous plane tree that grows in the shade of the mosque of Bayazit II on the third hill near the covered bazaar and the bookshops he loved.

It is known as the "mosque of the pigeons," pigeons having a sacred significance, and in the courtyard and amongst the tables of the open-air café hundreds of fat pigeons stagger around amongst the starving kittens, their eyes glazed with over-feeding. Under the black and white arches of the cloisters, between the pillars of jasper and porphyry, sits an old scribe with a prehistoric Underwood typewriter, waiting for custom.

Nuri bey placed himself carefully upon a rickety chair and ordered a narghile pipe into which he fitted his own ivory mouthpiece and settled into a long contemplative smoke. To watch the bubbles slowly travelling up through the faintly colouring water is known to be one of the most profoundly tranquil experiences available to man. It should have engendered wisdom and peace, but unfortunately he could only think shallow thoughts from the top of his head and all the time, through his mind, ran a jingle from the Oxford Book of Verse which had been haunting him for many hours and preventing him from more profound thoughts; a sickeningly sentimental verse which went:

> Jenny kiss'd me when we met
> Jumping from the chair she sat in;
> Time, you thief who love to get
> Sweets into your list, put that in!
> Say I'm weary, say I'm sad,
> Say that health and wealth have missed me,
> Say I'm growing old, but add,
> Jenny kiss'd me."

Nuri bey was entirely nauseated with himself but he had caught the verse as he might catch an attack of influenza, and that was that.

He sat for a long time. At a nearby table an old man and youth played two games of backgammon. The sellers of pigeon food rattled the maize about in their brown paper bags, hoping to attract custom. A kitten sat hopeless on the steps of the mosque, blinking its eyes, wishing it liked maize; pigeons walked round it and past it and almost over it but it never raised a paw; no one in Istanbul would harm a pigeon, least of all a kitten. The long arms of the Underwood typewriter were now flaying out wildly as the scribe typed furiously to the dictation of the old woman who bent over him.

It seemed that no amount of hubble-bubbling was going to help Nuri bey to reach a decision to his almost insoluble problem. Through the archway, opposite the garden where the Sultan Bayazit lies buried, is the bookshop to which Nuri bey now knew he was going, drawn there by an irresistible impulse. As he slipped his own mouthpiece into his pocket he looked up and saw that the old woman who had been dictating to the scribe was now coming down the steps of the mosque towards him and she was Miasma. He had to have a second look before deciding that it was definitely she because he had never known her to be out unchaperoned. As she walked past the table she looked directly at him; there was nothing to be done but to rise and greet her.

This he did, kissing her hand as usual and saying how astonished he was to see her here alone, and employing the services of the scribe!

"I was writing to Valance's sister in France."

"But I was going to do that for you."

"I am not sure about your French, Nuri bey. The scribe has a French colleague who will translate my letter for him. Valance had a sister Martine to whom she was much devoted; I have written at length to tell her of Valance's beautiful funeral. She will be distracted with sorrow, poor woman!"

The intuition for which Nuri bey had been waiting all day suddenly struck with a force which nearly knocked him off his feet. In all the years he had known her it occurred to Nuri bey for the first time that Miasma could neither read nor write. And this was why he was asked to visit her every week to read the news of the world to her and would account, also, for the endless time she spent on the telephone. She had probably used the services of the scribe many a time. It made explicable, suddenly, quite a number of things about her which he had never understood.

Miasma peered up into his face across which shadows of his thoughts were racing like cloud shadows across a bare fell. "We have been close for many years, you and I, my lion. And now, when I am in grave trouble, you seem to have become my enemy," she said plaintively. "I cannot understand. There is no more loyalty towards me."

"No, Madame," Nuri bey answered stiffly, "I cannot claim that we have been friends. Acquaintances only. One must know something about one's friends. I now understand that I have, all these years, known nothing about you. You have been to me as a closed book. I do not admire a book for its binding nor can I feel affection for a book I have not opened." Thinking how much he preferred books to people, his glance slipped over the top of her head towards the archway in the wall beneath the plane tree, through which he hoped to go to his favourite second-hand bookshop at the earliest possible moment.

"After all I have done for you," he heard her saying, "the arrangements I have made in your favour when I am gone!"

His face hardened, he did not now believe in those benefits at which she had hinted many, many times.

"Where do you think my money comes from? From Allah? Where do you think I get the money to pay for those two parasites Valance and Hadji? They have squeezed me dry, those two, sucked all the juice from me until I am as a used lemon." She then flatly stated and repeated, the amount of money that she had paid monthly to her two servants, and Nuri bey, listening in spite of not wanting to do so, was staggered to hear that each of them received in one week what he had to live on in a month in the way of rents from some half-dozen houses he owned.

"And in addition to all that they are kept by me. Each time Valance came back from her home in France, she demanded a rise in pay, *each time,* my friend. And, knowing how I had missed her when she was away, living as I was obliged to, in that hotel in Beirut and hating every moment of it, she could be sure that I would have to agree to her outrageous demands. Pay me more . . . or I shall leave, that was her attitude. And she carried Hadji with her, each time I raised her salary it was necessary for me to give Hadji more as well. Valance has a good sum of money salted away in France, let me tell you, and believe me," she raised her finger and her voice became shrill, "that sister of hers, to whom I have just sent a long letter, will demand Valance's salary to the end of this month, even though the poor woman is dead! Oh, the French are mean . . . mean . . . they would pick up the pigeons' corn, grain by grain, to make bread for themselves!"

With all his reading and all his profound knowledge of the thinking of the philosophers of the world, Nuri bey realised with a crushing rush of awareness, he knew little about people.

He also realised that there was a certain desperate urgency about the way Miasma was talking to him.

"Nuri bey, get me the case back, my lion!"

He could say absolutely nothing.

"Have pity, Nuri, have pity, you who never transgress. Try to understand that I, a woman of the people, have had to spend my whole life striving. No man ever kept me, I arrived too late at the harem, I was one the Sultan never even saw! Everything I have had in my life I have had to gain with cunning, brain work," she tapped her forehead now covered by the lace mantilla which she affected in the Spanish manner, "it all comes from here!"

The one the Sultan never saw! And she had always caused it to be believed that she was the mother of a son of the Sultan! Never even an *ikbal!*

"Nuri bey, get me back my case!"

Now he was feeling nothing but a gigantic bewilderment, greater than anything he had yet known. Furthermore, he had no idea where the case was, if it was in the Golden Horn, or somewhere in Jenny's hand, or in his own house. He did not know. He could never be sure, ever again, of anything.

"Five thousand dollars, Nuri, in boxes of *locum!* And now you have the truth, can you bear to carry such a burden? But not only that, but to lose it will be the end of my association with my friend in Hong Kong! They will say I am too old, too ridiculously old. The old are not often suspect. They liked me old once, old as I was, and a woman of some position, but now I am *too* old, as I have shown. Clumsy . . . unreliable . . . not to be trusted. . . . They will say I have lost control of myself, as the old sometimes do. 'She is in her dotage,' they will say, 'she is crazy, senile, incontinent, incompetent, importunate . . . too old!'"

Nuri bey looked round uneasily. The man and the boy were playing yet another game of backgammon. A group of American tourists, buying souvenirs on the steps of the mosque, were the centre of attraction. A pedlar passed crying his wares in what sounded like Turkish but was, in fact, English: "Coloured postcards, lovely coloured postcards!"

"Have pity, Nuri," she begged again plaintively, with her tiny claw on his arm, "have pity. That five thousand dollars is already partly spent! I am desperate."

He would have liked to shake her off and stride away through the archway into his own world of printed words, brutally telling her to live on Hadji. But he was not like that. Nuri bey had a fund of limitless kindness which was of great annoyance to him; it was like a fine well at which all comers could drink, which, in time, became everybody's well, thoroughly cluttered up with the litter of trippers and parasites; that which is free for all is never either appreciated or respected.

"Say something, Nuri bey, *say* something!"

He badly wanted to say something to help the poor soul. He thought she knew that Jenny existed but now he could not be sure. And anyway, how could it comfort her to be told that Jenny, the female accomplice, probably had the case?

"I do not know, Madame, I do not know where your case is, and that is the truth."

And then a hideous thing happened, something so ugly and degrading that Nuri bey could never again smoke the hubble bubble pipe of peace in the café in the precinct of the mosque of the pigeons.

She uttered a really low-class Turkish oath of slum origin and slapped him hard across the mouth, then, muttering to herself, she hobbled away.

It was only when he had gone through the archway and was standing looking down unseeing at the books arranged outside the shop near the Sultan's grave that Nuri bey brought out his pocket handkerchief and dabbed his mouth. He looked furtively at the handkerchief and found it had blood on it from the scratch made where one of her rings had caught it.

But, nevertheless, the pain had the effect of triggering off the latent energy that Nuri bey's dervish father had used up so liberally in himself when he danced himself into a frothing frenzy for the love of Allah and which his son had kept folded away in a drawer of his personality . . . until now.

Nuri bey quite suddenly became as the Winged Lion of the Book of Revelations, six wings about him and full of eyes, before, behind and within.

Chapter 10

HE SPRANG on to a bus going north along the Europe side of the Bosphorus and after a half-hour journey and a few minutes in a *dolmus* he came to Istiniye in Europe, a place famous in history where ships have been built since before Christ, where the Argonauts put up a temple and where Saint Daniel squatted at the top of a pole for thirty-three years, being forcibly taken down when he became too old, and dying at the age of eighty-four.

Though tiny, this is the largest and most flourishing harbour of the Bosphorus; it looks like an Eventide Home for old liners, which loll about in a broken-winded way and nowhere is there to be seen a lick of paint. He sought out the equivalent of the harbour master who was a friend and remained in consultation with him for some time. After which he picked his way over ropes and boles through the small forest of fishing vessels, where a fisherman softly tapped out with his palm on his drum the news that he was on his way. Tall and lean, Nuri bey moved amongst them with the strange grace inherited from his father who had danced in a waist-gripping coat with flying skirt, and everywhere he was greeted with the respectful touching of the forehead and the title "Efendim." Here and there he stopped to talk and when he had made his way round the little harbour he was satisfied that no young man of any nationality had been stowed away in any vessel going anywhere up or down the Bosphorus in the last few days or nights.

The skipper of an Arab schooner loading a cargo of

simple things for ports on the Black Sea greeted him with pleasure; he had, on occasion, taken Nuri bey to Trebizond to visit his favourite sister, a widow with a son a school teacher in that city. The passage of time being one of the least important factors in an Arab's life, it was necessary for Nuri bey to spend several minutes in the exchange of greetings and pleasantries. He was only able to interrupt the episode when he saw the ferry steamer coming round the point, and rushed to catch it.

He disembarked at Miasma's village, on the Asia side, but instead of going to Miasma's *yali* he stayed in the village square, sitting in a café and eating a dish of the splendid yoghourt for which that village is famous. As always in these villages a clutch of dark, dusty, Arab-like characters lounged around apparently aimlessly, as much part of the scene as the dying kittens and plane trees and dwelling places that look like decrepit cow sheds. Some of these had been hired as mourners for Valance's death, and Nuri bey, eyeing them sharply, knew that they were idling away their temporarily splendid affluence. It needed no more than a certain kind of glance to get two of them to sidle across to his table and squat upon the ground at his feet and talk about the things that Arabs do talk about, whatever that may be.

Then, led skilfully by Nuri bey, the talk drifted to the death at the *yali* and how they had been paid double the usual rates for mourning the Christian death because they had all objected to such an unusual procedure and Hadji had had to bribe them with much fine gold (in other words, dirty Turkish notes).

They told how many had left as the night advanced but that there were still a few who saw the arrival of a young man in a taxi from Uskudar, and how, almost immediately, behind the entrance door of the *yali,* across the courtyard, they heard strange sounds.

"What sort of sounds?" Nuri bey asked.

"Shooting!" they whispered. "Undoubtedly shooting." And, frightened and almost ashamed of what they had heard, they had crept away only to return at dawn to assist in the carrying of the bier forty steps towards the grave in order, as the Prophet had promised, to expiate a few of their mortal sins. The young man had not been one of the tiny procession which wound its way on foot up the hill to the newly-dug grave. No one had seen the young man since: the whispered words floated away like bubbles, to burst aimlessly into the air, full of emptiness. He had not come out of the main door of the *yali,* though it was always possible that he had gone out of another door. . . . They wrapped their arms round their scraggy, pin-stripe covered knees and rocked themselves almost imperceptibly to and fro, like the calamity-prone characters that they were, a human frieze denoting disaster. The only other door led out on to the Bosphorus. . . .

Abnormally superstitious, they were deathly afraid of what might happen to them in their connivance; that a Christian should have a Moslem burial was so unusual an event that they were not sure whether or not it was a mortal offence and naturally enough no one had dared to approach the *imam* with such a problem. So convinced were they that no good would come of it that Nuri bey, as he listened to all they had to tell him, tempered the information with common sense.

Immediately across the road, from the back of the *yali,* the ground rose sharply, covered with the styles or pole-like stones which take the place of ordinary Christian gravestones, leaning together like drunkards unable to stand, or fallen to the ground. Cemeteries are not tended in any way and weeds and bushes grow up amongst the styles in great disorder. A hedge of rhododendrons almost hid the melancholy sight of the rising cemetery from the road and it would be amongst these bushes that, all day and possibly all night, one or two of them would lie, keeping a constant watch upon the *yali,* because they had nothing else to do and nowhere else to go.

A young girl, they said, was now at the *yali,* last night there had been nobody there, unless the young man had been lying asleep, or drugged, or dead, the house had been empty. But they had returned an hour after dawn, Hadji driving the car and Madame in the back with a young woman who laughed and made much joyous noise as she was led into the *yali*. An American, perhaps, or an English young woman, or perhaps French, she had laughed very much and talked in English and French very loud, and Madame had hustled her inside. Since then Madame and Hadji had both left the *yali,* once more Hadji driving the motor car towards Uskudar. The young girl was not with them, and the woman who went in to clean had let herself in with her key, as usual.

The young girl had not left the *yali* by the main door. . . .

So either there were two young people now in the *yali* . . . or not.

And with these saturnine remarks they stared at Nuri bey out of their black cavernous eyes, full of apprehension.

Nuri bey ate steadily, ordering a second bowl of yoghourt and sprinkling it well with sugar. No lines marred the smoothness of his impassive silvery-tan face, he might not have been listening at all, though in fact not one syllable of what was being said escaped him. When it was clear that his source of information was now as empty as the bowls, he left the table and strode away towards the villa, scattering the proles at his feet, whilst some of them trailed after him to see the fun.

In Miasma's courtyard a splendid rhododendron flourished and now great crimson flowers hung forward over the marble flags. Nuri bey paused to pick some petals and eat them, as his ancestors had eaten such flowers on the eve of battle. Fortified, he banged loudly on the door and the followers, peering through the gateway, cringed nervously because it was clear that the Efendi was on the warpath.

The cleaner, a woman of such humble proportions as to be barely human, with her head and a quarter of her face wrapped tightly in an unbecoming black shawl, opened the door a crack and peered out.

Allah be praised, it was the Efendi! Mysteriously she drew him inside, closing and barring the door. As she did so, the new Nuri bey, being, as he was, full of eyes before, behind and within, at once saw the bullet marks.

She had something to show him and, as she hurried

off to get whatever it was, Nuri bey touched the bullet marks with his fingers. There were two of them on the door and one mark, which may have been that of a glancing bullet, on the wall beside the door. There must have been some pretty wild shooting.

What she had to show him was a pair of fine shoes in dark brown suede; she was clearly under the impression that they belonged to Nuri bey and handed them to him with the air of triumph. Nuri bey asked where she had found them and she readily confessed that she had found them "hidden" in Hadji's bedroom next to the kitchen. It would appear that the woman did not like Hadji, thought that he had stolen the shoes and was glad that she was able to do Nuri bey the service of returning them to him and at the same time implicating Hadji.

Nuri bey thought it expedient to admit that they were his and she immediately went on to tell him that a young girl was lying asleep in Valance's bed. There was nobody else in the house, Madame and Hadji had gone out before she arrived, she did not know where they had gone because it was not Madame's day at the *hamam,* and if it had been, Hadji would only have taken her as far as Uskudar, and would have returned long before now. It was now nearly nightfall and though she should be gone she had stayed on because she did not like to leave the young lady, whoever she might be, alone. And why was she sleeping so soundly? The woman was afraid the young girl was ill. She was pleased that Nuri bey had come so that she could hand over responsibility.

There was no question of deciding whether or not he should go into Valance's room to observe the young girl asleep; she forced it upon him, excitedly leading him up the stairs and into the room.

Jenny's healthy pink cheeks were the colour of goat's cheese, her hair straggled damply across the huge, French, square feather-pillow and she was breathing heavily, her mouth slightly open.

"Is she ill, Efendim?"

Bending over her Nuri bey smelt her breath, which

was far from fresh, as he had known it would be. He touched her bare shoulder and was embarrassed to find she was wearing only a bra.

The cleaning woman said darkly that she was in an unnatural sleep. Nuri bey took both her shoulders and shook her firmly but still she did not wake. He asked for water and a cloth and when the woman brought it he wiped her face with the cloth soaked in cold water. It was several minutes before she opened her eyes and several more minutes before she came round completely, wondering where she was but at once recognising Nuri bey.

"Stay here!" he sternly ordered the cleaning woman, and then he drew back the bedclothes and pulled Jenny from the bed. She was wearing an acid green waist petticoat of startling brilliance which he at once extinguished beneath Valance's best lace and satin-lined bedspread. He marched her across to the window and firmly held her standing in front of it whilst she took some deep breaths of fresh air.

It was some time before she said anything and then a number of disjointed sentences escaped her swollen lips. "Oh, my lord, what is going to happen to me next . . . oh, that ghastly hanging . . . oh, my lord, I do feel sick!" She retched into the pail of cold water. "Oh, Nuri bey, you are an angel . . . oh, my lord, whatever next!"

Nuri bey drew a chair up to the window and gently sat her down. The woman crouched on the floor by the door. "Stay here!" Nuri bey ordered again, though, fascinated by events, she had no intention of going. And then Jenny started to cry and Nuri bey took out his pocket handkerchief and mopped her eyes and put his arm round her shoulders, as though she were a child.

It was mainly about the hanging, she said, it was like a nightmare, she could hardly believe it had really happened, and listening, shocked, Nuri bey could hardly believe it either. He was probably far more shocked at what had happened to Jenny than she was herself. Kneeling on the floor beside her chair and listening to what she was saying, Nuri's heart cringed within him.

She went on to tell him how sorry she was that she left

his house the way she did, and why. It became so dark that the woman officiously switched on the light, a central pendant round which Valance had arranged a lace and satin-lined shade. "Do not leave," Nuri bey again ordered, unnecessarily.

"You must come away with me, Jenny," he stated. "I shall telephone for a taxi to take us to the ferry. You shall come back home with me."

But no, Jenny could not do that. She must stay. She was sure that Tony was here. She had searched the house and there had been no sign of him, but nevertheless she was sure this was his headquarters, and to prove her point she asked Nuri bey to open the top left-hand drawer of the chest.

He stared down at the photograph of the handsome, wry face of Tony Grand and tried to understand why it should be found in Valance's drawer.

"You see?"

Even his inward eye failed to function fully, so that he did not, in fact, see reason, he only guessed that Tony came to the *yali* from the airport, and asked for protection, with Valance already dead and lying on her bier in the hall ready for burial.

"You must come away with me," he repeated, looking round for her clothes.

"I can't, Nuri bey, really I can't. Madame has been quite kind to me since the hanging. I must show Tony some loyalty, even if he hasn't seemed to show me any. But maybe he simply couldn't help leaving me like that. Don't you understand? I must stay, if only to explain to him what happened to the case."

"What did happen to the case?" he asked grimly.

"I told you!"

"The case is worth thousands of dollars to Madame."

"I dare say, but if I'd been found with it I'd probably have been hanged. You must think I'm a bit of a fool, Nuri bey. I'm not the sweet and simple young thing you insist on thinking I am. Naturally I examined the case. I went into a public loo and opened it and I undid the packets of *locum;* they were neatly packed with all the

Haci Bekir wrapping and what have you, but inside they were solid blocks of heavy green stuff that smelt pretty horrid. Anyone with any sense could see it was raw opium, or something like that, mechanically compressed and cut into blocks the same size as a box of *locum*. That's why I went to the Turkish Delight shop near the bridge to have a look and see how it was packed. It was exactly the same and the boxes were made airtight by the Cellophane wrapping, so that the smell didn't escape till I opened them. Oh, my lord, what a sickly smell!"

She paused whilst a few involuntary indrawn gasps, the aftermath of weeping, shook her. "I did what anyone in their right mind would do; I threw it away! As I told you. Filthy stuff! And in the taxi on the way back Madame gave me a shot of it." She showed Nuri bey the small purple bruise on her forearm. "So I'm well on the way to being a heroin addict, old dear. It was marvellous, and according to all the books, I shan't be happy now until I get another shot. I could do with one now."

In the years to come Nuri bey would have much to say arising from all the information he had received but for the moment he had nothing to say other than that she must come back home with him at once.

And that was the one thing Jenny would not consent to do. Her argument was reasonable enough, she must get into contact with Tony; once she had seen him she would be satisfied and would then do anything Nuri bey wished. Until then she must stay near Miasma—if she failed to do so, she would never forgive herself. She would have all the rest of her life, during which probably nothing exciting would happen, to regret not having done all she could for Tony.

If she left with Nuri bey she might never hear of Tony again. An affair like this simply could not be left suspended, as it were, in mid-air. A decision must be arrived at, if only in her own mind.

Nuri bey, seeing the reason of what she had to say, made her promise that she would not allow Madame to give her another injection, and to this, seeing reason also on his side, she agreed. Neither, he said, was she to have anything to eat or drink that had been prepared by anyone but herself, in this house.

He pointed out graphically that throwing people into the Bosphorus was an old Turkish custom, and one, he regretted to say, still frequently employed. She could be doped into unconsciousness and put into a sack, weighed down with stones, and flung into the almost bottomless deeps within a few feet of the *yali* windows. And Jenny, having seen what she had already seen, could readily believe it. Furthermore, he went on relentlessly, to perform such duties with young girls of the Sultan's harem who had been unfaithful to the Shadow of God upon Earth, the Grand Signior (i.e. the Sultan), would fall to Hadji as one of those in charge of the harem in the first decade of the century. To undertake such a task would commend itself instinctively to Hadji.

"Doing what comes naturally," she murmured inexplicably with a frail smile.

"You're a brave girl," he said, "and, as I have always heard of the English, you do not take real danger seriously. You laugh in the face of death."

"Oh, no, I don't," she returned crossly.

He stared at her whilst the thought went through his mind of the diver who went over the side of a ship that was anchored in some shallows off the Seraglio Point, to do repairs, and was horrified to see half a dozen corpses of young girls, not long dead, standing upright, balanced by heavy stones at the bottom of sacks from which their heads emerged, nodding and bowing with the movement of the current, with eyes wide open and hair waving slowly to and fro. . . . The sight drove the diver out of his mind so that for ever afterwards he bowed and swayed in imitation of the corpses.

"Why are you looking at me like that, Nuri? You're giving me the shivers!"

Before leaving, he went himself to the kitchen and made tea, which he brought to the bedside with instructions that she must drink as much fluid as she could to clean out of her bloodstream the remains of the drug. After that the best thing would be for her to go to sleep again. He would return to-morrow, when he would see Miasma and ask her for an explanation. They could not go on any longer in this manner, he observed: Madame was behaving in an unwomanly way. As an old woman, within a few steps of Paradise, it was unseemly and he would insist that proper explanation for her behaviour be given him. And as for Tony, Nuri bey said, he had certain ideas as to what could be done about him. Unwilling though he was to have anything more to do with the affair, for Jenny's sake, and for that reason only, it might be that he could arrange for Tony to leave the environment secretly and go into hiding in a more secure place.

Nuri bey's sister in Trebizond was by no means well-off. If he telephoned to her, he thought she might agree to take a young foreigner as paying guest for a few weeks, and, in the meantime, something else could be arranged. He told Jenny all this but carefully avoided mentioning the shoes, without which Tony could not either have gone—or go—far.

It was obvious that the effect of the drug had not worn off, her eyelids were heavy with sleep, and patting her shoulder he told her to settle down and to remember: he would come back to take her away from this place.

Ordering the cleaning woman to stay until Madame and Hadji returned, he stalked stiffly from the room. The great empty hall was almost dark, the bird room silent. He stood at the foot of the stairs, absolutely still, and emptied his mind of every thought so that he became a kind of receiving set for any oscillations that might be in the atmosphere. He had had an aunt who was clairvoyant and by emptying her mind of thought she was often able to see things which had happened or things which were going to happen in the place where she was at the time. But, as so often in the past, when he had tried, no pictures were shown on the screen of his mind. He took the suède shoes into the salon and hid them behind a divan. And whilst he waited for the bus he had a few words with the proles of the market square.

Back again in Europe, he swung on to a tram on Galata

Bridge. He stood head and shoulders above the people in the tram who clung to it like flies in the autumn in the corner of an attic window. So much of his life was spent on a bus, or a ferry or a tram, hurrying from Continent to Continent yet going nowhere. He never ceased to travel and yet he had never left his country. It was a saddening thought which was with him till he reached his own front door, by which time he was assailed by an even sadder one. Someone had been in his house.

He went slowly round from room to room. Everywhere there were small signs that someone other than himself had been: opening and shutting, turning upside down and reinstating, pulling out, looking behind and replacing, standing up on chairs or looking on top of, kneeling down on the floor and looking underneath of . . . Hadji and Miasma . . . Hadji or Miasma . . . what did it matter which?

Lately he had been too preoccupied to take his carpet-bag of valuable books up to his bedroom: it was still behind the Shirvan carpet which acted as a curtain across his front door in winter-time. He pulled it out and opened it. They had been through it all right. Everyone who knew Nuri bey knew also about his carpet-bag of treasures. People whom he liked would be shown the entire fabulous contents which he would display somewhat in the manner of a conjurer, giving time between tricks for assimilation of the last before starting on the next.

Any other man would go to his sideboard for the whisky bottle to calm his nerves; Nuri bey's long slender fingers picked out from amongst his other treasures an early illuminated manuscript of the synoptic gospels. He took it into his study where he sat for a long time in his upright chair, turning the pages and looking at the strange representations of the first Evangelists.

When, finally, he went upstairs to bed he took with him from the carpet-bag the cream of his possessions. But as he lay staring sleepless up into the dark there came over him an active dislike of his bedfellows.

Chapter 11

EARLY IN the morning Jenny got up and washed as well as she could in the tiny basin in about half a pint of water, which the cleaner had brought the evening before, dressed, brushed her hair, camouflaged her pretty mouth and eyes with an abstract design of lipstick and eyeblack and went purposefully downstairs to make herself tea. The kitchen appalled her; a dingy cave with blackened ceiling and creeper-covered window, it was impregnated and reeking with the strange smell of the oil which is used for the cooking stoves in Turkey, a distinctive smell which often finds its way into the food. There was nothing that looked remotely like a kettle so after a small struggle to light the stove with the aid of her lighter, she half-filled an earthenware crock with water which she put on to boil.

She had a long thoughtful look at a door leading out of the kitchen which she was sure opened into Hadji's bedroom. A sound came through to her which she could not identify, having never heard anything like it but which she decided from the regular rhythm, was the sound of snoring. Whilst waiting for the water to boil she had a quick tour of the ground floor: beside the front door the dark salon with a strongly unused smell, the vast low, heavy divans lining the walls, the elaborate metal charcoal stove in the centre of the room; the prim Victorian dining-room with its faded Morris wallpaper, its upright chairs, the backs pierced with heart-shaped holes, the fumed oak dining-table with turned legs and white china castors. She lingered in the bird room; the birds were awake, lively and unaccountably busy in their cages. She opened the french windows and stepped out on to the terrace. It was a beautiful morning, the sky was of palest blue but the seething navy blue Bosphorus took no hint of gentleness from the sky.

Apart from what Nuri bey had said about the Bosphorus it frightened her. The thought of all that water pouring through that narrow channel from one great inland sea to another for thousands, perhaps millions of years, was impressive enough but the whole stretch of hurrying fluid somehow lacked the peace which a large expanse of water can engender. People sit placidly watching huge rollers restlessly moving up and down the sands, others find rest for the soul by the great still lakes of Sweden, but on the shores of the most historic waterway in the world there is no peace to be had, nor comfort. Stepping carefully down the few stone stairs to the extreme edge Jenny peered into the water to see if she could see the bottom. The bank sloped down almost vertically, disappearing from sight at a distance of two feet from the edge. How deep is bottomless? she wondered. As though at a cry of alarm she whipped round suddenly. She could see no one and there had been no sound but her knees were shaking.

I need some food, she thought, and going back to the kitchen she made tea, found some bread and oranges and stood by the table trying to steady herself by assuring herself that the situation was normal, or nearly so. She jumped violently, however, when the door of Hadji's room opened and he came out, fully dressed, a dust-ball with a small monkey's face.

Jenny stopped chewing, opened her eyes widely and stared at him as rudely as she could manage, which was quite rude. Not understanding that she was trying to insult him he peered anxiously up into her face. What he saw he evidently found satisfactory, for he nodded approvingly and murmured something which she did not get.

He then started a kind of muddled slow bustle, clearing a space on the table, bringing out a large basket; he told her something with regard to his preparations that she did not get either. Finally he left with the basket on his arm and his cloth cap on his head. Remembering Nuri bey's instructions to drink tea she refilled her small cup a number of times; she was still drinking tea when he returned with the basket full of what he had bought:

bread, butter, fruit, vegetables, and several small dishes of yoghourt.

"Hamam," he said once or twice and she realised suddenly that he was making preparations for Madame's visit to the Turkish bath.

In the bird room Jenny found Madame fully dressed, feeding and twittering at her birds. She gave Jenny a nodding, satisfied look. "You have had a good night, I see. You have slept very well, *n'est ce pas?* You are better."

Fortified by her breakfast Jenny swung into the heart of the matter; she had told Madame about the case and it was now Madame's turn to tell her about Tony. Tony was the only reason for her presence in the *yali,* if it were not for him she would not be here, an unwanted guest.

"I do not know . . . I do not know . . . I do not know. . . ." Madame answered, reiterating in an ascending scale so that her final denial came out a shriek. "And it is equal to me where he is, I occupy myself only with the case."

"But it is too absolutely absurd," Jenny reasoned "I do not know where the case is, you do not know where Tony is, we can both go on telling each other lies for ever at this rate!"

"Lies . . . lies . . . lies . . .!" Miasma held her head in the orthodox manner of a woman purporting to be driven to the edge of insanity by the imbecilities of the young. "To-day is Thursday. On Sunday evening my Valance died, on Monday evening your Tony ran away from you . . . hush, let me speak . . . on Tuesday morning early my Valance was buried . . . that event alone is enough to cut my life in half. But because of your miserable Tony my case of great value to me is missing. Perhaps it was wrong of me to take you to the hanging but I do not know how to treat the young, I do not understand you, and it was my method of shocking you into doing as I require!"

She put her box of bird seed down on the love-seat

and stood in front of Jenny, pointing and gesticulating with one raised finger. "Monday, Tuesday, Wednesday . . . three days of a kind I have never spent in my life. Three days during which the police are looking for your Tony. Any minute now they may find him. When they find him he will confess that he left the case with you. So you must understand that for all of us it is better that you stay beside me for the moment. You must also realise this it not an exciting adventure; it is a matter of life and death. You soft Westerners do not know how serious life in the East of Europe has become; pleasure-seeking and decadent, you laugh your way into terrible dangers and even to witness a horrible sight of a public hanging does not seem to bring you to your senses."

Hadji came in bearing an armful of soft-looking white Turkish towels and a short outbreak of Turkish talk followed. She turned back to Jenny who was now walking forlornly round the room, looking unseeing into the bird-cages.

"To-day is Thursday," Miasma hissed. "The day before Friday; on Friday Valance and I go to the mosque. On Thursday Valance and I go to the *hamam*. Eleven months of the year for many years Valance has gone to the *hamam* with me on Thursdays and to-day I shall have to take you with me for I cannot go alone."

"Why not?"

"Why not?" she repeated indignantly, "because I cannot go alone, of course! So get on your coat, Hadji drives us to the ferry and then a taxi to the best *hamam* in Istanbul. Come, my child!"

"Nuri bey is coming."

"Pfui!" She clicked her fingers with a gesture of dismissal.

Jenny shouted: "Take your hands off me, I hate you, I hate you! Oh, my lord! you're a horrible old woman!" she added in English.

Miasma could perfectly tolerate hysterical shouting. "You had better come," she murmured soothingly, "in that quiet, relaxed place you will perhaps see the futility of your stubbornness. You will perhaps tell me everything!"

"Oh, damn you, you old witch!" Jenny yelled futilely but feeling a lot better.

"Because," Miasma went on smoothly, "you know what the next thing will be? It will be to burn down the house where the evidence lies. . . ."

Enchanted with her own burst of rage Jenny hardly heard and she was sitting in the ancient De Dion Bouton before she started to figure out what had been meant.

So the *yali* was left empty and the front door locked with a large key which Hadji slipped into his sagging jacket pocket. A few minutes after they had gone one of the proles, a mere bundle of rags, arrived from the post office with a telegram. He or she, whichever it might have been was not evident, banged the knocker and waited, banged again and sat down on the step with crossed legs, resigned to a long wait with the tolerance of a human being who has never in a lifetime done anything other than wait.

Then a number of events took place which were of such unusual proportions that the bundle of rags with the telegram completely forgot about the telegram in its hand and simply sat where it was eating up the scene with its great eyes.

First a tumble-down truck arrived, stopping at the gate; two men climbed down from the cabin and rolled back the tarpaulin from an object at the back. It was a large, long, narrow wooden box with four elaborate metal handles. It was not exactly rectangular; being quite narrow at one end it grew gradually larger at the other. One of the men approached the front door with a delivery note to be signed.

"No one in," the bundle of rags volunteered.

"Urgent goods from the airport: came over on the first ferry," the delivery man announced.

"Leave it, the manservant will soon return."

The men drove away in the van and the bundle of rags stared and stared at the long narrow box lying on the flags of the courtyard with the rhododendrons nodding over it in the frisky morning breeze.

Next, the bus noisily passed the door and half a minute later Nuri bey appeared at the gate.

"No one in," the bundle of rags offered.

Nuri bey walked round the oblong box. He thought he knew what it was, having seen illustrations of such things in some of the strange books he read, as, for instance, Foxe's *Book of Martyrs*.

"A box for the dead," he murmured to himself and tried to remember the English word for it.

The garage was built backwards from the main road, taking off a corner of the courtyard and now, between the leaves of the rhododendrons, he could see glimpses of the De Dion being backed into it; he heard the doors being closed and Hadji appeared at the gate, having delivered Miasma and Jenny at the ferry. He saw the oblong case at once and shuffled across to it.

"Urgent goods from the airport," the bundle of rags announced, "came over on the first ferry."

A strange feeling which he could not define was enveloping Nuri bey. He went up to the front door and leaned against it with his arms folded, his lips firmly closed in a tight line, his eyes shining with an almost unearthly light. Hadji went round and round the box like a dog examining an unfamiliar object. He took one of the handles and lifted the box slightly to feel the weight. "Empty? Who sent it, Efendim?"

Nuri bey shrugged elaborately. "Where is Madame?"

"It is Thursday, Efendim, she is at the *hamam* as usual."

"And Mademoiselle?"

"There also." Hadji was so absorbed he showed no surprise at the Efendi's question. "But who would send an empty box, Efendim?"

"It is a box," Nuri bey announced, "for the dead."

Hadji raised a face of a thousand wrinkles. "For the dead?"

"In the West they put their dead into boxes before they bury them or before they burn them."

"Ah, so . . .!"

A low strange sound came from the bundle of rags which was now rocking itself slightly.

Nuri bey, arms still folded, looked up at the bright sky as though some tremendous thing had been proved, the sun shone down into the courtyard with early morning vitality, the stiff leaves rustled, sometimes a noisy car passed.

And then a taxi stopped and from it stepped a small, slight woman entirely encased in black and wearing an important hat, who paid the taxi-driver and, opening the iron gate, came briskly down into the courtyard with dignity and purpose.

"Ah, *bon, il est arrivé!*" she said, with a glance at the coffin. "Madame Miasma?"

"She is out," Nuri bey faltered into rather less than fluent French. "I am an acquaintance of hers; I have called also, to find her out. This," he indicated Hadji, "is her servant."

"Ah! I have no particular wish to meet Madame Miasma. I have come for the body of my sister. All arrangements have been made, there is nothing for me to do other than remove what rests of her. Later the arrangements for the sending of her personal possessions will be made. In the meantime, Monsieur . . ."

"If you would kindly repeat . . ." Nuri bey begged.

She did so. Valance's sister Martine!

"Hadji, open the door and let us inside. We cannot discuss this matter here."

Hadji was still musing over the coffin but now he brought out the key and opened the door. Nuri bey led the Frenchwoman into the cold hall.

"I do not wish to trouble you, Monsieur. Perhaps the servant can help me."

"He understands French but he cannot speak it well. I am afraid he will not be of much assistance to you, Madame. But I will try to help you as well as I can. If you will kindly explain once more, and more slowly, if you please."

"Bassompierre," she said and for a few moments Nuri

bey completedly failed to understand that she was not swearing but simply giving her surname.

Madame Bassompierre could see no difficulty whatever with regard to her visit. She had received a telegram on Monday morning informing her of the death of her sister Valance. She had wired back immediately that she would come by the earliest possible aeroplane and bring with her a coffin. Having arranged for the body of her dear sister to follow by freight, she was returning to Paris this evening; Valance's relatives would meet the plane at Orly when it arrived early to-morrow morning and the funeral would take place on Saturday as arranged at Père Lachaise cemetery.

She had arrived by jet late last night and had gone straight to a hotel where, for the present, she had left her hand luggage, which she would pick up on the way back to the airport.

Her son-in-law being, fortunately, the friend of a customs official, she had been able to make arrangements very quickly; the whole matter had been rushed through with the utmost smoothness.

"And now, Monsieur, if I could be taken to the body of my dead sister . . . or perhaps she has been removed to some temporary place of rest for the dead?"

She was clearly in for a very great shock indeed. To give himself time, Nuri bey repeated everything to Hadji.

It was impossible for the eunuch to pale or to show any signs of physical anguish other than those which were his standard pattern; but he did start to tremble.

Remembering how his Western friends flew automatically to the bottle in moments of uncertainty, or indeed any moment whatever, Nuri bey ordered *raki* to be brought to the salon into which he ceremoniously showed Madame Bassompierre, offering her, when she was comfortably seated on a divan, a cigarette from the case which he kept for his Western friends. She refused and seemed impatient. "You understand, Monsieur, it is a task which I wish to have done. If I had had a husband he would have performed this for me, but alas! we are a troupe of widows in my family; such men as we have are of younger generation and their work prevents their coming. Yes, thank you, a little of your national drink, if you please." She sipped delicately at the *raki* whilst Hadji cowered in the shadows.

"Did you have the good fortune to meet my sister, the companion of Madame Miasma?"

Nuri bey postponed the moment when he must tell her. Yes, he had met Valance. He came every week to the *yali* to read to Madame and he had often had a word or two with Valance on his way out. She had been a wonderful servant . . . that is . . . companion to Madame, who was going to miss her very much. So much, indeed, that he doubted whether she would continue to live here alone. She was old and it might be more expedient for her to live in a hotel.

Yes, Madame Bassompierre agreed, she was indeed old, and so was Valance, her elder sister by fifteen years. Valance herself should be too old for the work, if it had not been for her deep devotion to Madame Miasma she would have retired and returned to her own country long ago. "But Valance has never ailed a thing in her life, as strong as a little goat, and energetic . . . for her age she was a marvel. She has been sure she would not die before Madame and for the last few years, when we have begged her to stay at home with me, she always said she must return and stay with Miasma to the end. Those were her words, stay with her to the end. Alas, my poor Valance, she did not ever think it was she who would go first!"

Evidently finding the *raki* to her liking, Madame sipped more frequently until the glass was empty and Nuri bey, watchful, refilled it.

"Ah, the poor soul! It was not her wish that she should die in a foreign country. Long ago, and every time she has been home, I promised that if she were ill I would come at once and take her home. Perhaps we should all be thankful that her end was so quick. I suppose you can't give me any details, Monsieur? The telegram simply said 'died suddenly.' "

"I know that Madame Miasma has written a letter to

you with the details, but as it was written only yesterday you would not have had time to receive it."

"I have received no letter, only the telegram."

"Your sister was standing beside Madame. It was a warm evening and after supper Madame Miasma went out on to the steps beside the Bosphorus. Your sister complained of violent pain in her head and Madame went in to get her some remedy. She did not see your sister alive again; it is understood that she fell forward into the water."

"Alas, my poor sister."

"Her body was discovered within a few hours, washed into the shallows a mile or so downstream. They say she died before she entered the water."

A few small cries, a few sighs, another sip of *raki* and she had accepted the news but explained that to die unshriven, without the benefits of the Holy Church was about the worst thing that could happen to a Catholic. It was for this reason, perhaps particularly, that Madame Bassompierre had made this prodigious effort to bring her body home for a Christian funeral and burial in consecrated ground.

Miasma's visit to the *hamam* was an elaborate affair which took the whole day; she would not be back till evening. As Nuri bey saw it, there was nothing to do but tell Madame Bassompierre the worst and help the poor woman on her way back home in the kindest and most courteous way he could manage. Women in Turkey did as they were told and he had no experience of any other way of life. He formed sentences in his mind, trying to decide what form was the most suitable way of breaking the news.

But by now the *raki* was having an effect. Madame Bassompierre loosened the sable tippet she wore round her neck and undid the buttons of her smart black jacket.

"Not that my poor sister was a good Catholic as we understand it," she went on. "In fact there were many, many ways in which I could not understand Valance. But a sister is a sister, Monsieur, and what passes for affection towards a sister is of no value whatever if there

is not also loyalty. Family loyalty, Monsieur, you understand?"

Nuri bey, too, had a sister and he fully understood.
Why had he not told her immediately? he thought irritably; the postponement of the news of her burial had
simply made things more poignant; he was beginning to
like the Frenchwoman and to care a little about having
to distress her.

"Madame Bassompierre," he began.

"And moreover . . ." she went on robustly, "once a
Catholic always a Catholic. Our poor dear Valance,
though she sinned very much, was good at heart, Monsieur, good at heart!"

"Madame Bassompierre," he persisted, "your sister is
already buried."

The tiny *raki* glass, half-way to Madame Bassompierre's
mouth, was replaced on the tray. "I do not understand,
Monsieur."

"She received a Moslem burial; prayers were said for
her. The followers of Mohammed believe that the dead
suffer agony before they lie safely in the grave; the burial
always takes place as soon as possible. Owing to the
nature of Valance's death she could not be buried before
sunset on the day of her death but she was taken to her
grave shortly after sunrise on the next day. On Tuesday,
that is. The *imam* recited prayers and Madame Miasma
and Hadji followed her to her grave. There were hired
weepers round the house all night." Nuri bey hesitated.
He considered it bad taste to mention money but thought
it expedient. "Madame Miasma spent much money in
giving her old companion a funeral worthy of her devoted
service for so many years."

"Oh, *mon Dieu, mon Dieu, mon Dieu!*"

"The name of the dead was called over her body three
times when it lay at rest, and also the name of her
mother."

"Her mother! How could anyone know the name of
our mother?"

Nuri bey turned to Hadji who, though looking utterly

cowed, had seemed to follow the conversation. "Fatima
. . ." he croaked. "The *imam* called Fatima. . . ."

At which Madame gave a fairly piercing scream.

"We have no boxes for the dead," Nuri bey went on
smoothly, "they are wrapped from head to foot with
material which winds them tightly round and covered
with a green cloth."

"Mon Dieu, mon Dieu, mon Dieu!" Madame Bassompierre moaned.

Hadji plucked at Nuri bey's sleeve and poured a
torrent of mumbling Turkish into his ear. He was asking
him if he should go at once and fetch Madame home
from the *hamam* to attend to this crisis. No, Nuri bey told
him, he was to wait: it might be that Nuri bey himself
could deal with the situation and there would be no need
to bother Madame.

"Ayez pitié de moi!" Madame Bassompierre was beg-
ging her God, *"mon Dieu, mon Dieu, mon Dieu!"*

Nuri bey using the Turkish equivalent of "pull yourself
together," gave orders to Hadji. These orders caused
the eunuch's eyes almost to capsize in his skull. He was
to go out now, at once, to take the path up from the
village past the hovels, up and up through the burial
ground until he came to the new grave which Madame
had bought for herself, into which Valance had been
placed; he was to observe what the condition of this grave
was at the moment; was it still covered with the planks
which were put over the body immediately it was lowered
into the grave, or had the earth already been replaced?

"At once, immediately and now!" Nuri bey commanded and Hadji shuffled away, but very slowly.

Madame Bassompierre's hand came out and clawed up
the tiny *raki* glass, then replaced it swiftly but not too
swiftly for Nuri bey to observe the movement. Blandly
he refilled the glass.

"Fatima, as though our mother would be called Fatima!" she moaned as though this were the ultimate insult.

"Pauvre Madame," he murmured soothingly, "my poor,
poor lady. Calm yourself, my dear lady, calm yourself."

Presently Madame Bassompierre began to recover from her temporary defeat. Her resources were reforming themselves in newly discovered strength.

"I shall not return home without the body of my sister," she declared. "This body is my property. She has been dead only three days; there is nothing to prevent my taking her home. . . ."

"Except perhaps a weight of earth on top of her," Nuri bey reminded her, "and permission."

"Permission to regain my own property! Nonsense!" But it was not nonsense, as she seemed to realise during a long pause. "Then I must see the parish priest."

"We have no such person."

"Naturally I do not mean the Catholic priest, I know you have none here, but surely even Mohammedans have a shepherd of a kind?"

"If you mean the *imam;* he is the nearest we have to a parish priest."

"*Imam,* that's it. It was the *imam* who attended the funeral, wasn't it? Where can I find him?"

"The *imam* is usually to be found in the mosque. Between the times of prayer he can often be found instructing."

"Take me to him!"

Nuri bey was profoundly shocked. Though the *imam,* he pointed out, was a married man he was not particularly interested in women as parishioners. The mosque was, in the main, for the men, the women followed the men's example and went to the mosque but they sat apart from the men, at the back, in small pens round the back wall, and were of no account. Though Madame Miasma attended the mosque regularly and often Valance went with her, it was doubtful if the *imam* would know Valance even by sight.

"Shocking, shocking!" Madame Bassompierre declared, "like sheep, in pens round the wall! Alas, that our poor Valance should choose to end her life in such a barbaric country!"

But she was not to be deflected; she had come for the remains of Valance and she would not return without them. Permission would have to be given for Valance's body to be taken from the grave and put into the coffin she had brought. The quicker it was done the better, evidently. If necessary she would go at once to the French Consulate. There was no need to tell her that it could not be done; she knew there was nothing that money could not do. Valance had been a great saver and most of the money she had earned, over all these years in Turkey, had, against all regulations, been banked in France. She had left everything to her relatives and, as soon as the law permitted, the bills incurred for the whole operation would be paid in full. In the meantime Madame Bassompierre had supplied herself with enough cash to pay any immediate expenses.

"I have an idea," Nuri bey said and as he unfolded it Madame Bassompierre stared at him with incredulous scorn so that towards the end of his dissertation he faltered into silence.

"I understand, Monsieur, that you are suggesting I should return to my country with a coffin in which we have placed a few stones . . . have pity on me," she pleaded to a Deity who could allow her to be insulted by such an imbecile idea.

He had only half-believed in the idea himself and he had put it forward only to delay certain actions which he had known from the first he was going to take.

Swiftly he left the room whilst Madame Bassompierre took the opportunity of refilling her tiny glass.

He was back in a few moments and, like a conjurer with his ace trick, put down on the small table beside the tray, facing Madame, the photograph of Tony Grand.

Madame Bassompierre nodded, unastonished. *"Mais oui! Un beau garçon!"*

"Who is it?"

"Tony Grand. My great-nephew. Valance's grandson."

"French or English? Tell me about him, please."

"His father was an English soldier; he married my niece when the Allies were occupying the Maginot Line. He met her on leave in Paris and took her back to England. Later he was killed in the retreat to Dunkirk. His son was brought up by his French mother in England. Alas, she had to work hard to keep him and he had to be evacuated away from her. Monsieur, that boy had a hard childhood. My niece lost her head. She had far too gay a time with the American soldiers. In the end she married again and went to America; the new husband turned out to be a brute. Oh, things were terrible for my poor niece. However, she lives there permanently now and has found a job for herself. She is a naturalised American. Yes, poor Tony! He was fond of his grandmother. We will have to let him know about her death. She has left him well off."

"Where is he now?"

"Monsieur, he is an air steward at the present time, working for Zenobia Airways. We shall have no difficulty in finding him."

"Valance's grandson? She was married, then?"

"Alas no, Monsieur, she was not married. Valance had an illegitimate child, my niece."

"Ah, I see, I see. That explains a great deal."

"If by a great deal you mean her devotion to Madame Miasma, yes. Before the First World War, in our small bourgeois society, you understand, it was a disgrace for a woman to 'get into trouble.' Valance could not stay; she heard that she could get work in Turkey, and she left. Madame Miasma met her working as a masseuse in the Turkish bath, desperate, within a month of her delivery. She was kind to her and brought her to her house, here, I take it." She looked round in surprise. "Yes, to this same house. And here my sister had her child, and kept her beside her for years. Later she brought it home to France for a Catholic upbringing and would see her only once a year when she came home on holiday."

Nuri bey in desperation played his final trump. "Are you not aware, Madame, that the police of Turkey and of England are searching for your great-nephew? he is wanted for murder." If he intended it to be a superdramatic thunderbolt, it was a mere damp squib.

"That doesn't astonish me," Madame Bassompierre

answered. "Since he grew out of being a beautiful little angel he has been a fearful devil, Monsieur."

Nuri bey could not resist a smile at her emphatic manner, the way she said *"un beau petit ange"* with pursed lips and appropriate gestures and flung her whole self into *"un diable affreux."* "And furthermore, I don't think his mother cares. She is hard-hearted, that one, she loves only herself. But his grandmother cared. My poor Valance, she loved him dearly, she was proud of his looks, his success with women, his panache! I am so sad for my poor sister to hear this news. Maybe the shock brought on her stroke."

"Valance died before it took place. She did not know."

"A mercy. Tell me, please, Monsieur, since you seem very much at home here, what happened?"

"He shot dead an airline security detective at the airport and he has not been seen since."

Madame Bassompierre gave Nuri bey a long steady look. "You know the reason?"

"Why should I?"

"Smuggling, Monsieur. He was in trouble before but nothing was proved against him. Last time she was home Valance was very upset indeed about it all. She tried to talk him out of it, to frighten him but he only laughed at her. He took her out for rides in the fine little sports car he had bought, and to meals in expensive restaurants to tease her and when they got home he would say, *'Voila, grandmère,* how could I do that without a lot of extra money!' and then she would laugh—I can see her now. She would laugh and pat his face and tell him not to get caught! She adored that boy Tony!"

"Under these circumstances, Madame, would it not be better for you to go back home immediately and drop the question of taking the body of your sister?" Nuri bey said persuasively. "It is more than possible that someone, sooner or later, will connect your great-nephew with this house. It can't be much longer before they do. People in this village have seen him coming here. They are frightened of the police and it is because of that that no one so far has been to them with the information. But *sooner or later* someone will go."

"Then the sooner I get Valance's body away the better," she declared, getting up briskly and picking up her handbag and mink necklet. "Are you trying to frighten me?"

"Yes, in a way I am. I'm trying to frighten you out of doing something which I know you ought to give up trying to do."

"Nothing will persuade me, Monsieur. It is my duty. Please take me at once to your *imam.*" And to show that she meant what she said she stumped out of the salon. Though never guilty of pushing through a door in front of a lady, Nuri bey now nipped nimbly past her and managed to get one half of the front door open before she had time to study the panel at the back which clearly showed the blackened bullet holes.

On the top step the telegram bearer rocked itself slowly backwards and forwards, prepared to wait until the end of time. An extremely thin grey arm emerged with the envelope in its hand. Nuri bey took it and opened it, after a few puzzled moments he handed it to Madame Bassompierre; this was not a suitable time to apologize for his country's dilatoriness. It read:

> GEVIENS IMEDIATEMENTE APPORTEZ LECORESE DEM
> ASUR APARRIS
>
> MAR TINBAS SON PPEERREE

Chapter 12

FROM TIME to time Nuri bey made sudden temporary retreats from the world around him into a kind of spiritual communion with himself, and, as it was now clear that for the moment she had lost his attention, Madame Bassompierre gave the coffin a very thorough examination to assure herself that it was undamaged in transit.

Hereditary Moslems differ from other people in that

they are possessed of a kind of inner clock and compass outfit so that wherever and whenever they are, they instinctively know the hour of prayer and the exact angle at which to face Mecca for their prayers. During Nuri bey's unexpected withdrawal Madame Bassompierre finished her appraisal of the coffin and stood, restlessly tapping her foot and looking expectantly at him, when the air was suddenly full of a metallic hollow sound which might have been the noise of a herd of maddened elephants approaching with trunks raised, honking loudly in mass hysteria. It was the call to prayer from a nearby mosque relayed on a record through the Tannoy; though the same words are used, it is a different sound altogether from that of the cry to prayer of the *muezzins* from the minarets of the Blue Mosque.

Madame Bassompierre gave a shuddering shout of terror, signing herself with the Cross and taking some sort of instinctive cover under the rhododendrons.

Nuri bey came out of his trance to observe a strange phenomenon; Hadji flashed past the gate and Nuri bey could just see through the leaves the garage doors open and the De Dion Bouton being driven out and away towards Uskudar, well before the noise had ceased.

It was probably the only time in his adult life that Hadji had ignored the hour of prayer. He had overdone the lack of speed with which he had left the salon; once the door had shut behind him he must have carried out Nuri bey's instructions at the speed of sound.

So now all was easy: Nuri bey came down the steps smiling again as though something had been proved. He explained that it was the hour of prayer and it would be quite impossible for anyone, let alone a woman, to talk to the *imam*. What he would now do would be to take Madame Bassompierre to the grave of her sister. He pointed to the hillside rising steeply on the other side of the road. It was not far, a little walk up through the pines.

In the village he asked one of the Biblical characters exactly where the new grave was and, watched by many dark, thoughtful eyes, he guided the Frenchwoman up the stony path, past a few hovels, into the cemetery.

The stone styles which mark the graves are best described as stone posts, each carved at the top with a kind of funny hat, turban or fez which tells the knowledgeable the status of the person so commemorated. When there is no hat, the top foot or so of post is carved with Arabic writing. No attempt is made to keep the conventional shape of the grave; the styles, in the course of time, become loose and lean this way and that, in confusion; sometimes they fall down altogether and low shrubs grow over them. There are dozens of square miles of cemetery near the Bosphorus and up the hills behind Istanbul and along the shores of the Golden Horn. Rarely are people seen walking amongst the graves; relatives do not visit with flowers; once they are covered with earth, the dead are left to Allah, first expiating their sins which, according to the Prophet, will have been noted in a "glorious book in which all things are recorded," and then, with luck, are elevated to Paradise. Many believe that the worst offenders suffer tortures in the grave and it may be for this reason that Moslems avoid cemeteries.

The sunshine was now hot and the path rough going. Madame Bassompierre began to gasp with heat. She took off her black gloves, her fur tippet and finally her jacket which Nuri bey carried, and presently her face became screwed up momentarily and frequently with the twinges of pain from her feet.

"Not very much farther," he repeated from time to time, encouragingly. Once or twice he stopped and pointed out the view which, as they mounted, became magnificent with the Bosphorus as dignified and grand as becomes one of the great waterways of the world, and not merely a deep ditch between two continents.

"*C'est incroyable,*" she gasped now and then; Nuri bey did not realise she was referring to the distance and the discomfort rather than the view and assumed an air of placid pride in his country that was not quite justified under the circumstances.

She took her passport from her handbag and fanned

herself with it and Nuri bey took out his passport, looked at it, wondered whether to fan himself with it or not, decided it would be an unmanly act and replaced it in his breast pocket. It was certainly very hot indeed. The bees hummed amongst the wild lavender, the scent of thyme and other tangy herbs was intoxicating, but for Madame Bassompierre it now became an endurance test.

"Nearly there," Nuri encouraged. Finally, they reached the absolute summit and Madame Bassompierre gave a wild cry of distress as they began to descend.

"There it is!" he cried with joy hardly commensurate with the occasion. The grave was noticeable only because there was a pile of earth beside it. They stumbled over the rough ground and at the graveside Madame Bassompierre burst into tears and fell to her knees whilst Nuri bey with delicacy turned his back.

And whilst she prayed he had a strange experience, of a kind which he had known several times in his life and which was either a genuine faculty for clairvoyance inherited from his aunt, or a simple attack of *déjà vu* in which, at a time when it is overtired or overstrained, the mind divides.

It was as though he himself was drawn clean out of his body and sucked up into the ether some feet above him. Looking down he saw that Miasma's companion Valance was standing at his side, by the grave. She was dressed in her neat black as he always saw her, her pale silvery hair drawn back smoothly into a small bun. She was pointing down into the grave and looking up into his face as though to prove something.

And the grave was empty. He looked carefully to make sure he was not mistaken but no, he could see the stones and the clay-like earth at the bottom, a different colour from the heap of topsoil. He saw himself staring down and she stared down, too, and together they stood side by side and looked down into the empty grave. Nothing startling happened but it was more real than reality until Nuri bey was back in his body, feeling extremely ill. His legs gave way under him and he lay down in the sweet smelling herbs, his face was no longer the shade of a hazel nut but the more ordinary colour of a pale-green olive.

Madame Bassompierre presently finished praying; she also apparently finished weeping and tucked her pocket handkerchief away in her waistbelt.

"Eh bien alors!" she started briskly and then her tone changed to one of concern. "Are you all right, Monsieur?"

Loathing weakness of any kind in himself, Nuri bey tried to spring lightly to his feet but he pulled himself slowly from the ground like an ancient man.

"You have exhausted yourself, my poor Monsieur. I am an ungrateful creature. You are being so very kind and I am accepting everything without question!"

He staggered to the graveside and looked down. The rough-hewn planks with which the body is covered were firmly in place, wedged under a ridge of clay shovelled out for the purpose. A few handfuls of earth which the *imam* had thrown down, lay on the top.

"You see, it will be a simple operation," Madame Bassompierre observed, "God did not intend her to be covered by the soil of Asia. She can be removed easily, perfectly. I see they cover the body with wood until they can put the earth back," she observed with a flash of French realism, "so that the wolves cannot get at her."

After a rest, during which Nuri bey thought hard, they started to walk slowly back the way they had come.

It could be done, he said at last, and having considered the question from every point of view, he had decided that it must be done secretly without any reference to the *imam*. But it would have to be done at night, between sunset and sunrise. There were certain people, he went on, who would, for a consideration (frankly, for money) carry out the work. These people were unhappy about the Christian having been buried for a Moslem; they thought that much bad luck might follow. They could easily be persuaded that the spell of ill luck might be broken if the mistake were put right. He could arrange for the body to be raised during the night, for a mule cart to come up by the path up which hearses would come from the main road, not by the path they had just taken, through the square and past the hovels. The mule cart would bring the coffin, it would be loaded and taken back, down the hill to the next village. There it would be met by a truck which would take it to the airport via the car ferry to Europe. Taking the first early-morning ferry it could be at the airport in time to catch any freight plane leaving to-morrow. It would certainly mean that the arrangements for the funeral would have to be put back a day, but in the matter of transport of the dead the airline officials were always helpfulness itself.

The wooden boards now over the body would be replaced over earth in such a way that, when the gravediggers finally came to fill in the grave, they would notice no disturbance. It could be several days before gravediggers were sent to perform this task and if, by any chance, they were to come to-day, before sunset, the people who would undertake to do the task for him would be perfectly capable of removing a ton or so of earth, if they were properly equipped.

And furthermore, Nuri bey could promise that those who would perform the task would be far too afraid to talk about it to anyone.

She must understand, he said firmly, that what they were about to arrange might not be exactly criminal, but it was a procedure without precedent, against every rule, law, convention, moral standard and, in a word, unique; the people whom Nuri bey intended to employ for the operation would do so only if they approved of it; they could not be bribed into doing what they knew to be wrong.

Furthermore, a body must be buried after sunrise or before sunset; it was right that the reverse operation should take place in the hours of darkness.

A Frenchwoman can almost always be relied upon to listen to reason and, after discussion, Madame Bassompierre saw the point absolutely. It would be inconvenient to have to postpone the funeral arrangements at home but, as Valance would lie in the family vault in Père Lachaise and not in a newly-dug grave, it could be done fairly simply. In view of the way telegrams were dealt with in Turkey, Madame would not think of wiring the new arrangements to her brother; it was absolutely necessary for her to return on the plane on which she had a reservation, and make the new arrangements in person.

"And now," Nuri bey said, "we must hurry a little. I must hire the mule cart at once; the coffin must be removed from the *yali* courtyard before Miasma sees it."

With the practicality of her kind, she opened her handbag and brought out Turkish money with which she had been well supplied in Paris, and gave Nuri bey a stout bundle. "You will need this!"

He thanked her and then broke one of the rules he always tried to keep but was finding increasingly difficult to do so; he asked a direct question. Did she want to see Madame Miasma?

She answered that she had not left home with that idea in mind, though she wanted to discuss Valance's possessions and the best way of transporting them back home; her bed being one item about which Valance had been anxious. Her sister had hated travelling by air and every time she did so she was afraid it would be the last. Consequently she had made a list, which Madame had here in her handbag, so there would be no need to see Miasma. And under the circumstances it was very much better not. When she got home she would write all instructions.

Nuri bey agreed emphatically, much relieved.

"My sister was on strange terms with Madame Miasma," she volunteered. "I was never able to understand their relationship. At the same time she loved . . . and she hated. I have never decided what kind of person Miasma was or is. And now it is too late, it is of no interest to me."

"She is a woman who has had a hard life. She has never ceased, even in her old age, to strive; she cannot sit in peace with folded hands, counting back along the years as the Faithful finger their beads, each bead one precious year of a happy and contented life."

"I must pray for her," Madame Bassompierre murmured absently. "I am badly in need of some refreshment, Monsieur. I would like a glass of very cold water, many glasses of cold water."

The walk back was easier and much quicker; they were soon in the village. Watched by many bright black eyes, they walked across the dusty square to the café under the trees, within a yard of the Bosphorus. He saw she was comfortably seated at a tin-topped table, ordered yoghourt and many glasses of water, then he bent forward and asked another direct question.

"If you please, Madame, would you kindly remove your hat and veil?"

"Exactly what I wanted to do!" she cried, and pulling out skewer-like pins, she took off her hat and bunched out her mauve, smartly cut, short hair. "That's much better!"

Nuri bey stared. "You are not a bit like your sister."

"No, we are not at all alike."

Turning away, Nuri bey hurried with great strides across the square to make his arrangements.

Chapter 13

To ENTER a Turkish "Turkish bath" is to suspend voluntarily, for the duration of the visit, all connection with reality. Steam, warm marble, intricately carved fountains spouting hot and cold water and dim light filtering through tiny star-shaped windows in the domed roofs, combine to create a beatitude which extinguishes individuality and absorbs the spirit into a mindless elation. No wonder Mohammed disapproved of them and said that the whole world was suitable for prayer *except the graveyard and the bath*.

After being par-boiled in scalding water, drenched with icy water, rubbed with rough towels and prodded violently in a curious kind of massage, Jenny lay in naked abandon, as though tossed carelessly down, on a huge marble platform, about a foot high and warm. The marble had not returned to its native cold since it was first constructed and had been warm with the warmth of a charcoal fire below it for more than three hundred years.

All round her, women screeched and shouted platitudes at one another and the sound differed from that in the parrot-house at the Zoo only in that it was softened as it struck the marble walls and was muffled by steam. All tension, bewilderment, determination, anxiety, doubt, sorrow, uncertainty, indignation and regret had left her and she was as peaceful and mindless as a maggot.

Entry to the *hamam* was through the cool hall. This was a vast domed chamber with two tiers of marble benches arranged round the walls on which the women who had finished their baths lay resting, cooling off, gossiping and eating. When they had had enough, those who wished could return to the steam chamber and start the whole operation all over again. The female in charge was a lusty-looking woman who appeared to have a bit too much of everything. She had naked feet and legs and wore a thin blouse and a towel wrapped firmly round her middle, brought forward between her legs and secured over her stomach in a manner dating back through history to the days when the Romans brought their luxurious baths to their outlying bastion of Byzantium.

This splendid woman moved, in spite of her bulk, with grace and beauty inherited from her race of magnificent dagger-carrying Caucasian women who were as good on the field of battle as their husbands; she ruled her tiny world of the *hamam* with a quite superfluous amount of zeal, enthusiasm and sense of leadership which probably acted as a safety-valve and prevented her from eating her husband when off duty.

Miasma did not always visit the same *hamam* but over the years she had attended this particular one some hundreds of times and always Valance had been with her, carrying the towels and the basket of provisions. Valance had paid the entrance fee with money given her previously by Miasma; it was she who helped Miasma to undress, who went with her into the baths, who returned to lay out the food, who combed her hair, who, in short, performed the duties of the slave. The services of the superintendent were not, therefore, required and Miasma, in the manner of her kind, had treated this zealot with blatant contempt, never addressing her, or paying her any attention, or, worst of all, tipping her.

Now she had hobbled in, tossed down the money and passed the superintendent without a word of explanation as to why Valance was not with her; followed by a young girl carrying the gear, she had stumped to her usual place on the marble benches as though the place belonged to her.

All the *hamam* woman required was a chance to get her own back and this she had shortly before midday when a yellow-faced, over-excited, highly nervous creature who, though barely in the form of a man, seemed to be more a man than anything else, sidled in through the entrance and demanded to see Madame Miasma upon the instant. The *hamam* woman put her hands on her hips and laughed loud and long and without being in the least amused. A stream of language poured from her scornful lips and strong brown throat, the outcome being that, if Mohammed himself had requested to have Madame Miasma brought out from her bath, she would not allow it. When her ladies were in the *hamam,* they were inaccessible and out of touch with the world; if urgent messages were to be delivered to her clients when they were bathing, the whole purpose and sanctity of the *hamam* would be lost.

Standing directly in front of Hadji with arms and legs akimbo, she tore him, virtually, to shreds and he stared fascinated at the space between her splendid legs as though wondering if he should dive between them and make a run for it, and this he might well have done had it not been for the unnerving idea of surprising Madame Miasma actually in the process of bathing.

In vain Hadji tried to explain that something of very great importance had occurred and that Madame Miasma herself would be extremely angry if the news were not imparted to her immediately.

But on the contrary, the *hamam* woman argued, Madame Miasma would be disturbed and agitated to such an extent that her health might well be endangered if she were called suddenly from the hot room. An old lady in such circumstances might have heart failure and she was not going to be responsible. Not if the sun had fallen out of the sky would she permit the news to be taken in to Madame Miasma; a number of equally picturesque similes followed, of mixed application that might be translated: wild horses on their bended knees would not persuade her. Her great luminous eyes bulged to bursting point and Hadji stared fascinated like a cringing but still wily stoat.

A short silence throbbed between them before she became suddenly practical and suggested that, if Hadji wrote a note, she would see that Madame Miasma received it at a convenient moment. And there she had him. How could Hadji tell her that Madame Miasma, though gifted beyond ordinary women, could neither read nor write and that Valance and Hadji together had stood between this disability and the people who knew her and occasionally corresponded with her, for many years?

For the moment he was defeated and looked it and the *hamam* woman at once gathered what she had been certain of all along, the news could wait. With something that stopped just short of being a particularly well-directed spit, she turned on her way back to the cool room, telling him the Turkish equivalent of: go and get lost.

He went a few steps along the street and sat down at the entrance to an alley on the opposite side, from which he could keep watch on the *hamam* door.

He thought about fire because fire is never very far from the minds of the citizens of Istanbul whose city has many times been ablaze and once burned "from sea to sea." And as he sat with his arms wrapped round his knees, his thoughts lingered on fire and upon murder in a sad nostalgic vein. Murder was not what it had been in his youth. In those halcyon days, murder was quick and neat and clean; those whose presence was a nuisance would be disposed of and that was that. But in this so-called time of emancipation, murder was a much more complicated affair, it would seem. Whereas in the old days that a murder was expedient was all that was required, to-day there was a ridiculous sanctity about human life and, however advantageous the murder might be, authority was against it and so it was necessary to murder again and again and even again, in order to avoid being strung up at dawn on the football ground before the Sultan Ahmed Mosque.

Which all proved, Hadji was sure, how ridiculous it was to attempt to make one's countrymen happier and more contented by the modern methods introduced by Mustapha Kemal, whose memory Hadji, for one, execrated with all his shrivelled little soul.

Madame Bassompierre would have to take the same road to Paradise as her sister Valance; it was sad and made Hadji feel melancholy because he had nothing against the two Frenchwomen. Nothing at all, it was only, as he might have phrased it, that they stuck out their necks.

And though Nuri bey did not stick out his neck, he would die rather than admit that he was in possession of the case, which was valuable and, in addition, deadly evidence. Rocking himself to and fro and looking immeasurably sad, Hadji felt charitable enough to hope that, when his house was set on fire, Nuri bey himself would not perish in the flames.

Chapter 14

ONE OF the many delights of the *hamam* was that there was no hurry. After the morning session and refreshment which included delicious water ices, and a long period of attention to the *toilette,* the whole process was repeated. As evening approached, the thought of facing the hard cold world again, clothed and in one's right mind, was repellent; by then Jenny did not care if she stayed in the *hamam* for the rest of her life.

All afternoon the *hamam* woman kept a keen watch on the entrance, never leaving her position in the cool room to do her rounds of the hot chambers, but watching the entrance door as a cat watches a mouse-hole. Though it would have been possible for Hadji to peer round the door and create a disturbance at a time when Miasma and Jenny were in the cool room, had he attempted it the consequences would have been calamitous. He was obliged to wait outside, in an agony of impatience, for many hours.

When, finally, they came out, the dirt and dust and grey drabness of the old imperial city was transmuted; the sun had gone down and the sky, a deep, dark blue, wore one brilliant star in the east, and the massed buildings, down to the Golden Horn and up on the other side, round the Galata Tower, so uninspiring in full daylight, seemed now to be assembled in all their old glory.

Hadji was crouching, half-asleep, in the doorway opposite; the satellite which had, for once, acted on its own, was utterly spent and could do no more until remotivated.

Miasma waited on the edge of the pavement for a taxi and Jenny, carrying all the *hamam* luggage, was in a kind of dream. The happenings of the next few hours, however, though they had the same quality of unreality as a dream, differed in that her limbs were not weighed heavily, or her mind bogged down, as so often happens in dreams. The *hamam* had cleaned away all traces of drugs and she felt clear-headed and new as morning.

Hadji was soon reporting his news to Miasma in such an excited manner and fantastic torrent of language that it would seem impossible for anyone, even a fellow-countrywoman, to understand what he was saying. But clearly she got the gist of it because she uttered a loud exclamation and staggered back as though about to fall and Hadji steadied her only to continue his revelations.

"What is it? What has happened?" Jenny put in now and then but neither took any notice at all and tears came to her eyes with the frustration of not being able to understand. Miasma's exclamations soon tipped over into the hysterical, her voice rose to a shriek as both she and Hadji shouted together, neither listening to what the other said. Jenny heard the repeated word *"yok"* which seemed to be operating as frequently as a comma. And then it would appear that Miasma was blaming him for not telling her sooner and Hadji was making cowering excuses, gesticulating towards the *hamam* entrance and giving a poor reproduction of the *hamam* woman's implacability.

But in spite of the clamour, some decision was quickly arrived at. Miasma hailed a shabby car with the black and white checkered line round the middle which showed it to be a taxi and the pirate-like driver pushed his bristly face out of the window, apparently telling them, with hoarse cries, to hurry up and get in. Traffic halted behind, started to hoot and for a moment Jenny thought she was going to be abandoned on the pavement. Hadji snatched the *hamam* impediment from her and Miasma, having got into the taxi, now remembered her and leaned out.

"And you," she spluttered, "you are not *necessary,* my child, you have never been necessary. You—you . . . " French words failed her. "You are a silly girl to imagine that Tony Grand would bother about a stupid child like you. He only wanted to use you and now he has finished with you. Don't leave yourself lying about any longer. . . ." Her French became almost incomprehensible but the gist of what she was saying was: "Get the hell out of here."

She was about to slam the taxi door when she had another thought: "Go to the British Consul. Pretend you are half-witted, that should not be difficult! Say you have lost your memory; they will have to send you back home; go back to your mother, whom you should never have left!" With these few kind words the taxi door was slammed and they drove off as the traffic held up behind reached a frenzy of hysterical hooting.

Jenny took stock of herself. In the matter of her dress and immediate possessions she was intact; she was wearing her white raincoat, carrying her large handbag with all its contents, including her passport, and thrust into her pocket were her silk headscarf and her crushed cotton gloves. She had bought tooth-brush and paste and several small items of food, and she still had a small amount of the money she had changed into Turkish *lire;* there was no need for panic action.

Nuri bey had promised he would return to the *yali,* but he probably went earlier in the day. Since Miasma and she had left that morning, something of tremendous moment had happened; she felt sure the police had somehow traced Tony to the *yali* and had been making inquiries there; hence Hadji's panic. She was clearly no longer wanted there and it might be stupid pig-headedness to go back to that dismal Swiss chalet perched on the very edge of the sullen black water, at this moment, and it was something she preferred not to do.

Remembering Nuri bey telling her of his friend in the British Council with whom, on the evening he had been sent to the airport, he had arranged to have coffee, she decided to go there and ask for Nuri bey's address. Walking thoughtfully down the hill towards Galata Bridge she could see the newer city of Pera across the Golden Horn; somewhere up beyond the tower in the endless blocks of houses and criss-cross of streets at the top of the hill, Nuri bey's house lay but, even if she could find it after considerable search in daylight, she would never be able to find it at night.

Unsuccessfully she asked a number of people the way to the British Council and in the end she took a taxi. The offices were shut but an Englishman was standing around who, though not the friend of whom Nuri bey had spoken, knew of Nuri bey and looked up his address in a telephone book. He went further, going out into the street for another taxi, seeing Jenny into it and giving the driver the address: it was as easy as that.

As the taxi turned into the street where Nuri bey lived, she saw at once that a great cloud of smoke and flame was pouring up into the dark blue sky from behind the house. She saw the wooden house with the strange look-out room silhouetted against the conflagration, one window oddly red, like a sore eye. The driver brought his vehicle to a standstill with a number of deprecatory shouts and, bounding out, joined the handful of sightseers, staring apathetically.

Having spent some time regretting what she called her "tame" behaviour in the incident of the shooting at the airport, Jenny rose to this occasion. She tossed her white mackintosh over the front railings and, to the admiration of the crowd, dashed up the front steps, tried the front door to find it locked, and flung herself against it. She had seen cowboys do this in Western films and always the wooden panels of the doors against which they hurled themselves gave way. This time . . . not. She tore round the back and beside the back door she could see that a fire had been built against the wooden wall, the squarish sheet of metal which had been used for a dustbin lid had been propped against a support of the wooden wall, waste paper and household wood from the woodshed had been thrust underneath. Over the prepared heap had evidently been poured the fuel oil used for cooking, an empty tin lay on the ground nearby, dribbling the strong-smelling remains. Half the back of the house, right up to the roof, was burning briskly. Jenny laughed excitedly as she had done at the big bonfires they had had on Guy Fawkes day when she was a child.

A few brisk swipes with a stone broke enough of a panel of the kitchen door for her to put her hand in and undo the bolt. The kitchen was not yet alight but the sudden draught caused part of the stained-glass window in the hall to break and flames and clouds of black smoke poured hungrily in. She tied her scarf over the lower part of her face and ran through the hall, wrenching the Shirvan carpet aside and snatching up Nuri bey's precious carpet-bag. The black smoke rushed at her like an army with banners. She pulled at the green satin table cover and crammed it into the carpet bag.

It was smoke that killed, rather than flames; smoke would kill before the flames arrived. She knew there was no return through the kitchen now. Nor could she open the front door. Her eyes were streaming, she pulled the silk scarf up over her face and groped her way into the study. Here the smoke only wandered aimlessly and she could slip the scarf down again and pick up a chair; with all her strength, she thrust it against the window, which went with a splendid crash. Rolling the carpet-bag out ahead of her, she stood on the chair and tried to climb out. Willing hands from below stretched up to help her but she had to go carefully to avoid the jagged edges of glass. Now the smoke seemed to have got the hang of it and, in a purposeful billow, caught up with her, sending out long arms to catch her, impaled upon the broken glass. She shrieked as her sweater caught and she felt the sharp edge of glass running down her forearm. Then somehow, by two men standing upon the bent backs of two others, she was lifted clear and fell to the ground crying like a child at the sight of the blood pouring down her hand. It didn't hurt but there was so much blood that she felt it must hurt.

The window yawned smoke with the boredom of having lost its prey. Kind hands lifted her to safety, dozens of anxious faces peered into her own. A woman was fetched who evidently knew where to apply a tourniquet and a piece of material was produced which the woman wrapped tightly round her upper arm in a position which was evidently correct; the pulsating fountain of blood stopped almost immediately.

No one attempted to bring water for the fire but water in gallons, brought in any number of curiously shaped receptacles from earthenware pitchers to plastic washing-up bowls, was poured liberally all over her in an almost continual stream. Gentle hands were laid on her forehead, water was put to her lips, kind, if incomprehensible, words were spoken, she was propped up, petted, pampered and fussed over. Are these a sample of the people, she wondered dreamily, who turned out in their hundreds to watch the public hanging yesterday morning?

Chapter 15

WHILST Madame Bassompierre fanned herself with her passport in the cool shade of the waterside terrace café and watched the wavelets breaking lightly against the water-steps, Nuri bey carried out the business in hand in a hovel a few yards behind the square. It was a squat building, whitewashed, with two small and one larger apertures which, if they had been glazed and boarded, would have been windows and a door. As it was, sacks hung over the windows so that no light should penetrate the darkness within. It was an eminently suitable place for his purposes.

Arab-like, Nuri bey took up the position instinctively comfortable, cross-legged upon the hard clay floor, whilst six troglodytes of calamity and misfortune, sat in like manner, in a semi-circle round him, clasping their clean bare feet (clean because that was a part of their persons which many of them washed five times in twenty-four hours) and rocking themselves gently to and fro, as though keeping time to some astral music unheard by anyone but themselves. The consonant-less talk ran between them as easily and fluidly as a marble swung round an empty wooden bowl.

He began by praising them for their prescience in regretting the burial which took place from Miasma's house; an unfortunate mistake, he explained. Madame's companion had never mentioned her wishes with regard to her disposal in the event of her death, to Madame Miasma, as was natural; nobody likes to dwell unnecessarily upon that time. The poor woman having died suddenly, Madame Miasma had been anxious only to do her duty as a good Moslem and get her old friend and companion buried as soon as possible. Valance's body had had the treatment, as Madame had said, as she herself would wish her own body to be dealt with after death.

But her family in France, as was meet and right, had been repeatedly told by their dear sister that she wished only for a Christian burial and for her body to lie in her native soil.

In a short, rousing speech Nuri bey declaimed upon the impropriety of burying an infidel under the flag of Islam, the religion of warriors.

What to do? It was quite clear that neither Madame Miasma nor the *imam* would allow the removal of the body; such a thing was without precedent and the bare mention of it would cause the greatest distress to those two who had arranged the burial, and who believed, as they all believed, that once in the grave the dead body should be allowed to remain there until the end of time.

But the family of Valance, as represented by the poor French lady who now sat in the café, waiting the result of their conference, were expecting her body back in France to-morrow for the funeral which had already been arranged and the laying of the coffin by the side of her forefathers, as was seemly in the Christian Church.

Who would suffer the more if nothing were done? It was hard to say. Madame Bassompierre would undoubtedly raise hell; but then, so would Madame Miasma. And furthermore, either the Prophet or the God of the Christians was going to be seriously annoyed. It could not, Nuri bey said warmly, be pleasing to the Prophet that the Christian should lie in the Moslem burial ground in the grave where, later, Miasma herself would lie. Would it not be for the best to please Allah and the Prophet by putting right this terrible mistake and at the same time appease the God of the Christians?

The "Ayes" had it, especially when Nuri bey, at this crucial moment, brought forth part (though not all) of the bundle of notes which Madame Bassompierre had given him, and began thoughtfully to riffle through them.

One of the trogs appointed himself foreman and suggested that the present six of them should remove the coffin at once from Madame's courtyard so that there would be no danger of her seeing it. No need to wait for a mule cart to be hired, they would go at once and lift the coffin across the road, thrust it through the rhodo-dendron hedge, and carry it up to the top of the hill where they would guard it until after dark. One of them would then arrange for the mule cart after the exhumation to carry the coffin with the body in it back down the track to the waiting truck during the hours of darkness.

The foreman would take a bus to the next village and arrange for the truck to take the coffin across in the car ferry and to the airport soon after dawn. He would, furthermore, and if Nuri bey so required and would write it, deliver a note to Madame Miasma which would set her mind at ease with regard to the coffin, about the arrival of which Hadji had undoubtedly gone to report. It might well be that Madame Miasma was on her way back to the *yali* at the moment.

On the inside of an old envelope Nuri bey wrote to Miasma that, with regard to any news Hadji had brought Miasma, he wanted her to know that he had the situation in hand and that he would telephone her later in the day. The note was to be left at the *yali* when they went for the coffin.

He looked slowly from one to another, round the ring of inscrutable brown faces so close to his own.

"Can anything go wrong?" he asked, and answered the question himself. "It can go wrong if any of you talk about this to anyone outside the circle. Nobody must know . . . if the news leaks out, you will have half the village trailing up to the grave after you to-night; the *imam* himself will be told, and all will be lost; great disgrace will come upon you."

He tapped his lips with pointed finger and thumb as he thought. "And it can go wrong if you do not take with you everything you will require: spades, a rope, an instrument for prising up the burial boards." Unblinking, the bright black eyes stared at him from under the peaks of five cloth caps and one elderly felt trilby.

"And it can go wrong," Nuri bey went on slowly, "if any of you lose your nerve. Is there one amongst you who thinks that, when the time comes, he will not dare to assist in this terrible task? Remember, you are to raise a body whose soul may already be, as it were, in the arms of the Prophet, or maybe whose soul cries out for a Christian burial and still haunts the poor body. Do you dare?" he asked the foreman who promptly answered that he did dare. "And you? And you?" He went round the circle and got instant acceptance from all. Not once, as he spoke, did one of them drop his eyes to the money in Nuri bey's hand but neither did any of them forget it for a split second!

"And remember," Nuri bey went on, "you are committing no crime; as far as I know there is no law against it. As I understand it, it is an unusual deed but a good one because, if it is not done, a number of people will be very unhappy, and the doing of it will cause happiness and satisfaction. And who knows? it may bring good fortune to any of you, and it will certainly remove the possibility of bad fortune, to have that alien body removed from our midst. Here is your first stroke of good fortune," Nuri bey added unsmilingly, handing out what he considered rather more than a suitable amount of money to each of them, and an additional sum to the foreman who was to arrange for the mule cart and the truck.

They all stood up and bowed to the bey Efendi, touching their foreheads in the Arab greeting. It was on his lips to murmur, "Allah be with you," he also thought of "God speed" but decided, for safety, upon a secular valediction: "Good luck," he said in English and hurried out.

It was no time for smiling; Madame Bassompierre repressed her look of approval into a crooked pursing of her lips which gave her face a semi-humorous expression. The steamer which Nuri bey knew was due, now appeared round the point, coming down the Bosphorus on its way to town. By taking it here and now, they would avoid having to return to the *yali* at an uncomfortable moment. Nuri bey's heart sank; it was quite evident that he could not merely pack Madame Bassompierre into the ferry boat and say good-bye to her; he would have to go back to the city and help her to arrange for the transport of the coffin and further, as she could not return to the *yali,* he would have to stay beside her until he got her safely off into the sky. As she was the great-aunt of Tony Grand, he could not afford to let her out of his sight for long. It seemed to him that the question of Tony Grand had been dropped from their conversation altogether too easily. His helpfulness on her behalf ought to engender a similar helpfulness on her part.

She had put on her hat and adjusted the veil and now she sat placidly beside him, black-gloved hands folded calmly in her lap, and enjoyed the cool breeze as they steamed down towards Istanbul.

"You have been very kind, Monsieur Nuri bey. I don't know what I should have done without your magnificent help."

Nuri bey waved the thanks aside, murmuring that he could have done nothing without assistance from others. He very much hoped that they would not be discovered; humble people were often suspected of malpractice when revealed in unusual actions; though, in fact, their motives were innocent, the authorities would never believe that they were harmless but would suspect them of removing the body to sell it to a hospital, a practice that was often done years ago.

"I promise you, dear Monsieur, that I will never repeat to any living soul what has taken place between us this morning. I will take a solemn Christian oath on it," and so saying she signed herself with the Cross.

He acknowledged this with equal solemnity, adding: "But if I had thought there was the slightest likelihood of discovery, I would never have employed them. I assure you, Madame, that a Moslem cemetery is the most empty place in the world; I can think of no contingency at all which would lead to their discovery. And I assure you *they* won't talk about it!"

There was a considerable wait at the airline office but, on the whole, the matter was put through without any difficulty. The officials concerned maintained a nice degree of sympathy with the bereaved Frenchwoman, showing a personal understanding. There was a certain womanly dignity about her of which the Turks strongly approved, and, furthermore, her readiness to pay for everything without any argument about prices eased the way. It was arranged that the coffin leave the airport by the next freight plane, which would be on the following day, arriving the same day in Paris.

After that, luncheon was necessary and he took her to a small restaurant off Eminonu where Madame ate her meal with gusto. They went for a quick tour of the Hippodrome, the Cistern, Aya Sofia and, to the old Harem where they wandered about in the shade. Any normal woman, he thought, would plead exhaustion and beg to be taken back to her hotel for a rest; but the Frenchwoman appeared to have an iron constitution and boundless energy. He would stick closer than a brother, he thought; sooner or later she would have to mention the urgent question of her great-nephew.

But when they had sat in a café and sipped tea until it was time to go to the hotel to collect her overnight case and on to the airport bus terminus, she had still not said anything further, Nuri bey knew he would have to bring up the subject again.

Tentatively, he took it up where they had left off. Now that the question of her sister's body had been satisfactorily arranged, he began, would it not be as well for Madame to consider the question of her great-nephew, wanted by the police of two countries? He went on to say that after all that had happened between them to-day, Madame could surely feel that he was to be trusted?

Indeed, Madame said emphatically, she trusted Nuri bey perfectly and completely.

Well, then?

Madame Bassompierre turned her chair and looked at him long and steadily, saying nothing.

If, Nuri bey went on, Tony Grand was to be left well off, as she had said, by his grandmother Valance, it would, surely, be of importance to the family to know where he was hiding. Or whether, in fact, anything serious had happened to him.

"Monsieur," she answered grandly, "I—and I speak for my family, do not wish to be associated with this matter in any way. We have a certain position in our own country: a friend of my son-in-law, as I told you, is a customs officer. It is absolutely impossible for us to associate ourselves with this matter."

"Then you don't care," (in simple French: that is to you equal) "that your great-nephew is perhaps already dead?" It was crudely put but there was no time for niceness. "I must remind you," Nuri bey went on, "his death, if he is dead, will have to be proved before anything can be done with the money left him by his grandmother."

It was a good point and Madame Bassompierre saw it instantly. *"Voyons,"* she said at last, "Monsieur Nuri bey, it is important that you understand how we look at this. . . ."

"It is indeed!"

"Last time Valance was home, she told us the whole unhappy circumstance and wept many, many tears before she left us. In the course of time Tony Grand would often come to Istanbul to see his grandmother. He knows that she intended to leave him her considerable savings; besides, I think that he is truly fond of her in his way. When he visited her he also met Madame Miasma, and it is there that lies the whole cause of the trouble."

"How?"

"How?" Madame Bassompierre turned her thoughts over carefully before answering. "I make no accusations, Monsieur." There was a finality about the way she said it which kept Nuri bey quiet but she added, as an afterthought: "Whatever the exact situation may have been, it made Valance extremely unhappy. She could not mention it in her recent letters, of course, but it is my private opinion that what was worrying her when she was home last summer finally killed her. The English have an expression to 'worry one's self to death' and I am sure that is what my poor sister did."

"Then you have really no idea where your great-nephew could be?"

"If I had, I should tell nobody. But I have not and I do not wish to know. I want nothing whatever to do with it, and my sister wanted nothing whatever to do with it, either, poor soul. If the boy is dead, it will be no surprise to me. The money due to him from Valance will be divided between the great-nephews and nieces, amongst whom are my own grown-up grandchildren. I know you think I sound hard, Monsieur, but Tony Grand is, yes, I shall have to admit it, even though the boy is my own flesh and blood, a scoundrel: I am only thankful he does not bear our family name!"

Nuri bey could see no point whatever in mentioning female followers of the family scapegoat; to do so would be to complicate the situation even further.

"You should leave the matter alone," Madame Bassompierre advised kindly, "you don't want to get mixed up in it. As you must know, Monsieur, it is not ordinary smuggling which is in question." She tapped her fingers nervously on the table and looked extremely pained. "Pardon me, Monsieur, but the thoughts I have cause me such anger and pain I cannot keep quiet. Imagine . . . please use imagination . . . pay attention . . . every ounce of drug which is smuggled is used . . . for what? For what?" she demanded angrily.

"We do not use drugs here," he answered, trying not to sound smug. "We have other escapes to Nirvana!"

"Nirvana! Every ounce, my friend, of smuggled drug goes into the blood stream of some poor wretch who is slowly destroying himself. To commit suicide is a crime . . . Monsieur . . . and yet slowly and surely to destroy the body and soul by the most disintegrating and degrading method known to man is not considered to be a crime."

Nuri bey shivered, he simply could not help it.

"So what do they do, the authorities? They prohibit the use except for a little for a few regular addicts; they restrict the sales. So the commerce of this devilish substance goes into the black market, naturally. Murderers are executed, are they not? But yes. And yet those who help to take drugs into a country are murderers of the worst kind: that is, those without imagination and common humanity!" She gave a loud exclamation: "Pcha! Don't mention Tony Grand to me, if you please!"

"Vous avez raison, Madame," he murmured absently, lost in admiration for a mind which could strip a situation of all inessentials; nobody had ever talked like that to him in his life and he found it a stimulating experience; though he had known her only a few hours, Nuri bey felt he was going to miss Madame Bassompierre. He thought her a necessary person in the same way that Madame Miasma had thought Jenny unnecessary.

"I must try to be more of a realist," he said out loud. But Madame Bassompierre did not hear; she was drumming her fingers on the table and humming a tune. "I trust," she said at last, "that nothing will go wrong with our plans. It is at least a beautiful evening, Monsieur; there will be no mud."

"Mud?"

"In the grave. A beautiful fine, warm, dry evening. They will be able to raise the body of my poor sister as cleanly and easily as I can remove a truffle from the ground and transfer it to my basket when I am staying with my relatives in the Perigord."

Nuri bey hoped it would be so.

"Once her body lies at peace in Père Lachaise, there will no longer be any need to worry overmuch about her soul, though one will, of course, pray for it. She will rest in peace all right, my poor sister."

Nuri bey again hoped it would be so.

At the bus station, with the moment of departure impending, they were like two old friends, depressed by the imminent separation, making the conventional last-minute remarks on the "mind-you-write" and "give my love to Aunty" lines. Nuri bey said how much he had enjoyed meeting her and she thanked him for all his kindness. He said that when she came again she must not fail to get in touch with him and she, in turn, invited him to her home in Paris whenever he could find time to come. They exchanged cards with their respective addresses. Nuri bey said he had plenty of time (refraining from mentioning it was money he lacked) and that perhaps it might happen that he would come." And Madame said that, though they lived near St. Augustin, a bus passed their flat which could take him across Paris to the door of the mosque which was not as big as Aya Sofia but very nice. And Nuri bey said that would be very convenient. Madame thanked him again and Nuri bey waved the thanks aside airily and said any time . . . any time. They shook hands, clasped warmly and firmly for several seconds like two people in no hurry to leave each other, and then Madame briskly climbed into the bus and waved to Nuri bey through the window whilst he stood at attention until the bus moved off down the street.

And that was that. Exit Madame Bassompierre, who had flashed through his life like a meteor, leaving him slightly altered so that in the years to come Nuri bey would think of his life as "before Bassompierre' or "after Bassompierre"; two distinct periods.

Nobody would have thought, to see him swing himself on to the crowded tram going up the steep main road of Pera, that he was going home to fetch the dagger which was kept on his hall table and used as a paper-knife.

Chapter 16

IT HAD burned like a dry packing-case; when the first stage of fire passed into the second stage, there was no hope for the house at all. Three red and white fire engines arrived with a set of impressively large hoses which poured what appeared to be a vast quantity of water into the conflagration. But nothing less than the entire Bosphorus would have quenched that blaze. The look-out room was the last to go; tottering, intact, in the top corner of an incandescent edifice, it hung on until there was nothing left to hang on to, and then crashed down and gave the fire a final mouthful to consume.

Jenny sat hugging her wounded arm, her back against the wall of a nearby house, the carpet-bag safely beside her, and thought how much she would have been enjoying the sight under different circumstances.

The whole house fell together in a sickening black mess from which emerged charred wooden uprights like totem poles. And the firemen, with great enthusiasm and energy continued to pour hundreds of gallons of water into the black mass, subduing every tiny wisp of escaping smoke until nothing living remained of the fire but an extremely nauseating smell.

And back came Nuri bey, striding along the road with great purposeful strides, to find his house no longer existed. But he was surrounded by friends offering help, advice, sympathy, encouragement. He was told about Jenny's heroism, her near escape from death and her grave injury. He was led to her and shown the wound and told how it had been dealt with. Offers of hospitality were showered upon him.

Whilst the firemen packed away their hoses and the helpers picked over the rubble and tried fruitlessly to find one whole intact object, Nuri bey walked up and down and round what had been his house. He showed neither rage nor sorrow; sometimes he stooped and picked up a fragment of carpet, a section of stained glass, the sodden corner of a ruined book, and threw it back into the morass. Finally, with extreme tact and sympathy, everybody left the stricken owner to his sorrow; everybody, that is, except Jenny, who went to him with the carpet-bag and took his arm.

"It's all because of me," she murmured, "I'm so terribly sorry. I've brought all this down on you and ruined your life."

"Yes, Jenny. It is so. But it had to happen. I see that now."

"How do you mean?"

"I mean I paid too much attention to my possessions and not enough to my soul."

"That sounds quite ridiculous. Look, Nuri bey!" Triumphantly she held up the carpet-bag, the satin tablecloth bursting from it. "All your best treasures."

"No," he shook his head mournfully and slowly. "No."

"What do you mean, *no?* They're here. Look, here!"

"No."

"What do you mean?"

"My most valuable things are not in the bag, Jenny. I took them to bed with me." The occasion was too vital for the words to sound absurd.

"You what?"

He repeated it. "Last night, when I came home from seeing you in the *yali,* and discovered that my house had been ransacked, I took my best books to bed with me!"

She nearly laughed but instead hid her laugh in his coat lapel saying: "Darling Nuri bey: is that all you had to take to bed with you?"

"No," he said violently, avoiding self-pity as though it were a dangerous adder, "I did it because I loved them, my wonderful old books! I see now that one must not love *things* to excess. I would not sell them, but if I had done so, I would have had money to do what I have always wanted to do, to go to Oxford. As it is, now I shall never go because I have nothing left to sell."

Jenny pulled the satin table-cloth out of the carpet-bag. "But look what's here!" She held up some old volumes, taking them out one by one.

"Yes," he agreed, "there are a few good books there which I can sell for something. But not priceless, like some of my others. However, I shall sell what I have; it will keep us for a few weeks."

"Us?"

"You and me, Jenny."

"I have been quite enough trouble to you, Nuri bey. I must go."

"It would be a great deal more trouble to me if you left me now; that would be what you in English call 'the last straw which breaks the camel's back.' You have nowhere to go, Jenny."

"Back to the *yali* to wait for Tony."

"That you cannot do. I have a great deal to tell you about what has happened to-day. But now I can only say you cannot go back. And, Jenny, I am almost sure your Tony is dead. Almost, but not quite."

She nodded. "I knew you thought so."

"So, for the present, your home is where I am!" He took a few steps back and looked at her in the dim light from the street lamp: "Jenny, you are in what you would call a mess. You have ruined your skirt and sweater. Your stockings!"

"But there's my mac, over there, quite safe!"

"You look like a tramp!"

"Don't rub it in; what can I do about it?"

"This!" With a few skilful twists of the wrist Nuri bey had wrapped her sari-fashion in the satin table-cloth and tucked in the ends. "Extremely alluring," he said coldly. "Come!"

"Where?"

"To the only place to which I dare take you in this state. We shall get a taxi to the Hilton Hotel!"

"Oh, my lord!"

"American, expensive, brash and very comfortable. I know the manager, he will let us stay to-night, and to-morrow I will sell my remaining possessions to pay the bill!"

"Oh, my lord!"

"What is it, Jenny?"

"It . . . it's like this: I'm not as free and easy as I was! . . . Oh, my lord, don't look so angry! You're frightening me!"

"I hope I am. I should hit you if it were not for your sore arm."

He went off to get a taxi and Jenny drooped like a discarded flower.

When he came back and held open the taxi door and helped her in, she dared not meet his eyes. She crept into the far corner and dragged up the edge of the table-cloth towards her chin as though trying to disappear.

The arrival porch at the Hilton might have been specifically designed to dispel coolness between arriving couples. Absurd and exaggerated, the great canopy with wavy edges, supported by four elephantine pillars standing in pools of light which fire the magnificent underside made entirely of gold mosiac, it is like something erected in a pantomime for the "At The Palace, Night of the Ball" scene rather than a hotel entrance.

As he handed her from the taxi Nuri bey gave one of his rare laughs: "If you could only see yourself," he said, "the dirty Princess!"

They waded, ankle deep, across the golden-coloured carpet of the entrance hall to the reception desk, followed by a porter carrying Jenny's white mackintosh and the Victorian carpet-bag.

"Two single rooms," Nuri bey commanded, loudly and clearly. "On different floors!"

Chapter 17

GOOD MORNING! the breakfast menu shouted: HAVE YOU SLEPT WELL? WHAT'S NEW? And amongst the recommended new breakfast suggestions were: BOILED PORRIDGE AND FRESH MILK and TOASTS AS GRANDMA MADE THEM.

Nuri bey, fully dressed, and Jenny (because she had washed her clothes and they were drying) wrapped in the green satin table-cloth, sat at breakfast in Nuri bey's room in front of the window.

He was enjoying the selection of jams and honey, the variety of bread and buns and the excellent coffee. She drooped over her coffee, her hair hanging dismally forward. The fog-horn sounded its forlorn moan through the mist which still shrouded the Bosphorus.

"Come, Jenny, you had better eat. It may be the last good meal we have for a long time to come!"

"Tell me, please, honestly, are you really as badly off as you make out?"

"I haven't 'made-out' how badly-off I am yet but since you ask me so frankly, I will tell you. I have a small amount of money which comes to me at the beginning of every month from a few houses which are my patrimony. Slum property, you would call it. An agent collects the rents for me. That is enough for me to live on, alone in my house. I have never earned money; I chose, instead, not to marry and have a family but to idle, if you like, my life away with my books. There you have the truth, Jenny. One of the idle poor, am I."

"Oh, my lord, Nuri bey, what are you going to do?"

"Let us consider what you are going to do, Jenny. Your state would seem to me to be worse than mine."

"When I think," she answered, "when I *think* what has happened to me in less than one week, and how I've changed . . ."

"People don't change. We are all of us complex, full of contradictions, we can never truly, as Socrates encourages us: know *ourselves*. It is impossible. Montaigne, a Frenchman and much more realistic, discovered: 'There is as much difference between us and ourselves as there is between ourselves and others.' Socrates was Greek and things said in Greek sound more important than they are."

"And that goes for Latin, too!" she agreed gloomily. "But honestly, Nuri bey, when I think of me a week ago at this time!"

"Tell me."

"Well, about this time last Friday I was lying in bed."

"Alone?"

"Alone. Tony had a room reserved for him at what he calls a '*recherché* little hotel' in Soho. I suppose it's pretty squalid, really," she murmured thoughtfully. "Anyway, I moved in, to save money. I have an afternoon typing job (I suppose I should say *had* because I'm pretty sure to be sacked by now). I used to lie in bed most of the morning, thinking."

"What about?"

She chuckled. "About me being a Kept Woman and whether it felt any different and, you know, it didn't! I was just beginning to get bored with it. Anyway, this time last Friday, I was wondering when Tony would be back. I went to work in the afternoon and was paid for the week and to a movie in the evening with a girl friend and when I got back . . . there was Tony!"

Nuri bey looked pained.

"But he didn't tell me about the trip to Hong Kong till lunch-time on Saturday. He'd been out all morning 'on business' and came back at lunch-time full of what we were going to do. Naturally, I was thrilled. But now, looking back at the last few days, I don't think I'll ever be bored again. Too much has happened, too quickly. I seem to have had all my life crammed into a few days. Honestly, Nuri bey, I'm old and stale, a squeezed-out orange, me!"

"You should go back home to your family!"

"Oh, my lord! Everybody harps on that! But I'll tell you something: I'm not going back to that life in Soho. I've *had* that. Shall I tell you something else? It was curiosity."

"What do you mean?"

"Curiosity and a kind of feeling that I was getting left behind . . . about sex, I mean. Every film you see, every play you go to, every book you read, every magazine you pick up . . . you get the feeling that if you're not absolutely up to the neck in a love affair, or married, by the time you're seventeen, you're a complete, out-and-out flop; there must be something frightfully wrong about you. So I jumped into it with both feet. Bonk! There I was; a sort of amateur tart!"

Nuri bey was so shocked that he stopped eating the delicious iced sultana buns.

"I suppose the beastliness of that hanging was a kind of therapy; I hated it more than I can possibly express; I felt a kind of frightful guilt, as though I had assisted in some obscene and thoroughly wicked rite. But, somehow or other, it's cleared my mind of a whole lot of unimportant things. I can't explain it better than that. Let's stop talking about me, Nuri bey, and talk about you because it seems to me you're in a pretty awful mess. Worse than me!"

He started to eat again. "Breakfast is the time for philosophy," he observed, "I shall not bother you with my friend Montaigne any more, Jenny, but he did say this: 'There is no knowledge so arduous as to know how to live this life well and naturally.' I was, as I thought, living my life well and naturally but that has all been taken from me."

"All through me. . . ."

"So now I shall have to find another way to live my life well and naturally. In'sh Allah!"

Jenny looked round the luxurious room. "What's worrying me now is how you're going to pay for all this."

It was worrying Nuri bey, too, though he would not have admitted it. After the meal, he opened his depleted carpet-bag and laid out the contents, his hoard, his treasure trove and a shabby enough collection it looked.

"I came back home last night for my dagger," he said thoughtfully, "I felt sure you had gone back to the *yali* with Miasma and I needed the dagger because I believed I would have to rescue you from there. I considered it a matter of life and death . . . and I still think so . . . but you are safely here. I do not understand why Miasma left you like that."

"I was a nuisance. Unnecessary, she called me. She suddenly dropped me like a hot potato!"

"I do not understand. That is, I do not *quite* understand though I have a much better understanding than I had. I am going out now, Jenny, to see friends who will advise me about selling these few remaining valuables."

He opened the carpet-bag and satisfied himself with regard to the contents. "But I have had quite enough of finding that you are gone; you have the disappearing qualities of a small slippery fish and I do not want to be shocked out of my wits yet again. Shall I have to ask the chambermaid to keep you locked in your room upstairs?"

"Don't be ridiculous! Anyway, how can I go out dressed like this?"

"I still have your white raincoat, which I shall lock up in this room. You see, I don't trust you, Jenny. I believe that if Tony Grand were to appear and say: 'Come!' you would go."

"Don't! You're frightening me! I can't be as unreliable as all that!"

"And now I have no dagger. It is somewhere in that stinking black wet pile of rubble which I do not wish ever to see again. So if you go . . . for any reason . . . it will be forever, this time, Jenny."

She did not raise her eyes but fidgeted with a tassel of the satin table-cloth in which she was wrapped.

"It is time you grew up and stopped playing with your life as though it were some kind of game. It may be the only life you will ever have, Jenny, so you should cease to treat it like a toy balloon, one of those rubber things filled with air which are amusing to toss about but which explode suddenly, pouf! and there is nothing left but a tiny scrap of crumpled rubber!"

As though she were not listening, she was now assessing the movement of her wounded arm in which, the previous evening, the hotel doctor had put five stitches.

"Yes, it works all right, but you had better rest it. Come!"

She tottered along the passage beside him like a Japanese in her tightly-wound wrapper. In the lift, the attendant, used to startlingly unfamiliar sights, gave them a barely curious glance. Not a word was exchanged as they went down the endless golden-carpeted passages. As she meekly opened the door of her room, still without looking at him, Nuri bey had some difficulty in keeping the expression of grim determination on his face, but he succeeded and left her without another word.

Chapter 18

IN THE tram swinging down the Istiklal Cadesi, Nuri bey tried hard to invoke a proper image of Tony Grand, the key person in the whole strange and violent situation which had developed so suddenly. "Just one of those things," he had said lightly, and "be seeing you." A careless swagger, a kind of self-assured insouciance was the impression he had left. Short, dark, his physical attributes were so negligible that Nuri bey thought he would not recognize him if he were to meet him again in the street except that he would be outstandingly dressed, in this particular city, with his sports jacket and his smart black tapered trousers.

Bullet marks on the inside of Miasma's front door and a pair of brown suède shoes didn't by any means prove that he was dead but Nuri bey passionately hoped that he was, otherwise he must find him and he would be obliged to kill him. Without his dagger, it would be a disgusting proceeding but to leave him alive, ranging about the world with raw opium, carelessly depriving young virgins of their virginity would be a great deal more disgusting, and not to kill him would be cowardly. He had shown himself to be part of the world's lumber. Nuri bey's eyes flickered over the crowds who moved up and down the main street endlessly, closely avoiding the traffic as they overflowed from the narrow pavements into the gutters. If he were not at the bottom of the Bosphorus in a sack weighed down with basalt rocks, where was he? And if he were at the bottom of the Bosphorus, a fine and safe place for him to be, how could Nuri bey ever be sure? And so long as he was not sure, how could be ever have a peaceful hour again?

He hurried up the third hill towards the mosque of Bayazit II and through the courtyard where the smug pigeons waddled about, monarchs of all they surveyed, and the tiny starving kittens mewed out from the shadows as they died standing up, under the branches of the great and splendid plane tree, through the archway and into the bookshop.

"Good day, good day, Efendim." The bookseller bowed and even remained bowed, possibly less humbly and more dispiritedly, when he heard that Nuri bey had come not to buy, this time, but to sell.

But Nuri bey's heart was uplifted because he at once noticed that a dark corner of the shop was filled with the huge, toad-like figure he had been hoping would be there.

This character, whom Nuri bey always thought of as the Toad because he was shapelessly dark, mysteriously lumpy and throbbed with clearly perceptible regular throbs in the region of his neck, if he had a neck, exactly like a toad, was important because he was a kind of scout, or agent for dealers who bought and sold important books and incunabula to the great museums and libraries of the world.

For years this person had been waiting for the time when Nuri bey would use the word "sell." One or two of the books in Nuri bey's possession were well known by many to be most rare and would fetch glittering prices in the world markets. He did not start excitedly at Nuri bey's words but he did what was his nearest approach to it: he opened his eyes, an action which happened in two stages so that his lids were raised first to display a red nictitating inner membrane which, in turn, was slowly raised in the manner of a heavily sleeping dog at night. When the operation was complete, his eyes were fully open and were seen to be big and bulging and greedy. In his horny grey fingers he held a short string of blue beads, the Moslem rosary or *tespyeh*, which dangled incongruously on his protruding stomach. He fiddled with the thirty-three beads, running them through his fingers as his eyes bulged out over Nuri bey.

And now the winged lion of the Book of Revelations had not only his six wings about him, but his wits also. He gave a short but important speech, listened to in such complete silence that the imaginative might think they heard the throb in the Toad's neck. What he said was to the effect that the time had come for him to travel; he had never left his country but had sat in his study and read and read and read, all the wisdom and all the history of other countries of the world. Now, he felt, with the coming of spring, the end of Ramadan, that he had read himself to a standstill. His library had nothing more to offer him. He now intented to travel and to take with him a small selection of his most valuable possessions: to Paris, to New York, to Oxford. In order to live whilst in these cities he would be obliged to do what he had, up to now, sworn he would never do; in short: sell, to the highest bidder, one by one.

The bookseller's eyes and the Toad's eyes were lowered from Nuri bey's face to the carpet-bag, where they stayed. After a good many more words, flowery and a little off the point, he said that his first requirement was ready money for the journey and for his immediate needs until such time as he was able to get in touch with the actual buyers in the museums and libraries of the world. And as he talked he lifted his carpet-bag on to the counter and opened the top, slowly and deliberately, and brought out the best of what he had with him, the excellent illuminated psalter.

The Toad spoke for the first time and his voice sounded like a small fall of rock. "You have much better than this—this pigeon food!"

"Naturally, but I seek to sell my best in the world markets, as I have said."

The bookseller and the Toad were knit together in silent, mutual consternation and the blue beads passed a little more rapidly from finger to finger. The psalter, barely medieval but colourful, lay disregarded.

"Our culture here," Nuri bey proclaimed, "is limited; our interests are narrow; our outlook restricted. It would be foolish of me to sell my best . . . locally." And the last word fell with dismal effect upon the straining hairy ears.

The Toad said that the prices that would be offered . . . *locally* . . . might well be equal to anything that might be offered abroad. And Nuri bey asked how that could be. When abroad, he would go from expert to expert, taking their advice; he need be in no hurry to sell; he would get in touch with the people who interested themselves exclusively in any one particular book that he wished to sell at the time. Clearly this way he would get the best possible prices.

"Efendim!" the bookseller said reproachfully, "I have always strived to sell you my best at my lowest price. I have kept aside for you anything which I thought would be of interest to you."

"My friend, you have always served me excellently well, and I thank you. However, over the matter of the things which I inherited, they are of such importance that I hesitate to burden you with them. Who knows, I may come back from the Western World with my valuables intact? They may be found to be not so valuable as we have thought."

That was ridiculous. Everybody knew Nuri bey possessed a very remarkable, if tiny, collection of books: they had been inspected more than once by those interested, in the city, and by visiting experts.

"I know where I could get a very good price for your illuminated manuscript of the synoptic gospels," the Toad croaked.

"Thank you. But before selling I would like to satisfy myself as to the highest price I could get."

There was a heavy silence but not complete deadlock. The door was evidently not yet slammed in their faces. Thoughtfully the bookseller flipped through the pages of the illuminated psalter. "You have never sold me anything," he murmured mournfully, "you have never tried me for price. I may be able to offer you just as good prices as your foreign experts."

Nuri bey looked interested but doubtful. He, too, fingered the psalter, leaving it open at the most showy of the exquisite paintings.

"Consider," the Toad rumbled, "consider carefully, bey Efendi, that what you will do is for the best."

"If," Nuri bey said carefully, "if you are, indeed, in touch with world markets and can offer realistic prices . . . but until I have studied the situation for myself, how am I to know? I confess to being an amateur on the subject of the value of my possessions."

"Apart from your synoptic Bible there are, if I remember rightly, five items of great importance . . ." the Toad enumerated them on his stubby fingers, the beads dangling from his thumb as he did so, ". . . worth anything from, let me see. . . ." The amount of *lire,* when he heard it, gave Nuri bey a sick feeling in the pit of his stomach; all five and the synoptic Bible lay, an unrecognisable black mush in the place where his house had been; as disgusting as camel-dung and not as useful.

"I hope to get a good deal more than that," he stated calmly. He watched in vain for signs of frenzy in the slow throbbing in the Toad's neck.

"However——" he paused, *however* being a release word from tension.

"In the meantime I need many hundreds of *lire* for my immediate plans." He took out his passport and looked at it thoughtfully. "I shall travel by Comet," he boasted, "and that costs much money, I am told. . . ." He wandered off on the subject of travel to give time to the bookseller and the Toad to examine all he had brought to sell, which he now took out of his carpet-bag and laid on the counter beside the psalter. They fingered through his few possessions in the sneering, deprecatory way used by dealers about to buy. One of the Korans he had bought from that same shop many years ago, but now the bookseller pretended he had never seen it before and examined it thoroughly, stopping just short of smelling it.

In the end the price they offered was three times in excess of what Nuri bey had hoped for in his most optimistic moment. He took a tremendous risk, making a small smile that was more of a grimace and slowly, slowly, put the things back into the carpet-bag. "These, too, I should perhaps reserve for the world market," he murmured. It was a dizzy, sickening moment: it was so certain that the Toad would stir restlessly in his chair, as though anxious to see the last of him, and the bookseller would sigh, as though he really minded whether Nuri bey took it or left it, and all would be over.

"If, of course, we could have any assurance that the Efendi would give us the opportunity of marketing his *other possessions,* no doubt the price could be raised."

It was a matter of principle. Nuri bey was no George Washington, who could not tell a lie, but the truth was important to him. After a long struggle with himself, interminably long, the words jerked themselves out, half-truths because the meaning behind them was untruth. "I cannot give you that assurance."

If they had asked directly "why not?" he would have answered truthfully, but mercifully they didn't. The shopkeeper said in an offended way that only last week a titled English gentleman and his wife had been in; they had left a card and here it was! the bey Efendi must read it; the curator of a musuem in Cambridge, England, no less! How, then, could Nuri bey possibly imply that he, the shopkeeper, was not in touch with world markets?

"Did he buy?" Nuri bey asked, and the shopkeeper had had to reply that no, he had not bought because he had not, at the moment, anything that interested this particular gentleman. But he had promised he would get in touch with him if something worth while did turn up. The shopkeeper was so impressed himself by the card that he could not imagine Nuri bey was not equally impressed; he believed that he had produced the ace of trumps and acted on that premise.

"So you will bring me your things, Efendim?" He abandoned dignity altogether and almost pleaded as an old friend who had always attended to Nuri bey's interests.

"Double the price you mentioned," Nuri bey suggested absurdly, "and perhaps . . . I will see. . . ."

Some kind of almost imperceptible tick-tack was going on between the shopkeeper and the Toad and the beads were swinging about in a lively way. The shopkeeper didn't exactly say "Yes" or "Done" but somehow the books Nuri bey had were taken out of the carpet-bag again and spread on the counter and money was being brought out, not with a crisp crackle because Turkish money is dirty and limp, but notes were being quite definitely slid out of wallets, pockets, drawers and boxes. A lot of them. Nuri bey looked out through the shop door where the Sultan's grave lay in the bright sunlight; it was an emotional moment.

After all, he thought as he hurried down towards the covered market, his carpet-bag empty and his breast pocket full, he and his father before him, had spent quite an appreciable amount of money in that shop in the years. He went into the market and bought a soft black leather hand-made jacket for Jenny; it was lined with sheepskin

and smelt rather because it had been incompletely tanned.
If she had gone, he would give it to the chambermaid.
He hurried over the bridge and swung on to a tram.

It was a day with a ring round it, a shining little lacuna
of a day, a day when nothing could go wrong. With the
jacket hanging over his arm, Nuri bey stood outside
Jenny's room and listened to the laughter. When he rang,
the door was at once opened by the floor waiter who,
with two of the chambermaids, were having an English
lesson. With Nuri bey's appearance the merriment ceased
and there was a general stiffening-up and pulling together;
a few murmured words of apology for existing and the
staff had disappeared as swiftly as the last of the bath
water running from a bath.

"Oh, Nuri bey, they can only speak about six words
of English! They're longing to learn; the ones who can
speak good English get a rise in pay and a more important
job. Do you know, I'm sure I can earn enough money to
live on if I give English lessons!"

The jacket was an immediate success. He was an "absolute angel" to buy it; she could wear it over her blouse and
get her sweater washed. It was just what she wanted: "A
sheep-minding wesket!" She disappeared into the bathroom in her satin sari and came out in her slim skirt,
wearing the jacket with an air which gave it a certain
chic which gratified Nuri bey with a strange new kind of
pride.

"Now I'm presentable," she said, "we can go and explore this gorgeous, luscious, palace of a hotel."

They chose one of the four exotic restaurants in which
to have lunch and afterwards they sat on the terrace
under a sun umbrella and drank strong, sweet Turkish
coffee and watched the fountain splashing below and
looked over the Bosphorus to Asia.

"Nobody knows where I am, except the manager,
who is my friend," Nuri bey remarked.

"Nor me, but what does it matter?"

Far from mattering, Nuri bey thought, it was, probably,
all for the best. When he tried to imagine what might

be happening at the *yali* he felt extremely thankful that he was out of reach. He hoped the exhumation would have gone well, and could think of no reason why it should not have done so. As Madame Bassompierre had pointed out, the weather had been ideal for the operation.

The coffin should, by now, have reached its destination. The grave might well have been filled in, either by those who removed the coffin or by the official grave-diggers, but even if this were not so, the replaced boards at the bottom of the grave would have nothing to tell.

Hadji would be wan and worried and Madame Miasma would be excitable, hysterical even. After the fantastic information that Valance's sister had come for her body, had produced a container for the body, had been left with Nuri bey: now sister, box for the body and Nuri bey himself had vanished and nobody either could, or was prepared to, tell Hadji anything about what had taken place after he left the *yali*. Possibly he would have scrambled, in his panic-stricken way, up the hillside to the grave and found it filled in. Would that reassure him, or otherwise? The grave had, in any case, to be filled in within the course of a day or so.

And the proles in the square! They were the only certainty; they would be sitting and standing about, watching and listening, their eyes bright and all their mysterious Seljuk impassivity in their smooth expressionless faces.

Undoubtedly at that moment Madame Miasma and Hadji would be suffering from their wicked panic measures in setting fire to Nuri bey's house, hoping finally and forever to destroy the damning evidence in the small fibre case. Miasma would know that amongst all her chattering friends there was only one friend who would be any good to her now, and that was Nuri bey. And he was the one person with whom she could not make contact, owing to her own viciousness.

Jenny was enjoying herself and, watching the constantly changing expressions on her charming young face, Nuri bey began to sense a deep inner content which did not come from the pleasant contents of his stomach but from a growing feeling that things were working out all right.

Madame Bassompierre and Valance's relatives would soon have the dear departed amongst them and be preparing for decent family obsequies; the calamity-proners would have money tucked about their persons, which would make a change; and as for himself, his house was in ruins and he had lost his possessions but he was on the move; furthermore, he was staying at the best hotel in the world with an entrancing girl and his pocket was stuffed with money to pay for it.

"You know, old dear," she said, "this sheep-minding wesket of mine smells. It's not unpleasant; it's the smell of Istanbul. And when I'm a dear old lady, I'll be able to take it out and sniff it and everything will come back to me and when I try to tell my grandchildren about the adventure I had, they won't listen! They'll say the poor old dear's in her dotage!"

"That smell you notice and which we who live here do not sense at all, is the smell of the primitive tanneries. It pervades the entire city, I am told, and is the first thing people notice when they come. Some think it is the smell of decay as the old imperial city slowly drops to pieces."

"All except the Hilton Hotel!"

So they walked down the hill and bought presents for Nuri bey's sister: material, coffee and china tea. Then they got on a bus and went to Istiniye where Nuri bey saw, to his delight, that the Arab schooner was still loading at the harbour side. He sought out the captain, who seemed pleased to take the presents for the bey Efendi's sister. They were to leave when loading was complete, sailing the Euxine for Samsum, a slow, slow journey in the fore-and-aft-rigged vessel and, given fair winds, would be at Trebizond within a week.

They took a *dolmus* to the last village but one on the European side and there they climbed the wooden steps into the mosque, a tiny square room, the floor covered with rich rugs, in which there was a strong smell of Wesleyan chapel. They watched the *muezzin* climb a ladder up the plane tree, the only minaret, and proclaim the greatness of Allah from its lofty branches.

They went to a primitive restaurant on the quay, amongst fishing-boats and nets, and each chose a recently dead fish which was cooked on charcoal and eaten with an accompaniment of numerous glasses of *raki*.

After this they light-heartedly took the footpath, now being made into a road, over the hill to the last village on the European side. The Bosphorus is at its narrowest and it was here that Darius built across it a bridge of boats a very long time ago.

Sailing the sixteen miles back to the imperial city, they sat close together facing the prow and after they had drunk numerous minute glasses of tea, sold by a youth who continually cried, *"Çay, çay, çay"* (a sad and lonely sound), Nuri bey was not surprised to find they were holding hands, and put it down to the magic of that day with the ring round it.

He pointed out the *yali* of Miasma as they passed. It was not yet dark enough for the lights to be on, the door of the bird room stood wide open. Behind the house, up the steep hillside, rose the graveyard.

"It could be depressing," Jenny remarked, "all those miles and miles of neglected graves and all the black pointed yew trees. And as for the *yali,* I think it is just plain ugly! I wonder what they're doing, Nuri bey? I bet they're up to no good!"

And perhaps somewhere, not so far below, the body of Tony Grand swung and lurched with the movement of the tide. Would they have had a sack big enough to take him? Or did they wrap the rocks in sacking and bind them round the legs in the old, old way? But here no corpse could stand upright on the bottom, as in the shallows below the Seraglio. One day in the sky thousands of feet above, and the next, in the water, thousands of feet below: he was a great one for the elements . . . Tony Grand.

Chapter 19

THE NEXT MORNING, on waking, Nuri bey had a unique experience, that of lying in a comfortable bed, against luxurious pillows, between fine linen sheets with nothing whatever to do other than to marvel at how comfortable he was. During the day the bed was a neatly tailored divan, scattered with bright cushions, but at night it was pulled away from the wall and became a four-foot-wide bed and the occupant could then admire or otherwise the frameless modern abstract painting which, in endless variety, hung in every room, tastefully blending with the particular colour scheme.

He had a strange feeling of deprivation, like a soldier unarmed, an admiral without his ship or a trick cyclist without his bicycle. He had no book of any kind, either within reach or anywhere else. He stretched forth a long lean arm and turned on the radio from which broke Turkish music which is not tuneful, nor rhythmic, nor haunting, nor erotic, nor even pleasant, but a harsh, uncouth, grating sound, its main quality being that of persistence. He stared at the abstract, wondering what it represented. He saw his best and only European shirt, which he washed every night, on a hanger in the balcony doorway and thought about hanging in general. And then, as so often recently, his thoughts came to rest on Tony Grand.

". . . the body of Anthony Francis LeGrand, known as Tony Grand, the Englishman for whom an International police search had been going on was found late last night by Security Police at Le Bourget Airport, France. No further information has been released but it is understood that investigations with regard to the circumstances of his death are proceeding."

It was not Nuri bey's thoughts but the actual words were coming from the radio which was now giving the news in Turkish. He ceased to breathe in case he should miss a word. Then, having lost touch with his breath for too long he had the greatest difficulty in getting it again, as though life had been shocked out of him altogether as in a vagus inhibition, of which people do sometimes die and which is, literally, death from shock. If anybody has ever nearly died of shock it was Nuri bey at that moment.

He tried to take a breath but he had no mechanism for drawing it in. He believed that he did, in fact die, lying there against the pillows, a nothing, a nobody, with a film of darkness over his eyes and nothing working but his hearing, which was unimpaired.

And when the news was finished he wanted to turn a knob so that he could hear it all over again and reassure himself that he had heard aright. He reached for the telephone receiver with the intention of ringing up his detective friend to confirm what he had heard. He stopped in time and instead ordered tea and lemon to be brought. Reality must be regained somehow. Before the tea arrived he was seized with a rigour which shook him like one in the grip of malaria.

The waiter asked if he were ill and Nuri bey answered that he had a touch of *la grippe,* at which the waiter asked if he would like to see the doctor and Nuri bey answered that he would be better presently: it would pass. After the tea he had a shower and made all the movements of getting dressed.

Who knew that he was connected with Madame Bassompierre and the coffin for the body of her sister Valance? Madame herself and the proles in the market place, and to these latter the information would be as though it did not exist. When an Arab chooses to keep his own counsel, he keeps it, and in this case they would be far too frightened of their own participation in the events to profess to any knowledge of it at all. He tried to remember whether anyone who knew him had spoken to him when he had been helping Madame Bassompierre to make the arrangements at the airline office, and decided not.

If I had not been a kind of useless satellite, he thought

bitterly, an unemployed man, gigolo, dogsbody, one who has nothing better to do than to read newspapers to old ladies on Monday afternoons, all this would still have happened but I would have been outside, marvelling, instead of within, shaking from head to foot with fright. No, not quite correct, because the grave in the cemetery would never have been disturbed; or would it? Would Madame Bassompierre, with her immensely persuasive personality, have talked the *imam* into the act of violation?

What a woman! Nuri bey thought; she would out-mother-of-the-Sultan any *Validé Sultan;* what a terrible waste that a woman of such immense power and drive should be simply a French housewife; the pity of it! What, Nuri bey thought, what, in the name of Allah, would she be doing now? Here, surely, was a situation which would defeat even a Bassompierre.

For one fleeting spindrift second he thought of spending all the money in his wallet and flying to Paris for the pleasure and satisfaction of watching her deal with the situation. The main lesson to be learned from her, he told himself, was economy of action. She swooped, fully equipped, into the particular set of circumstances from which she wished to obtain something; obtained it by impressing those concerned of the impossibility of *not* obtaining it and withdrew in triumph.

There was much to be learned, he brooded darkly, from her example. Much. And slowly, slowly, the Winged Lion came to life, a mode of action was evolved and, whilst he thought, Nuri bey turned the wallet over and over in his hands: the first money he had ever earned, and earned by his own cunning.

Cunning equals earning power.

Here was his chance to squeeze from the lemon the juice which he had for a short time, five days ago, believed would send him to Oxford. And as he thought, the light came back into his eyes; not quite so pure and so guilelessly grand as before but a bright light, seasoned by dexterity.

After studying the menu, he lifted the telephone receiver: "Please wake Miss Jenny Bolton in Room 701.

And please serve breakfast for two in Room 94." He read out: "Oven-hot rolls, ice-cold Jaffa juice, fragrant hot coffee, honey from Mount Hymettus and . . ." thus striking down an ancient shibboleth . . . "sizzling pork sausages and frizzled tomatoes."

Believing that it is better to be shocked on a full stomach than whilst fasting, Nuri bey urged Jenny on to eat. And whilst they ate, he felt the need for some kind of conversation and could think of nothing to say. Instead, in an endeavour to entertain, he quoted from memory from an English book of what he believed to be philosophy:

"Yes," said Sir Thomas, speaking of the modern novel, "it certainly does seem strange; but the novelist was right. Such things do happen." "But, my dear Sir," I burst out, in the rudest manner, "think what life is—just think what really happens! Why! people suddenly swell up and turn dark purple; they hang themselves on meat-hooks; they are drowned in horse-ponds, are run over by butcher's carts, and are burnt alive—cooked like mutton chops."

but even as he spoke he was struck by the ineptness of the quotation.

"What on earth are you talking about?" she asked, in mild surprise.

"A thought from a great English *penseur,*" he said apologetically.

She said: "To-day I am going to see about teaching English. If I could get about five lessons a day at the equivalent of a guinea a time I could afford to go on living here! Or I could keep us both in some more ordinary hotel."

Discouraged by his lack of conversational success and determined to tell her nothing until she had eaten a good meal, Nuri bey stared out of the window and automatically ate his own breakfast, for which he had no appetite.

From time to time, she threw small rhetorical remarks into the silence: "You're very quiet this morning, Nuri bey," and "What shall we do after I've fixed up about the lessons?" and "Couldn't we go and explore those islands in the sea of Marmora?" and "When I get back home I'm going to the R.S.P.C.A. to tell them about all the kittens here."

When they had both quite finished eating, Nuri bey said gently: "And now I must tell you that your Tony Grand is truly dead."

"Do you know that for sure?"

He nodded, watching her face crumple in sorrow and the tears burst from beneath her creamy lids in great drops. Then she really cried with the overall wetness of a severe summer shower. Such uninhibited weeping, he mused, was healthy and excellent. He waited. He wanted to go into the bathroom and fetch one of the many luxurious fluffy towels which the hotel lavishly supplied to each customer but was afraid of striking the wrong note. Like all really good, drenching summer showers, it passed quickly. With gasps and shudders and lids no longer creamy but pink and swollen, she recovered quickly.

"Well, that's that!" she said at last. "Poor Tony!" She went to the bathroom herself and swilled her face and dried her tears and came back, sniffing. "It has its good side, really. At least Tony won't live to become an out-and-out crook, spending most of his life in gaol; that's something to be thankful for!" And after a few more minutes during which she sat and thought, sniffing from time to time, she said: "And as for me, I suppose I'm lucky. I haven't had to experience that slow cooling-off that was bound to come, have I? He shed me, just like that and it may have been because of . . . of events rather than sudden hatred, and much less painful really."

And after a while the question which was bound to come, came: "How did it happen, Nuri bey?"

He was in a schizophrenic state: strangely elated at the news of Tony Grand's death, yet deeply depressed by the circumstances of the finding of the body.

"That I cannot tell you, for the present."

In due course, he said, she would know everything but for the moment her position, apart from Nuri bey's participation, was extremely delicate, not to say dangerous. Now that Tony's body had been found, investigations as to how he met his end would be more widespread. The airline who employed him would be obliged to give the police all the information they had about him and there would be inquiries at the hotel in London which, no doubt, he would have given as his permanent address.

"No, I think a bank was his permanent address."

"But he would have to give an address at which the airline could get in touch with him."

She looked at him thoughtfuly, her entrancing baby's mouth in a pout.

"The Three Diamonds Hotel, Greek Street, Soho, for instance?"

"Well . . . yes."

"And at the Three Diamonds Hotel, Miss Jenny Bolton would also be well known?"

Pause. "You're being beastly."

He shook his head, smiling thinly. "I do not intend."

"Very well then, I suppose you'd better have it. We had a double room so we had to register as Mr. and Mrs. Grand."

Nuri bey sighed heavily. "Oh, if anyone ever wanted a good whipping," he murmured. The tiny smile she gave was a delicious mixture of agreement and a faint suggestion of conspiracy.

"I suppose it did not even occur to you that Grand was not his real name!" he said repressively. "It was Anthony Francis LeGrand. And it will not be very difficult for the police to trace Mrs. Grand, the widow, to Jenny Bolton. Your ticket from London to the Far East would have to be in your own name, the same name that you have on your passport. They will now have the full information that the young woman who flew on the Zenobia Airways jet, known to be a friend of Anthony Francis LeGrand, was Miss Jenny Bolton. I have no doubt that they are already in touch with your people.

It will be known that you did not arrive in Hong Kong, that you did not return to the jet after the shooting incident on Monday night; that you are, in fact, in Istanbul . . . 'at large' . . . 'on the run' . . . or perhaps in hiding. Though Tony Grand was a murderer, he himself was murdered. There are gunshot wounds in his back, Jenny. To-day they will do a post-mortem examination and the bullets which killed him will be found."

"Nuri bey, you must tell me what happened to Tony. If I'm going to be mixed up in it all, I'd better know something. It's ridiculous keeping me in the dark, like a child."

"Not at all! It is far better that you should know nothing if and when you are questioned. Yes, you were a friend of Tony Grand, yes, you flew in the aeroplane in which he served, for a holiday with him in the Far East; yes, you went into the transit lounge at the airport simply to stretch your legs after the long flight from London. During the wait you saw a young man, whom you *now* know to be Tony Grand, shoot another man and run away. Since that time you have seen or heard nothing whatever. That must be your story. If the Turkish police have anything to do with it, you will have to tell it over and over again. So you must be quite sure to keep as near to the truth as possible, Jenny. Tell me, have you got it all straight in your mind?"

"Perhaps you're right," she said after some thought, "perhaps it would be best for me to know nothing more now."

"It is very unfortunate," Nuri bey went on, "that we had to register your name when we came here the night before last. But it was inevitable. It was on your passport, which they always take from foreigners when they arrive at the reception desk. And by the way, Jenny, you should get the passport back from them this morning, and hold on to it carefully. You must not lose it because I do not think it would be wise for you to stay in this country much longer, for all the reasons I have just given you."

"Go on, then. Say: 'Go back home.' Say it!"

Because she ordered him to say it he said nothing, staring at her, wondering.

"I can't go back home yet, Nuri bey."

"Why not?"

"Because . . ." There was a long pause.

"Why not?"

"I must . . . that is . . . I've got to . . . I mean, it would be rather crawling back, wouldn't it? I've got to march back, with my head up, as it were."

"I see."

"If I've got to go from here, maybe I'll go to the family I lived with in Touraine."

Nuri bey brought out a note-book: "Give me their address, please."

And whilst he wrote it down, Jenny watched him, then said: "But why all this? Do you think I really will have to go? I'm just beginning to like it here."

Nuri bey brought out his pregnant wallet and his passport. He also wrote down the address of the agent who collected the rents for him and the address of his sister in Trebizond.

"What on earth is this? Last rites, or what?"

"Will you keep these till you next see me?"

"Oh, Nuri bey! What on earth is it?"

"If I am not back here to-morrow at this time I want you to do several things, Jenny. You will pay the hotel bill with this money. You will send a note to my sister. . . ."

"Saying what?"

"Saying that my house is burnt down and that I am probably dead."

"Oh, my lord!"

"And another note to my agent, telling him the same."

"What on earth are they going to think?"

"They will think I am in the Bosphorus, where so much that is redundant goes. . . ."

"Don't talk like that, you're frightening me, Nuri bey!"

"And lastly. I want you to promise me something."

"That depends. What?"

"Jenny . . . have I been kind to you?"

"Of course. You've more or less saved my life."

"Well, then. Can you now give me a blind promise?"

"Oh . . . all right then."

"That you will not leave your room all day?"

"What if the police come for me, as you seem to think?"

"I don't think they will *come for you* quite so quickly. You'll have to be tracked down to the Hilton; it will take them some little time. Come now, your promise."

"All right . . . I promise."

"And one more. If I am not back here to-morrow at this time, you will go to the station and buy yourself a ticket and leave this city to go to your friends in France?"

"Oh, Nuri bey, that's all very well. We were going to have another lovely day together. Is all this mystery and 'Famous Last Words' necessary?"

"I think so."

"But you're only looking at it from one side, Nuri bey."

"How?"

"You're not seeing this thing from my point of view at all."

"I thought I was seeing it only from your point of view," he said, a trifle grimly.

"I'm sorry. Of course you are. If you hadn't met me by the merest chance, on Monday evening, you would be living in your fairly nice house, perfectly contentedly, surrounded by all your books and the things you have known all your life. Quietly and peacefully leading your life. On Monday evening you met me and helped me and what happens? Five days later you are more or less a pauper, homeless and without a possession in the world. It's a wonder you have any clothes! And all because of me! Do you really think it likely that I am going meekly to carry out all your careful instructions and get myself off by train until the excitement has died down?" She waited for an answer which did not come. "If you did, you've got another think coming, old dear."

"It is not altogether quite like that."

"It is."

"No. I needed the wind of change to blow through my life, I can see that now. If it had not been so, I would have jumped on to that airport bus and watched you struggling into a taxi without giving you another thought. I see now that I was on an island, but that I was beginning to shade my eyes and look along the horizon for the sight of a sail."

"Oh?"

"And I understand, too, that people are not just something to collect like you would collect birds' eggs or incunabula. People *is* life, or do I mean *are* life? Anyway, I could not put it better in my own language."

"You aren't making out a case for me going and leaving you."

"No."

"And anyway, it wouldn't be very hard for me to guess where you are going to-day. Why not take me with you?"

Nuri bey got up and came over. "Please turn up your sleeve." He unwrapped the bandage and examined her wounded arm. "Quite nice. You will have to have the stitches out soon."

"Listen, Nuri bey," she went on impatiently, "why can't I come?"

"Because I should be worried for your safety and should not, therefore, feel myself free."

"I'd be a nuisance?"

"Yes."

"I see. Well, listen. Why go and do anything? Why not come away with me? If you really think the police will find me here within twenty-four hours, then you must know that they will find you, if they want to. Why not let us both go? You have plenty of money here to get you to England and keep you for a bit, probably. I would come back to England with you and I could take you to Oxford and introduce you to my brother, who will know someone doing modern languages. And he could put you in touch with the people who would soon find you a job teaching . . . Turkish," she said doubtfully, "or any of the Middle-Eastern languages you know. . . ."

With a strange rapt look on his face, Nuri bey was looking at the ceiling as though, in its glossy paint, he could see himself walking over Magdalen Bridge with Professor Toynbee, and they were deep in discussion. Only five days ago he had believed: *when she dies I shall go to Oxford.* Miasma was not dead, and evidently far from it, and yet the possibility of going to Oxford was nearer than it had ever been.

"I cannot get myself to Oxford with five pounds left over, so that I am an indigent foreigner, hanging by my teeth on to the fringe of that precinct. No, if I go to Oxford I must go as a representative, not a beggar."

"A sales rep? What of? Turkish Delight? Oh, I'm sorry, Nuri bey!"

And once again, warmly and impulsively, Jenny kissed him.

Chapter 20

IT WOULD SEEM that Turkish people of a certain class sleep naked and put on their night attire when they get up. Thus when you surprise a Turkish family unannounced, the women are wearing elaborate nightdresses and the men striped pyjamas more often than not. When you arrive, they hurry away with flustered cries of apology and reappear in a marvellously short time, fully dressed and bearing small fragments of a loofah-like eatable, deliciously soaked in golden syrup, as an act of reparation.

Miasma had actually assisted in the childish game of lighting the fire at the back of Nuri bey's house. Crouching low, her old knees cracking loudly, to fan the flames with a discarded tin lid. The primitive actions came to her across an enormous span of years with great familiarity; her first ten years of life had been spent in such absorbed squatting, lighting the fire for the family meal, sometimes in the bitter wind and at other times in the burning heat of the Anatolian plain. No troop of Boy Scouts could equal the speed and efficiency of Miasma and Hadji when getting a fire going. There was no anxious moment when they stood back: would it or would it not go? From the first flicker, the fire knew where it was going, it was up and away, and so were Hadji and Miasma, a slow elderly couple, hobbling away in the dusk, round the corner to the waiting taxi. And the taxi was down at the ferry-station before there was any fire visible to passers by the house of Nuri bey.

But home at the *yali* there was no comfort; no Valance to hurry her to bed, bring her a tray of supper, draw her curtains against the chill wind from the water, stand gossiping with folded arms at the foot of the bed until such time as Miasma felt sleepy. It was a dank, comfortless place and Miasma took more than usual of the sleeping pills given her by Dr. MacPherson.

The shock of Hadji's news, his extreme agitation, indeed—panic, kept sleep from her until the small hours of the morning. The result was that she awoke late, feeling ill and quite unable to do any clear thinking.

She was awakened by Hadji rushing into her room, crying out the news he had heard on the radio. It had been a continuation of the ghoulish night she had spent and, in order to make life tolerable at all, she had dismissed Hadji and taken out her syringe and given herself a shot of heroin of the same mildness as the one she had given Jenny. It was only after this began to have effect that she felt able to go downstairs and have a cup of coffee.

She went to her birds as into retreat, letting them sit on her shoulder whilst she filled their water and food dishes and put her shrivelled old lips against their smooth beaks in silent, secret communion.

An indefinable relationship existed between herself and Hadji; now, as she went from cage to cage, she cursed him in a long stream of peasant-Turkish, doubtless repetitive, and certainly untranslatable, and the air was striped and crossed and blotted with black awful talk over which the birds spun flimsy threads of twittering and piping.

Nuri bey did not mount the front steps and bang the heavy knocker. He took the door through the wall in the courtyard and walked between the dismal beds of periwinkle and London Pride, round by the rockery to the water steps, where the door of the bird room stood wide open to the Bosphorus.

If the Bosphorus had given up its dead, they could not have been more shocked and Nuri bey, on his side, was, perhaps, as shocked as they. Madame Miasma, the famous Miasma, who had nearly achieved the position of *Sultan Validé,* who had talked with Kings and was supposed to have slept with Sultans, was standing in her nightdress, birds in her hair, cursing her faithful servant, yellow and sickly, his European clothes hanging round him like rags, and not a fly-button to his name.

With the last setting of the sun behind the Sublime Porte, these two had flown the Imperial flag, tattered and faded, but still recognisable. And now even this symbol of the old glory had left them and they were nothing more than a couple of indigent malefactors.

But old—old!

That was their defence, the only one they had and, sick with himself, Nuri bey realised it. He could take no revenge. Angry because it was so, he swooped in like an avenging eagle: what terrible actions had they been up to?

"Nuri, my lion," Miasma whined in a pathetic attempt to keep up her habitual manner of talking to him. "I trust you have come to help me. I am flung into the greatest distress by the news Hadjl has given me. How is it possible that this insane English gunman should have been found in Valance's coffin?"

"You know as well as I that the gunman was Valance's own grandson, half-English, half-French and a drug-runner, acting steward on Zenobia Airways. One of you killed him, or both."

A shocked and complete denial followed.

He went to the front door, the two hobbling after him,

and pointed to the bullet holes. "From my little personal revolver," Miasma said, triumphantly, as though she had proved her innocence.

"Exactly. Are you in the habit of firing at your own front door?"

"Those marks have been there for years and years. Since the First World War, when I had to learn to use a revolver, and so had Hadji and Valance. Many, many years they have been there, Nuri, my lion."

"I have not seen them until now."

"That does not prove they were not there," she snapped out. Her mind was like mercury still, it was impossible to pick her up; at every turn she evaded the straight answer, ignored the direct question, explained away damning evidence. Certainly that wicked boy had been Valance's grandson. Certainly he had come here from the airport, clamouring for protection. Certainly they had told him his grandmother was dead, had slammed the door in his face; they wished to have nothing whatever to do with him. He had gone away and they had no idea where he had gone. The scene at the front door, when he arrived, in front of the people gathered to mourn the passing of his grandmother, had been unseemly; they had wished to terminate this argument which took place almost over the dead body of his grandmother.

Hadji had been up to the graveyard early this morning; he saw that now the ground had been replaced over the grave and, down below, Valance's body lay, now at peace with Allah (or God, if he preferred) and nothing would disturb it. If the coffin which Valance's ridiculous sister Martine had taken back to France contained the body of Valance's grandson, it was no concern of theirs.

"Do not deceive yourself, Madame. The coffin rested here for several hours, and Valance's sister Martine will undoubtedly tell the police this. Furthermore, to-day the body will be examined, the bullets with which he was killed will be found. Within perhaps a few hours the police will be here, examining the whole house and its contents. Your revolver will be examined and will, of course, have been found to have fired the killer shot.

These bullet marks will simply add to the information."

"No concern of ours," she chanted, like a refrain; meaningless but persistent.

"Furthermore," Nuri bey went on relentlessly, "your judgment is terribly bad. You have burnt down my house, certain that it contained evidence of your dealing in raw opium, Madame."

"Nonsense, Nuri bey. You can never prove it!"

"And it was needless. Your great fault is to under-estimate the brains of anyone other than yourself, Ma-dame. The young English girl, Jenny Bolton, was speaking the truth when she said she threw the case with everything in it, into the Golden Horn at the earliest possible oppor-tunity. If you had understood what the English are like, you would have known that what she said was true. And I should have been spared my house."

"The Golden Horn," she repeated with a shudder. "You hear that, Hadji, all that money, thrown into the Golden Horn!"

"Who are you to deplore such an action? We Turks have made a habit throughout history of throwing any-thing which is of embarrassment to us either into the Golden Horn or into the Bosphorus. The English girl showed great common sense in her action. Madame, I must beg of you to understand that you are at this moment in a terrible position."

"Then you must help us, Nuri bey, since it is through you that we are in such a position."

"How can you say that, let alone think it?"

"If you had not interfered with the young girl after the shooting, if you had come away from the airport as quickly as possible, nothing would have happened to involve us. It is all your fault."

He was dumbfounded and for a few minutes could say nothing but walked angrily up and down the room; he passed and re-passed the cages, whilst the scorching eyes of the two followed him.

At last he told them that, wherever the fault might lie, the police would very shortly be here and, as they knew, in Turkey people were arrested before questioning:

"Though even in this barbaric country," he added grimly, "they will have to have a warrant before entering and searching the house."

"We are in this together," Miasma said. "You cannot get away from it. Nobody will believe that you knew nothing of what you carried in the case, I myself do not believe it. I asked you to take the case to the airport for me. A clever lion like you, Nuri bey, would never take it without knowing."

"Then, if I knew what the case contained, why should I take it without demanding payment, Madame?" he returned sharply, and scored a point. Then, taking advantage of the moment, pressed home: "Tell me, Madame, who else is in this drug trade with you? You must tell me, otherwise I cannot help you."

"This I swear to you, Nuri. I am a link only in a chain of which I know none of the other links."

"What about the friend in Hong Kong?"

"I have never seen her. I think it is a husband and wife, but all I know is that I address my consignments to her."

"What is your part, then, exactly?"

"I receive the raw opium, Nuri. It is left for me in a parcel in the courtyard, ready wrapped, by someone who grows it here and prepares it in the form of packets of *locum*. Don't ask me who they are, because they have been to the greatest pains not to allow me to know. The opium is Turkish grown and packed here . . . beyond that I know nothing."

"You are the link who receives the opium and gets it on to the aeroplane, then?"

"Yes, that is so. It is only the last few years that have made things dangerous for me. Before any aeroplanes called here on their flight to the Far East, getting there so quickly, I sent it by boat. One old skipper obliged me for years. Then he died and I had to make other arrangements. Some of these young stewards on the airlines are known to take contraband goods of every kind; it so happened that Valance's young grandson could easily be persuaded. He, also, was paid from Hong Kong."

"Then, I take it that in Hong Kong the opium is converted into the heroin supplied to drug addicts everywhere?"

"Mostly for Japan, I understand."

"It doesn't matter who gets it, it's . . ." he searched for an adequate word to describe his disgust.

She shrugged. "If I did not play my part, somebody else would," she said. "I ought, by now, to have received an airmail letter containing Turkish notes, in payment for that consignment of eight pounds, *eight pounds* of raw opium, now at the bottom of the Golden Horn." She wrung and twisted her hands in agony at the thought. "It's no good your looking so disgusted, Nuri, my lion; so long as there are human beings there will be those who cannot face up to life and who resort to narcotics, and there will always be people to supply it. Do you not recall, my lion, reading something out of the newspaper to me, some three months ago, about an Ambassador from one of the South American States to a European country, who was dismissed because, with two other men, he was accused of arranging for drugs to be taken into the United States to the extent, when broken into heroin in small quantities, of twenty-one-and-a-half-million dollars' worth? You don't remember? I do, I remember it well!"

"Nothing you can say makes it any better!" he snapped. "And I can prove that I took that case to the airport in absolute innocence. I have many friends and acquaintances who will speak for me. But above all, everyone knows that I have never had any money, other than my patrimony."

"I see. Then you will let me be taken away by the police and cast into prison until they have built up a case against me. Is that right?"

"No. I will help you to get away but first I must ask you for money; money to pay the heavy expenses that will be incurred and money, my dear Madame, to pay for the loss of my house." As he spoke Nuri bey turned to look at Hadji, a cipher of dejection and fear. "You made a big blunder in that act of incendiarism, you must pay for it."

"But I have no money, Nuri. At least, very little. If I had, why should I be so upset at not receiving the payment for the last drug transaction? When I met you at the mosque on Wednesday, I told you something of my finances, you should understand that there is nothing."

"Then I shall do nothing."

"How can you be so wicked?"

He smiled grimly. "Wicked? I have lost everything, all my books, which have been my life until now. Everything except what I now appear before you wearing. Everything."

"You still have youth, my friend."

"Hardly."

"Whereas I am old."

After a few moments' thought, Miasma signalled to Hadji to follow her and the two stood out in the hall, conversing in low voices.

Nuri bey thought about his sister in Trebizond, who kept rooms for school teachers and who might be glad to take the old woman as a paying guest for a short time. Hadji could sleep in any doorway or beside any fountain, until Miasma had time to make her own arrangements to leave the country. The most he could do was to save them from immediate arrest and imprisonment which might last for months.

Miasma tottered back into the bird room. "You will have to persuade Hadji to part with some of his fortune," she said harshly, "I cannot get the dirty rat even to admit that he has thousands of *lire* hidden away not a hundred miles from here. What he hopes to do with it, only Allah knows. Only you can persuade the filthy dog that he must spend it to save his rotten pelt. When the police arrive, it will be too late for him to do anything but cower."

"One cannot reason with creatures such as he."

"Then beat him, Nuri, beat him senseless."

At which Nuri bey became extremely angry, a lion at

last and a wounded one. He shouted so loudly that the vibration shook the crystals hanging from the chandelier above the love-seat. The content of what he shouted is not important; a roar of angry Turkish sounds a lot more dire than the same things roared in English. The anger of one who is slow to wrath is more calamitous still. Hadji crept back and crouched, terrified, by the door.

Finally, in order to stop the noise, which could, surely, be heard over a good part of Asia, and in Europe, across the water, as well, Hadji produced a flat wad of filthy Turkish *lire* from some nameless region of his person and thrust them into Nuri bey's hands.

This lump of material smelled of sweat and dirty rags and essence of Hadji which was surprising, coming from one who washed parts of himself usually five times a day before prayer. But it was, nevertheless, dirty paper printed in a certain way which meant that, in return for it, things could be acquired which could not otherwise be obtained. Slipping it into his jacket pocket, Nuri bey immediately felt the need to wash his hands.

"I shall go," he said in sudden calm, "and see what I can do. You must not leave this house, Hadji, for one minute, not to buy bread or yoghourt or anything at all. You must bolt the front door when I leave and shut and bolt the outside door of this room and, if anyone comes, you must stay quiet and not let them know that you are here. Neither of you deserve to be spared what may be coming to you; but I shall do my best to see that you are, though the Allah to whom you, Hadji, are always praying, will, no doubt, know why. I don't."

And so saying, he left by the way that he had come.

Chapter 21

IF THE proles, lounging, squatting and merely existing, had heard anything they did not like, nothing of it showed in their faces. Nuri bey swung through the square, turning sharply to the right and swinging upwards past the hovels to the cemetery. It needed nothing more than a glance from him for the original six to pull themselves to their feet in a leisurely manner and, one by one, to follow him up the steep hillside.

Up the dusty, rough path, between the sweet-smelling tangy herbs, the wild lavender and thyme, in the bright sunshine, Nuri bey went, with his great scissor-like strides, thinking of Madame Bassompierre teetering along beside him on her ridiculous high heels. Up and up and up until the great fabled Bosphorus lay before him in all its so-called beauty. Up to the top and over the top. For a few moments he could not see the grave of Valance but presently found the newly filled-in oblong grave and sat down beside it, cross-legged.

What price a *déjà vu* now? How did it happen? How could he voluntarily repeat the experience? He leaned back against the style of the grave next door and tried to get himself into a psychic state. If once, why not again? He made his mind a blank and waited. But nothing happened except that the proles who had caught up with him, stood at a respectful distance and allowed the Efendi to commune with himself, or Allah, or whomsoever he was communing with. And Nuri bey became a mental nothing, a blank slate upon which the future or the past could scribble and nothing was scrawled thereon.

What he wanted to know was: who or what is in the grave, and the answer, correctly enough, was nothing.

And when he had had enough of nothingness, Nuri bey turned and beckoned the proles to come, and they squatted down on the scented herbs, in a semi-circle round him and became discursive.

Everything had gone according to plan. It had been a beautiful evening; dry, warm, and no wind and they had waited in the square and watched the Pleiades mount in the sky and mount and mount, and when they were nearly overhead they had taken the coffin from its hiding place in the rhododendrons and carried it up here. And here the mule cart had been, already waiting for them. They had brought ropes and shovels with them, as the

Efendi had instructed, and within the duration of a nightingale's song they had loosened the boards, had lifted the body, no longer stiff but rendered unyielding by placing two of the boards underneath it, and they had raised it with the ropes slung beneath the wood and placed it in the coffin, wrapped in the pale green winding cloth, as they had found it. Quickly they had fixed the lid of the coffin down with the latches already supplied. They had replaced the wood in the bottom of the grave exactly as they had found it; no one could possibly know by simply looking into the grave that the body was no longer there. Early this morning the official sexton and his assistant had come and hastily shovelled back the earth; one of them had watched from over there. Nothing had been suspected. All had gone well and the mule cart had gone slowly away, they following at a distance to find the truck already waiting at the lower end of the main pathway, towards the next village. They had watched the coffin being put on the truck and had seen the truck drive away towards Uskudar and the car ferry.

Nuri bey praised them in the flowery language which they expected. Furthermore, he brought out a few notes and handed them round as a little extra to show his pleasure in a job well carried out.

There were dark deeds at the *yali,* he said. There were undertakings of the most sly and clandestine; deeds and actions which Nuri bey deplored in his deepest self. But they knew nothing and when the police came they must continue to know nothing. *No* and *nought* were to be both operative word and action; and that went for all of them. Nuri bey looked round from black eyes to black eyes and knew with comforting certainty that they would *"yok"* their questioners unconscious.

Where now cumbersome boats with donkey engines, flimsy and unreliable outboard motors, or simply heavy oars, ply from village to village, the Bosphorus used to be gay with enchanting caiques, those grand, coloured, high-powered boats which are said to have inspired the Venetian gondolas, and which gave glamour to that dark and melancholy channel. Barely a generation since the last caiques were pulled ashore for ever, the descendents of the magnificent boatmen who manipulated them so skilfully, still use their boats on the treacherous surface with immense skill.

Nuri bey went in search of one such boatman whom he knew personally; it took him some little time because it was important to go about the task inconspicuously. In the end he took a bus to the next village downstream and found the boatman at the Sweet Waters of Asia, once a famous pleasure ground for Ottoman society, where the women would promenade along one bank and the men the other, sometimes throwing flowers across to each other as they walked. There is no romance now, except in the name; a bathing *plage,* dusty cafés, and a squalid fairground make it unattractive. Nuri bey's friend seemed to have little to do other than chew little bits of string, spitting the torn-off scraps as far as he was able to project them. Nuri bey offered him an alternative, that of taking him up to Istiniye, immediately, at once, upon the instant, which did not mean anytime from now on. But now.

There was nothing doing at first, incentive must be produced and this took the form of dirty note after dirty note which Nuri bey slid from his pocket, one by one, keeping an impassive face. When he had made the movement enough times the boatman sprang into action with alacrity and a great exertion of energy, suddenly taking his engine to pieces, banging and screwing them together again; sending some two dozen ragged boys with a rusty can full of holes for petrol; playing a hurried pithy phrase upon his highly-strung drum whilst he waited for their return; tying himself up in acres of fishing-net like a fly which has got entangled in a web; freeing himself with an easy movement which showed that he had not been entangled at all; wiping the seat where the bey Efendi was to sit, with a bunch of dirty cock's feathers; throwing out a hot-water bottle and some old sacks; borrowing a pair of oars from another boatman and, finally, taking down his personal washing from where it hung drying on a line rigged up in the prow.

After a few preliminary gasps and splutters the engine roared into life in a business-like way and Nuri bey climbed hopefully aboard. Leaving the engine revved up in agonising noise, the boatman pulled on the fairly clean white trousers he had taken from the drying line and a reasonably white polo sweater, and then brought out a yachting cap with a shiny black peak and a dazzlingly white top which he put on at an angle which would have rivalled the dash of any smart R.Y.C. member on the club lawn at Cowes, and they were off . . . or nearly so, for twenty yards or so off shore the engine puffed to a standstill.

It would make depressing reading to hear how often the engine died out, how many times it was reinfused with life only to fizzle out again. And because he was apparently determined not to have to return any of the lovely money the Efendi had given him, the boatman gave up struggling with mechanical vagaries and wrestled with the oars instead. It was a gigantic task, requiring great strength and skill, to row across that mighty stream, with its cross-currents and underflows which had nearly proved too much for the Argonauts some years before, but Nuri bey was not too restless nor too strung-up because when about half-way across he could see, with his perfect sight, that the masts of the Arab schooner were still there, in port, distinctive amongst the other masts, and he remained calm and tranquil until they arrived. Indeed, the boatman had shown himself to be so splendidly capable that Nuri bey would have embraced him if he had not been in a hurry.

The skipper of the Arab schooner was sitting in the bows, leaning against a pile of evil-smelling sacks, his legs apart in a wide V which brought his knees well above his head; he was thoughtfully picking at the quick round his thumb nail, and very much relaxed after the ardours of loading. He struggled to achieve a more respectful position when he saw the bey Efendi but Nuri bey at once put him at his ease by sitting down beside him amongst the sacks of sheep skin. They were sailing at once, immediately and now, which meant any time between now and midnight. There is no need to wait for the tide in the Bosphorus, the wind was favourable and had been so for some days; no storm was expected. They should be sailing the Euxine at dawn.

"Thalassa! Thalassa!" the Greeks had cried when they saw that murky stretch of wind-swept water and Nuri bey felt a similar cry of triumph rise in his throat at the thought that, with the help of Allah, Miasma and Hadji would also be sailing the Euxine at dawn, and it wouldn't do Madame any harm at all to bed down for several nights on piles of evil-smelling sacks filled with sheep skins.

This time the bargaining was done as became a couple of gentlemen, and not with notes produced one by dirty one. An initial deposit was made and Nuri bey promised that the rest of the fare would be produced, probably by the male servant, when the two old people were finally pulled on board, shortly after midnight.

If this were not so, Nuri bey declared, the skipper had his full permission to refuse altogether to take the old couple on board. "Drop them into the Bosphorus," Nuri bey said soberly, but in such a way as to tell an Arab that it was not intended seriously, "because they can well afford almost any sum you care to ask."

The old lady was as nimble as any of the best octogenarians but, Nuri bey advised, it would be as well to have all hands at the ready for that final haul. Further, Nuri bey suggested, it would be as well if landfall at Trebizond could occur during the hours of darkness. He would telephone to his sister and make all arrangements for the old woman's arrival; it was but a short walk to her house from the port.

"The Madame will be an infernal nuisance to you as a passenger, asking for attention all the time, so you must keep her out of your wheel-house and do not encourage discourse. She takes drugs and can easily become hysterical, so you will be ready to deal with her promptly should there be any trouble."

They discussed all these matters gravely and there was only one thing left which worried the captain. It was the question of time. As the Efendi knew, anchorage in that part of the Bosphorus was impossible; to pick up passengers at the least possible distance off shore, in the dark, could be done but would require absolutely accurate timing. The skipper knew the village and even the *yali* well by sight but it was not possible to say, until he had tried it, how near he could get to it.

Still stimulated by the superb exhibition of boatmanship which he had just experienced, Nuri bey promised that, if the skipper would come inshore as far as he could, Nuri bey would have a boatman ready with boat tied up alongside the water steps of the *yali* to set out with the passengers immediately the signal was received. The skipper then showed him the lantern with green glass shutter, which he would swing to and fro when he was ready for them.

Standing up, Nuri bey looked into the splendid hawk-like brown face of the Arab captain. He said, not to excuse himself but because he would not wish there to be any wrong thoughts behind that fine-drawn façade: "They will pay both of us well for this but, when you see them, you will understand that it is not only for money that one undertakes to get them away from here. It is because they are both so old and both so wicked; it would be undignified that they should hang, undignified for us as a people, I mean, not for them; they have been quite undignified enough as it is. If I do nothing, they will hang, and, though they deserve it, I cannot allow it to happen."

The Arab understood perfectly. He bowed gravely to indicate this. Nuri bey bowed back.

There was only one more thing. If Allah wished it and they were not to escape, if, in simpler words, anything went wrong, Nuri bey would switch on and off rapidly, five times, one of the electric lights in the *yali*. The Captain would know that something had gone wrong and would sail at once. When he returned to Istiniye, Nuri bey would make a point of looking him up and talking over the whole affair.

"For the present . . . my thanks."

Chapter 22

IN THE meantime the boatman, with the help of two engineers, had got the engine of his boat going, tearing the air into great jagged strips of nerve-racking sound and ejecting a thin stream of poisonous vapour. They screamed back across the water as though the long-boat had become a speed-boat, with the prow bouncing in and out of the water and spray fanning away to either side in fine style. Arriving back at their starting point, the engine was turned off with such an air of triumph that it was evident that the boatman was now in a very good mood to be persuaded to undertake the midnight operation. As they slipped into the shallows, where Valance's body had been found, where the Sweet Waters of Asia emerge into the Bosphorus, Nuri bey put his proposition.

What the boatman might or might not have thought was not important; there was no need for any explanation, as there had been to the skipper of the schooner. His intelligence was of a low order, as was his vessel, and all that was required of him was his services in conveying an old couple from the *yali* to the schooner. It was sailing about midnight and the operation would, therefore, have to take place during the hours of darkness and would involve considerable risk, for which Nuri bey was prepared to pay in full. To give the boatman the necessary shot of enthusiasm, Nuri bey dwelt upon the dangers it would involve and the skill that would be required. To tie up at the water steps of the *yali*, Nuri bey pointed out, would be no mean feat.

Incited to do his best, the boatman said that between

now and darkness he would borrow and rig up a swivelling headlamp, such as the ferry boats used, in the prow of his boat. If the male passenger, sitting in the prow, could handle this, the task would be simple. Nuri bey had, unwillingly, to reject this proposal as too likely to attract attention, explaining to the boatman that the operation was a secret one about which it would be best if no questions were asked. As an act of goodwill, Nuri bey gave him all the money that remained and assured him that he himself would hand over the balance when the boat arrived at the *yali,* and before the task was completed. Which munificence satisfied the boatman completely.

Since the splendid Hilton breakfast, the Bosphorus had been crossed three times, much important discussion had taken place and now the sun was dropping down the sky. Before returning to the *yali* for the worst part of his undertaking yet, Nuri bey went into a restaurant which was more or less another hole in a wall and ate a great deal of delicious white fish sprinkled with herbs and lemon, which had been alive when he walked in. Thus fortified, he approached the *yali* fully prepared to find the police already there, Miasma in hysterics and Hadji in a trance of fear.

No doubt the police headquarters in Paris, having issued the news of the find in the coffin to the Press, were awaiting the pathologist's report. Deprived of the funeral in Père Lachaise, the Bassompierre family and friends, in their deep mourning, would be swarming round the offices in the Quai des Orfèvres like a lot of angry bluebottles.

"I promise, dear Monsieur, that I will never repeat to any living soul what has taken place between us this morning. I will take a solemn Christian oath on it." Nuri bey shuddered: how strong would that Christian oath sealed with the sign of the Cross be when she learned that the suspicious customs officers had opened the coffin, searching for contraband goods, and discovered the body of a young man and not of an old woman? The young man who

was a blood relation, returned to them like rejected, sub-standard goods, and without an enclosed invoice!

If she acted as the sort of person she was, true to herself, she would simply fold her hands and say calmly over and over again: "I know nothing whatever except that I went for the body of my sister and made arrangements for its return, leaving the coffin for that purpose. If I had been allowed to bring the body of my sister in the coffin back with me, this would never have happened. I have no explanation whatever as to what happened to the body of my sister." She might grumble extensively about the nonsense of not being allowed to bring a dead body back with her in the aeroplane, the stupid superstitions of the officials of Zenobia Airlines and the ill-placed regard for the feelings of their passengers. A body was a body, an empty shell, she might say practically, and so on, and so forth, confusing the issue and talking the police into a kind of trance, as she had talked Nuri bey himself. But giving nothing away.

Waiting for the bus which would take him back to the yali, Nuri bey heard the hour of prayer being proclaimed by gramophone record from a nearby minaret. Before the next hour of prayer, Miasma and the eunuch should be on the high sea, with no one but the Arab crew to listen to their tune of a thousand lamentations.

It was but a single stage to the yali stop and, as Nuri bey descended, he saw at once two of the proles lounging against the railings. They made no sudden start forward to greet him and Nuri bey behaved equally casually, strolling slowly back in the direction from which he had come. They soon caught him up and, in a short series of indirect Moslem metaphors, told him that the police had called at the yali, had knocked loudly and often upon the door, had gone round through the garden to the water steps and peered in through the locked french window, had returned to the courtyard where they had had a short conference and had gone, but, since their departure, a motor had brought to the village a spy of the police, in simpler words, a plain-clothes policeman, who was now standing at the corner of the square, on the opposite side from the *yali*, reading a newspaper, with his back against the wall, whilst at the same time keeping a watch on the *yali*.

The Efendi could not return to the *yali* without being observed by this ill-gotten character. If he so wished, they could create a diversion which would, momentarily, divert the spy's attention and, in that fragment of time, he could slip into the courtyard, through the side-door and round to the water steps, where he would no doubt be let in. Nothing else of importance had happened. The cleaning woman had gone to the *yali* but had also been unable to get in, even though she had turned the lock with her own key; the door was bolted inside, therefore there was someone there. Nobody, other than Nuri bey himself, had left the *yali* since dawn. The police had questioned nobody, and if they had, they would have been told nothing.

Thanking them, Nuri bey professed his appreciation of their suggestion and sent them off ahead to create their diversion. What exact form the diversion took he never discovered; the proles acted in their own mysterious way, and, sure enough, in the five minutes which Nuri bey gave them, they had kicked up a row of such proportions that, when Nuri bey strolled into eyeshot, a fuss of a kind that presaged a major revolution was taking place in the square and the plain-clothes policeman was certainly no longer leaning against the wall reading a newspaper but probably in the heart of it all.

He slipped through the courtyard, evidently watched from the window by Hadji because, when he got round to the water steps, the eunuch, with trembling, fumbling fingers, was undoing the bolts and chain securing the french window.

"Come in, Efendim, come in," he begged, "the police have been and tried to enter. They have gone away but they will surely return with their warrant, to break in. What are we to do?"

With clammy hands the old man pulled him inside and secured the door behind him. Miasma now trailed into the bird room. She had decked herself in a splendid creation of purple velvet with a frontage of sequins; her sable stole was thrown round her shoulders, but her hair was a tangled mess, as it had been since the last time Valance had dressed it. Nuri bey had difficulty in checking an exclamation of impatience at her childishness, realising that she had dressed in her best for her interview with the police, possibly to give herself some badly-needed confidence.

How was he going to cause to hurry two old people whose lives had been frittered away in inessential activities. They had never hurried nor made the swift, economic movements of necessity.

To bark pithy instructions at them would be entirely useless. He opened the operation with ambiguous and sonorous remarks from the Bible, saying things about a time to plant and a time to pluck up that which is planted, a time to keep and a time to cast away . . . and a time to get going, which was now.

"You must cast away everything," he said, " and go, and I have made arrangements for you to sail away from here secretly at midnight. You will go to Trebizond, where you, Madame, will stay with my sister until you have been able to make plans to leave the country. And I want to hear no wailing and gnashing of teeth now; you will have plenty of time for that when you find yourself in gaol, probably for the rest of your lives, waiting trial. For if you go to the prison island now, you will certainly never leave, but will die there."

"But I am innocent," she screamed.

"Can you prove it?" he asked calmly.

"I want to live, Nuri bey. Can you not understand? I do not wish to end my life now; I should still have happy years ahead, amongst my possessions, I wish to live . . . I must . . . I shall not give up, nor die!"

"But, Madame, you shall live. It is with this very object in mind that I have been working for you all day, and have spent all the money which Hadji gave me." He then outlined the plan which he had laid for their escape. "It will cost much money but I know that Hadji has it, even if you have not."

A magnificent sight in her finery, she trotted up and down the room, past her bird cages, holding her face between her hands. He knew what was worrying her; it was Hadji, without whom she was as someone without a limb; Hadji whose miserliness had now put him in the position of pay-master; whose very servility, over the years, had now altered the balance of power. She longed to be rid of him but could not do without him; they were as two old trees whose roots were so entwined that they could not be divided.

"Come," Nuri bey said briskly, "a small handcase each, your jewels, Madame, the relevant papers with regard to your possession of this house, any important bank documents you may possess, a change of clothes, and that is all."

"Impossible," she shrieked. "All my beautiful clothes, everything I have is *all* I have; everything you see around you. How can I go with nothing?" and so on and so forth until Nuri bey became angry and once more shouted so loudly that the crystals on the chandeliers tinkled softly and the old wooden boards shivered imperceptibly and the *yali* might well have slipped to its knees and away downstream with the current.

The next three hours were the most painful Nuri bey had ever spent. His difficulties combined those of Zoo attendant with male nurse in a lunatic asylum. As darkness fell no light must show in the *yali* windows. In any case, the watcher on the corner might well have instructions to telephone for the police to return as soon as he knew someone was in the *yali*. Hadji found a couple of rusty Aladdin-like lamps of such incredible antiquity that they might even have been handed down from the vestal virgins themselves. These had to be trimmed and filled with oil, which operation, undertaken with trembling fingers, took Hadji the best part of an hour in semi-darkness. Nuri bey shut the doors of the rooms with windows overlooking the courtyard and the street so that no light would be seen.

During his absence from the bird room, Nuri bey found that Madame had piled a great heap of papers into a suitcase, the lid of which would not come down over them. Other suitcases lay about with a trail of finery tumbling from them. Hadji trailed in and out with a succession of baskets and carpet-bags containing bulky and clanking objects from the kitchen and, once again, Nuri bey had to get angry. Finally, though even *in extremis* Madame did not divulge that she could not read, she asked Nuri bey to pick out the relevant papers and stow the rest away "in safety, where I shall find them on my return."

Nuri bey had no watch, he told the time instinctively, helped by the sun, moon and stars, to within a few minutes. He knew that, though the chaos in the *yali* had increased a hundred-fold since his return, the time left them had shrunk and was shrinking rapidly.

In order to get Madame to make the final preparation of wearing suitable clothes for a week's sea voyage, Nuri bey had to pretend to compromise about the amount of luggage they might take and, helping to close them, banked up a heap of miscellaneous carriers and cases beside the door to the water steps. It was a real achievement to get them both assembled in the bird room at what Nuri bey judged to be a quarter of an hour before time. He looked them over. Madame had changed into her smart black coat, over which she clung to her mink wrap. A huge crocodile handbag hung from her arm and she wore her best hand-made crocodile shoes and a silk scarf round her head and tied under her chin.

"Nothing can be done without money," Nuri bey said. "Let me have the money for the boatman, it must be given to him before you climb on board." With a quick comprehensive look at Hadji, Madame fumbled in her handbag and brought out Turkish notes of the amount Nuri bey required. He told them that, as they climbed on board the schooner, a sum of money five times the amount of what he now held, was to be given to the captain, otherwise they would have to return to the *yali*. That, too, was understood. And finally, Nuri bey said, his sister must be well paid for her room; he would telephone to her as soon as he knew they were well on the way, and would arrange the payment with her for Madame's keep.

"Furthermore," Nuri bey went on, "there is a time to keep silent and a time to speak, and now is the time to speak. If I have helped you, you must help me by telling me what happened."

Madame was sitting on the love-seat, looking worn out. She said nothing. Hadji, who was wearing a leather satchel with a strap round his shoulder and a torn plastic mackintosh, allowed his eyes to slip away from Nuri bey's.

Nuri felt tired, exhausted with the awful frustration of it all. He wanted to shake the information out of them and yet, if he were to do so, he had no guarantee that what they would tell him would be true. He went across to the window, looking out at the black, rushing water a few feet away. When the time came they were going to be frightened; it would not be easy to get them to clamber and scramble into a madly rocking boat, tugged from before by the boatman and pushed from behind by Nuri bey. It was a terrifying rush of water on a summer's day; at night it was so frightening that it might well petrify them into refusing to leave. If that happened, Nuri bey decided, he would walk out and leave them to it. If Madame Bassompierre were true to herself she would also be true to him.

As he stared out across the water, Nuri bey realised that it was not totally dark; he could make out against the paler north-west sky, the dark form of the schooner, rigged fore and aft, drawn wonderfully near, riding the current with prow high, northward pointing. He smiled with pure delight at the success of his scheme. The skipper had been well paid; even if, at the last moment, the old people refused to leave, as well they might, nothing would be lost. He would signal to the ship and it would sail away without them. Later they would sail away in the other direction, down to the prison on an island in the Sea of Marmora; a pleasanter journey but a more final one.

As he stood thinking these things and watching for the little boat to come chugging along the water's edge, he was aware of a disturbance in the room behind him.

He had nagged, chivvied, scolded, ordered, organised and manipulated long enough, he was tired of it. Whatever it was they were doing, it didn't matter. They would go without anything but what Nuri bey threw into the boat after them, or they would certainly capsize the ill-balanced craft which was to take them to the ship.

He heard the blessed sound of the engine before he saw the boat and within a minute it was slipping past, to circle round and try again.

"Come," he said, and turning round to the room lighted only by the two tiny oil flames, he saw the full enormity of what they were doing. From cage after cage Hadji was catching the birds and thrusting them into a smaller cage, but even the small cage was by no means tiny. "You can't take that!" he cried sharply.

Far from not taking it, Miasma said, they could not go without it. How could she possibly leave her birds? Who would look after them? With Hadji holding one end and she the other, they staggered past him bearing the wire-fronted cage which now contained some fifty frantic birds, disturbed from their sleep and in a major panic.

A time for reason and a time for nonsense, Nuri bey thought, opening the french windows and letting them totter out to the top of the water steps. After they had gone, he would push the whole cage into the Bosphorus and let it bubble to destruction; he had never believed with his countrymen that birds were sacred.

Now the engine of the boat had been stopped and the boatman was bringing it closer by the use of his oars. Closer, closer and, finally, he threw the rope which Nuri bey missed because he could not see it, but what he could see was the green light, from the deck of the schooner, slowly being waved to left and to right.

They would have to have some light, and now that they were nearly gone, Nuri bey realised he must take the risk of turning on the lights of the bird room and of Madame's bedroom above, which would help the whole operation immeasurably. He sped upstairs and the light from the windows sprang out across the stretch of water in front of the *yali,* almost as far as the dark shadow of the schooner, waiting off shore. The bird room light, too, added to the splendidly illuminating beam but, as he hurried back to the water steps, Nuri bey saw that Madame and Hadji had, with incredible speed, thrown into the boat at least half the pile of baggage and now, at the water's edge, he heard a furious argument taking place with the boatman and much hissing reference to the money he would be given if he were to allow the bird cage to top the rest of the baggage in the already laden bows. The boatman was lying face downwards as he clung to the old mooring-ring to which the caiques had always tied, the prow was swinging away and round in a great circle. Nuri bey, crouching, used immense strength to force the boat back parallel with the steps.

"Get in," he cried, and taking Madame by the waist he lifted her and almost threw her into the seat which the boatman had prepared. Hadji cowered against the steps but Nuri bey picked him up and cast him less gently aboard after Madame. Both of them shrieked and moaned and lamented loudly and the boatman swore that he could not manage the bird-cage.

"Throw it in," Nuri bey told him, "the old woman is half mad. Here is your money, I have got you double what you asked."

It was clear that the boat was considerably over-loaded but, persuaded by the ghoulish threats of what would happen to him if he did not leave the bird-cage where it was, the boatman conceded; the boat immediately swung away downstream briskly and there was no time even to start up the engine. The boatman snatched the oars and got the unwieldly little craft under control but, though he was working with superhuman effort and using immense strength, they were making no visible progress towards the waiting ship.

"Throw the luggage away," Nuri bey shouted. "Lighten your load! Quickly, you will sink! Throw it away!" The boatman was now at least holding his own against the stream but it was impossible for him to cease his effort even for a moment. A wave, backwash from the schooner,

caused the boat to rock and Miasma, with a more piercing shriek than any that had gone before, lurched forward to
steady her swaying bird-cage.

Unsuccessfully, as it happened. What had been normal
swaying of a small overladen boat ceased to be a sway.
A pendulum always swings back, unless it is held. And,
as a pendulum is held, so was the boat held so that it did
not rock back but stayed in mid-rock, held by the ill-
balance of Miasma, the bird-cage and the rest of the
luggage which had lurched to one side. It had to go one
way or the other; for a terribly long second it was undecided whether to resume its rock or go over altogether
and over it went and, as it went, Nuri bey, eyes fixed
upon the scene, took off his jacket, and threw it behind
him. He slipped off his braces and stepped out of his
trousers, removed his shirt, vest and pants, and not once
did his eyes move from what he saw.

Whilst limbering up he could not see what the exact
position was and he would not dive in until he could see
who was where. He felt, rippling through him in splendid
waves, that immense physical power (from the Circassian
youth who had grown immensely tall through being
breast-fed by a series of wet nurses till he was ten) and an
almost pleasurable anticipation of bottomless water and
a life and death struggle with vicious currents.

There was a deathly silence. The boatman was the
first to come out from under. He had no thought for his
passengers but struck out at once, downstream, and that
was the last Nuri bey saw of him. The boat stayed keel
upwards for a few moments, also drifting downstream
and then, with a gulp, vanished as first one, then two
heads appeared. Nuri bey could barely make out which
was which, but he was in no doubt when the screaming
started.

"Nuri, Nuri, save me!" and then a ghastly bubbling,
water-choked noise. And from Hadji . . . nothing . . .
no sound.

"My lion—my lion . . ." And still no sound from
Hadji, who might have been making some attempt to
swim. Then silence again. She had disappeared.

"Hold on, Hadji, I am coming," Nuri bey shouted and at once clove the water in a beautiful scimitar-shaped dive.

But suddenly, there was Miasma again, like a bobbed-up cork. "Nuri . . . Nuri . . . save me . . . I want to live . . . help! . . ."

If one can truly be said to think whole thoughts in such a position, Nuri bey thought: "Which shall I save? I clearly cannot manage both. Which shall it be?"

As he got nearer to them, with great strong overarm strokes, she went down once more but incredibly soon was up again and shouting: "My lion . . . save me . . . save me . . . my lion!"

Afterwards he told himself that he had thought coherent thoughts. He thought he thought: I will not save her; she had no mercy on others, I will have no mercy on her. But in fact it was not thought but instinct which turned him from her to Hadji. He caught hold of the strong strap which Hadji had round his shoulder and pulled.

"Lie on your back and keep still, old man!" He set off for shore.

The Bosphorus did not want to leave go, it caught at his legs and pulled, it tore at his shoulders, it pushed him bodily away from the shore. It was hungry and it fed on human beings. It pulled and tugged; it beat and kicked and even when, exhausted, Nuri bey grabbed for the rusty ring and pulled himself on to the bottom step, it snatched at Hadji and tried to get away at least one tough mortal.

"I want to live . . . save me . . . to live . . . save . . ." And between each cry the hideous, soft, bubbling, gasping sound of someone drowning.

If there had been time he might have gone back for her then, half dead though she was, with lungs already water-logged and only the will to live left. But Hadji had to be pulled from the water; and once out he was not like a drowned rat but as heavy as a sackful of drowned beavers. By the time he was dragged up the steps far enough not to slip back and vomiting water on to the marble, it was too late.

She had gone down for the last time, and there was nothing more to be seen and nothing to be heard but the gentle sound of the dark water as it hissed past.

Chapter 23

HE DRAGGED the miserable, sodden bundle of human being into the bird room and left him lying face downwards on the floor whilst he went upstairs to put out the bedroom light. Back in the bird room, he switched the light on and off five times but there was no time to stand on the water steps watching the schooner sail away; it was the creature on the floor to whom attention must be paid. If anyone could ever be said to be in a frenzy of grief, it was Hadji; he beat the floor with his fists and banged his head repeatedly against the marble tiles; froth poured from his mouth and he howled like a dog. He was beside himself. Nuri bey handled him as he would a sick child, stripping the wet clothes from him and wrapping him in a blanket from Miasma's bed. He left him on the love-seat and, taking one of the Aladdin-lamps, he went in search of alcohol, returning with a bottle of *raki*, some of the contents of which he poured down Hadji's madly resisting throat and some down his own.

Thoughtfully he put on his clothes and it was as though he could still hear and would continue to hear all the rest of his life, that dreadful choking cry: *I want to live!* He was stunned with awe at the fitness of her end: that she should die as she had caused Valance to die! It was as though the hand of Allah had been seen actually to move and Nuri bey was struck with reverential fear at what he had witnessed.

There was an eerie silence in the bird room which he always associated with sound from the birds. The fronts of the cages hung open, the room seemed vast and empty in the light of the two small lamps. Shuddering with sudden chill, he closed the french windows and went back to Hadji, who was calmer but still whimpering.

Exhausted by the immense physical feat he had accomplished, Nuri bey, slumped uncomfortably beside Hadji on the love-seat, fell suddenly into a deep sleep. He woke as dawn was breaking and he could hear, faintly, the *muezzin's* cry to prayer. He expected Hadji to fall to his knees and looked at the old man, sitting with his chin sunk into the blanket in which he was wrapped, making no movement. Had he died of shock from immersion? Nuri bey shook his arm. "Are you all right, old man?"

"It is I who should be dead, Efendim, drowned. Not she. You saved the wrong one, it is I who should have drowned."

"Say not so," Nuri bey returned sharply. Five hours earlier had been the time to speak. Now was the time to keep silence. What had happened had been a fit and tidy ending to what had begun exactly a week ago to the hour. It was meet and right and proper; the wheel had turned full circle and the circle was rounded off as only Allah could make a circle.

In the grey dawn-light, as the lamps flickered and went out, the yellow, monkey-faced neuter, neither male nor female, was not keeping a fit and proper silence but was talking.

Said Hadji: when men were castrated they did not, of necessity, lose their desires as men; in fact, it could happen that they fall in love and, because they were without effective pistils and stamens, that love had no natural outlet but could burn them up, scorch and damage them to such an extent that they could become tiny spiritual monsters. Such a one had he become because he had loved the girl attendant in the *hamam*, called Miasma, daughter of a gipsy and later a member of the harem of the last Grand Turk, not an *ikbal*, but one whom the Sultan never even saw!

Nuri bey shook his arm. "Sh . . . sh! This is the time to keep silence, you will be sorry if you tell me any more!"

Said Hadji: all these years he had loved only her, not

any other person, nor idea, nor possession, nor object, but only Miasma. All these years he had taken from her all the money he could get her to give him and for what? To keep them both in their old age because Miasma was the most spendthrift, extravagant and wasteful girl ever to toss her black hair at prudence.

"Sh . . . sh!" Nuri bey hissed, "these are the secrets of your heart. It is the time for silence, old man!"

Said Hadji: she loved all things of no real value, clothes, jewels, furs, scent, rich food. She spent and spent. And so it was necessary for her to make money and the only way she could make a lot of money easily was to join the drug traffickers. He knew it would lead her to disaster but, so long as only she and he knew, he could protect her. It was only when Valance's grandson got himself into trouble and Valance told her what he had been doing that she said Tony Grand must work for her. Hadji knew no good would come of it but Valance was weak, she was also greedy and loved money. She was afraid Miasma might one day no longer be able to afford to keep her. She allowed it. And that is what has led us to disaster. Hadji had been warned that the police were tightening up their investigations into drug traffic. Last Monday Valance had to go to the airport with the drug. The day before she told Miasma that it would be the last time, that she would warn her grandson that he must not do it again, either for them or for anyone else, and that, if he did not obey her, she would send his name in to the security police as one of those who carried drugs in the course of duty as steward in Zenobia Airways. There was a terrible row; Miasma and Valance would often quarrel and last Sunday evening was the worst Hadji had ever known. Afterwards when Valance was standing out alone at the top of the water steps, sulking, he went up behind her and pushed her in. It was all for the best.

Nuri bey gasped: "And did Miasma know?"

Hadji shook his head emphatically.

Nuri bey still thought it was the time for silence but now he had to hear the rest: "Go on," he urged.

Said Hadji: on the Monday evening, Valance's body, wrapped in the winding cloth, was left on the bier beside the front door covered with the pale green cloth of death.

The bey Efendi had obliged Miasma by going to the airport. Around midnight Tony Grand had come, no longer the loving grandson but a desperate hunted gangster. Miasma had been in bed. Hadji also, but he had got up to open the front door and the young man had rushed in, demanding to be hidden. Hadji had told him that his grandmother was dead, and pointed to her body, ready for burial after sunrise, but young Grand had said he must stay and be given shelter and, when Hadji had strongly objected, he had threatened him with his revolver.

Hadji had gone upstairs to Madame's room; having taken sleeping tablets she was soundly asleep; Hadji had taken the revolver from her handbag and loaded it. In the hall the young man had been standing by the bier, with his back to Hadji, who had fired twice from close range. He had not fallen dead but had turned and staggered across the hall; Hadji had retreated, panicked and fired again, this time wide. The young man had fallen and Hadji had left him, dying, and run to hide. Then, a few hours later, he had gone back to the hall to find him dead. He had undressed him with the idea of tying the body into a sack weighed down with big stones from the rockery, and casting it into the Bosphorus, as all unwanted corpses were cast. But he had been too heavy, too unwieldy. Hadji had had the cunning idea of wrapping him tightly in the winding sheet in which Valance was wrapped.

Said Hadji: he should not have pushed Valance into the Bosphorus in the hurried, crude manner he had employed. When erring women went into that stream, they went in in the way he had described and, because she had not done so, she had reappeared, down by the Sweet Waters of Asia in a most unseemly manner, with clothes above her head and general disorder. The worry of it had nearly killed him and, given another chance, he seized the opportunity to carry out the obsequies as was meet and right. For years he had had a suitably large sack ready—made almost to measure, and for an equal number of years had marked the large pieces of basalt rock he would use for the operation. It had been a matter of five minutes to do what he had visualised doing, so often; her body had gone into the water, her head protruding from the tied neck of the sack in the old, old way. He had kicked her down the water steps and now she lay, a distance of not more than two feet from the bottom step, but a long way down; food for the Bosphorus.

Said Hadji: it was, of course, Allah who had sent the Frenchwoman, Valance's sister.

Nuri bey became deeply thoughtful. He was ready to subscribe to the splendid ambiguity of assuming that Miasma knew nothing whatever but that did not prevent him from thinking that she certainly made a first-class accessory.

He said: "Hadji, you are a wicked, little . . ." he paused for a second before saying: "eunuch."

And after a long silence and much more thought he said, "And only now I begin to understand. In her way, I think Miasma loved you, Hadji, though she never ceased to abuse you. The fiendish idea of taking the young English girl to the public hanging was not one which suddenly dropped into her mind. She had been thinking about it with regard to you, Hadji."

"How so?"

"She wanted you to realise that, if you were discovered, you would hang."

"That may be so. She was frantic to have the money for the opium, Efendim, and I think now she wished to go away, and to take me, possibly to the hotel at which she stayed in Beirut when Valance was away, and where she first met her contacts. That may, indeed, be so."

"And if you are discovered you will hang after all, Hadji!" and Nuri bey's heart sank because he knew he would have to do something more to help him to escape death on the gallows.

Said Hadji: "A life without my mistress is no longer of any use to me, I no longer need it, or need the money."

He pointed a trembling finger at the sodden leather satchel, still lying on the water steps. "Take that, Efendim. It is all the money I saved for her in all the years I have served her. I owe it to you for the loss of your house. There is quite a lot of it. It is wrapped carefully in water-proof material, you will find it quite dry."

"Hadji, the police will surely be here soon with a warrant. There has been someone in the road watching the gate all night. They will come without any doubt."

"Let them come, I will tell them all. It will be a relief."

"But you will be hanged!"

"I wish for the *idam sehpasi,* the tripod of death, astride my miserable body and to hang at dawn before the Sultan Ahmed Mosque," he murmured.

And that was that.

Nuri bey made tea which they drank together without another word being spoken by Hadji, who sat in absolute apathy and dejection. When the police finally arrived, they banged loudly on the door and Hadji spoke:

"Leave me, Efendim, I beg you. This has nothing to do with you any more. Go quickly, and leave by the small gate at the end of the garden which has not been opened for years. It is bolted on this side and will be rusty. Go and catch the bus in the square. I do not wish you to see me leave the house in this . . . unseemly . . . condition . . . wrapped in a blanket."

They exchanged the Moslem leave-taking and Nuri bey went to the french window. "Farewell, Hadji," he said, turning round.

Hadji was walking towards the door; oddly enough, wrapped in his blanket, the creature achieved a strange dignity; he had instinctively wound it about him in the traditional way and now he looked like one of the original Wise Men.

"Don't forget the money," he called over his shoulder.

If he went back to the Hilton Hotel, he would be lost; he would fall for sentiment and a fairy-tale ending. So he strode the streets, damp satchel hanging over his shoulder, until it was time to go to the station.

And when he saw her in her sheep-minding wesket and saw her face light up in her enchanting smile, he nearly changed his mind.

"Darling Nuri bey! Thank goodness you're there!" She clung to him and Nuri bey trembled at his own weakness.

"It's all over," he told her. "Miasma is accidentally drowned in the Bosphorus and Hadji will soon be hanged for the murder of Tony Grand and Valance his grandmother. And you have had some narrow escapes and must now go back to your own country where I hope nothing more will happen to you."

They talked a lot more, as they walked to the train, found a single seat and stood side by side on the platform, watching people settling themselves for the long trans-European journey.

In desperation she said: "But, Nuri bey, I love you!"

"I love you, Jenny!"

"Well, then . . .?"

"If you love me you will do something for me?"

"Anything in the world!"

Nuri bey shook his head. "A blind promise! Jenny Bolton, you love too easily." He opened the satchel and took out the thick bundle of Turkish money. "You will take half of this!"

"Oh, no, I couldn't!"

"You must. You promised! I want you to take this and do not declare it. When you get home to England go to this address." He wrote on a slip of paper. "They are friends of mine and will give you English money in exchange."

"But what are you going to do?"

The guard was shooing everybody into the train which was about to leave. Jenny flung her arms round Nuri bey's neck and kissed him. He pushed her away and into the train. She let down the corridor window and leaned out.

"What *are* you going to do?"

"I still have my land. I shall clear it and rebuild my house. I shall live in it and study my people, whom I have never noticed before."

"But what about Oxford, Nuri bey? You've always longed to go."

"I longed when I had not the money to go. Now that I have, I dare not go. I dare not . . . in case the substance does not equal the shadow."

"What on earth are you talking about?"

"Let us say, I would rather stay here and . . . be a big fish in a small pond."

A kind of child's trumpet was blown and the train gave a jerk.

"Oh, Nuri bey!" she cried. She stretched out a hand and he caught it, running along beside the moving train. "I've been ditched again!" Her face was crumpled and tears were streaming from her eyes, her enchanting baby's mouth was stretched to an impossible shape. He ran faster but at last he had to leave go and stood with arm raised until she was drawn from sight.

He stayed on the spot where he had stopped running and, fumbling a little, brought out his passport which she had returned to him and stared down at it.

"Or, perhaps," he said aloud, "like Potemkin, I only wanted to long for something."